Nostalgia
The Forest and The Tree
M.J. Bauer

To all those who have supported me throughout this entire
process. I would not be here without every one of you.

I AM WRITING THIS *so she will not be forgotten.*

PROLOGUE

S HIMMERING OF METAL IN the dark. The hotel room is in disarray. Two silhouettes stare each other down. Far away, the sounds of hustle and bustle whisper beneath the scene. The entity with a lashing reptilian tail breathes raggedly.

"You can't keep running from us forever," hisses the wounded reptilian.

"Does it look like I'm running?" the other figure retorts.

The lizard-man snarls. Then, he lunges.

BANG — The other figure's shot goes wide. Claws and teeth gnash and slash, held at bay by that shimmer of metal: a blade. With a lift and a toss, the lizard-man goes careening into an armoire, knocking it over, and sending a third figure, a scrawny teen with tousled white hair and pale skin, spilling out onto the floor.

It had been a good hiding spot, giving them a good vantage point of the entire conflict. But it also didn't give them many ways out when the fight came to them.

"Keera, RUN!" the sword-wielder barked.

Without a second thought, the third figure scrambles up and out the door. Bursting into the lit hallway, they look around frantically, their short white hair flipping back and forth. Trying to remember the route through labyrinthian hallways they only just entered a few hours prior, the sound of footsteps approaching behind them jogs their memory. The teen takes off, careening from wall to wall like a pinball down the opulent red and gold hallway. Keera just keeps repeating the same mantra in their head: *Just keep going, she will find me. Just keep going, she will find me.*

Bursting into the main lobby, Keera's eyes dart around the space. Hotel guests, all dressed to the nines in gaudy attire, recoil at her sudden intrusion. Keera doesn't acknowledge them. The front door looks like a promising exit, until three heavily armed reptilian badlanders burst through it. Each scaly skinned monster is decked out in what was likely all they could scavenge for protective equipment: scraps of leather, bits of metal, and other detritus. They scan the crowd, their forked tongues flicking, until one of them locks eyes with Keera.

"There's one of them!" the lizard calls out. Keera barely manages to duck and scurry up a nearby staircase before a barrage of bullets force her behind a banister. The gawking crowd panics, fleeing in all directions, with some unfortunate souls being caught in crossfire. The child keeps scurrying along the upper catwalk. *I just need to find a way out, she will find me. A way out, a way out.* It's then that they see it: an open window. *No, there has to be another—* Another buckshot just misses Keera's ear, leaving it ringing for a moment. Heavy, boot-clad steps thump their way up the staircase. They are coming. A decision has to be made.

Fuck it. They sprint for the window.

Time slows. Bullets whiz by, but the sound of their beating heart drowns them out. The dark void beyond draws closer. And closer. Until... Keera jumps. It feels surreal. Shards of glass shower over them, cutting at their skin along with the cold night air. But they aren't thinking about that right now.

Because they just looked down.

Big mistake. Just hard, rain-soaked concrete down there. *Do I tuck and roll? CAN I tuck and roll? Oh shit, this was a bad idea.* Instead of tucking, the gangly teen flails wildly to grasp for something that doesn't exist. *This is it. This is how I die. Like a fucking idiot.* Keera closes their eyes and winces, trying to brace themself for whatever death feels like.

It's to their surprise, then, that, instead of a cold, uncaring ground greeting them, they are caught in the equally cold, yet concerned arms of their guardian.

"Radley!" Keera squeaks.

Realizing they are no longer going to die, they feel the need to explain their actions. Keera starts to apologize for jumping out of a second-story window with no actual plan, but the woman cuts them off: "We'll talk about this later." She sets them down.

It's then that a hoard of reptilians pour out from the building Keera had just defenestrated themself from. The two turn to flee, only to be cut off by more lizard-men surrounding them.

"Stay behind me," Radley orders. Keera isn't going to argue.

A deep, raspy cackle emanates from within the hoard of reptilians. Out from the crowd steps the largest lizard yet: at least a foot higher than anyone around, this hulking behemoth of muscle, scale, leather, and steel wields an absurdly large shotgun. To him, this gun is proportional, but that doesn't make it any less intimidating. Various scars interrupt the gray-green scales on their face and chest. The reptilian stops just in front of the rest of the hoard.

His booming laugh rolls into a cocky snarl: "The great and savage Radley of the Wastes! You and your little charge have been tough ones to nail down. But, lucky for me," he glances at his goons around him, "I've got my fair share of hammers." This elicits a raucous jeer from the surrounding mutants, those with melee weapons tapping them menacingly.

"This is your last warning:" Radley states, "Leave now, and don't look back."

They seem unshaken by this display of bravado. Another loud laugh bellows from the boss lizard; "You still think you're in a position to negotiate, huh?! Well, unfortunately for you... I like to let my Boombox do the talking."

The lizard levels the massive shotgun toward the two, and fires.

Chapter 1

K EERA DOESN'T REMEMBER THEIR life before the Canary Bridge. Not for lack of trying, as they often find themselves wandering away in their mind to whatever far away place that may be. Today, they imagine being born in a lush forest. Not like the ones in Canary: grown artificially under UV lamps, carefully cultivated to yield a crop of valuable plantlife, while still making the attempt to appear like a naturally grown forest. No, they imagine a REAL forest, under the warm sun, with plants growing where and in whatever way they deemed it necessary to grow. Animals of all shapes and sizes find a home amongst the foliage. None of them are doing so for any particular reason. There is no intentioned utility to nature. Just living in a way that feels... right. And doing so with an enthusiastic fervor.

Somewhere, deep within those woods, far from the bunkers and the caverns that comprise Canary, Keera imagines a young, beautiful couple with snow-white hair. And a little babe in their arms.

"Keera!" their instructor bellows. They jolt back to the present, the glittering green glade giving way to a fluorescent-lit, drab classroom. They return the gaze of the gray-haired woman, their adopted mother. The woman's dark, wrinkled brow is further creased in annoyance. "Where'd you go this time, girl?"

"Sorry, Mrs. D," Keera mumbles.

The woman sighs, continuing on with her lecture, "As I was saying: After the Fourth Incursion, and the subsequent wars that followed, much of the northern hemisphere was rendered uninhabitable due to intra- and extra-universal radiation. This forced our founders, as well as many other community's founders, underground..."

She continues on, but Keera's attention is drawn to a tap on their shoulder. It's Bri, her big brown eyes bright with curiosity. "Where did you go this time?" she whispers.

"To the forest," Keera responds.

"I love that one," Bri sighs, "Do you really think that's where you're from? Like, are there any forests left up there?"

"I don't know," they say, "But it's my daydream, I can be from wherever I want. I can be the bastard of a slime and a reptilian if I want."

"Ew!" Bri giggles, but silences herself to not alert their teacher.

"You know, if you wanted to see a real tree... you could go down to the deep caves," Autumn, the girl behind Bri, chimes in. The preppy teen has mischief in their slate-gray eyes.

"Wait, there's a tree down there?" Keera asks.

"You didn't know? What are you, new?" Autumn sneers. Keera rolls their eyes.

Bri twists around, retorting, "Knock it off, Autumn. There's nothing down there."

"There is, my brother told me so last night," she says. Bri tries to continue arguing, but the redhead cuts her off, "What are you doing tonight, Keera?"

"Nothing"

"Wanna go down there tonight and see for yourself? There'll be booze."

"No!" Bri responds, a little too loud.

The trio turn to see Mrs. D scowling at them. "Do I need to separate you all?"

"No, ma'am," the three respond almost in unison. There is a tense moment of silence before the teacher continues lecturing.

Autumn whispers one last time: "Tonight?"

Keera, more motivated by seeing a relic of the outside world than alcohol, nods.

Bri scowls.

***

"Why did you agree to that?!" Bri demands, running up beside Keera.

"I want to see if she's full of shit," Keera shrugs, shuffling down the sidewalk.

"It's Autumn, she's ALWAYS full of shit! "

"Yeah, but her brother usually isn't."

"Her brother is about to be tried for drinking at his job."

"Right, so then why would he be lying about something like that?"

Bri steps in front of Keera. High above, on the ceiling of the cavern in which the entire town exists, ugly white light emanates from dimming UV lamps. This signifies that evening is approaching in Canary Bridge. There are no pretty sunrises deep under the earth, only slow fades into pure darkness.

"Why do you need to see this tree so bad?" Bri asks.

Keera looks out to the rows and rows of stale, boring homes they have been walking past. They are the same houses Keera has seen in all sixteen years of their life. Save for a few decorations or graffiti here and there, they are identical. Same with the stores, the school, the community center, the gates between the districts. Always the same, never changing.

Eventually, Keera responds with, "I just want something new."

"Trees aren't new, Keera, we have trees here," Bri gestures to some of the sad, lollipop-looking trees spaced evenly along the sidewalk.

"No, a *real* tree! A tree that grew where it did just because, and not as some calculated decision by the city people. A tree without a purpose, without expectations. Just... a tree."

"You're weird, Keera," Bri sighs, as the two continue walking, "I just wish Autumn wasn't going to be there."

"Why do you hang out with her if you don't like her?" Keera asks.

Bri tucks a bit of her brown wavy hair behind her ear. She murmurs, "Well, I like you, and you hang out with her."

"I guess, yah," Keera says. They walk in silence for a while. It's not awkward; the two have known each other for years, so they can exist around one another without a conversation, enjoying their shared company. Of course, still being young, they often have a lot of new and interesting things to share, but sometimes those thoughts and feelings can be hard to understand, and silence feels like the only solution at the moment.

Keera, reaching one of the many identical apartment complexes, begins peeling off. "Alright, well, see you later tonight!"

Bri mutters, "See ya," as she continues down the path to her home. Keera pauses and allows their gaze to linger on their friend as she walks away. Part of them regrets making these plans. They know Bri isn't the biggest fan of adventures like this. The girl is much more interested in her historical fiction and craft hobbies. Keera likes those, too. Well, they're more fantasy fiction than historical, but hearing Bri emphatically talk about the new book she's reading is just as enjoyable as any story about elves and dragons. Anything with Bri is fun. But... something about the idea of this strange, misplaced tree is calling to Keera's wanderlust. A little taste of the outside world, something they believe they will never get to see. They hope their friend will understand when they get there.

Inside the apartment, the smell and sound of freshly cooked bacon immediately assault Keera's senses. It is a small space; the front door opens straight into a living room, which is open to the dining nook, and a kitchen just around the corner. To the right, a short hallway leads to the bathroom and two bedrooms. The space would be comfortable for one or maybe two people, but is just too small for three.

The sizzling and popping of grease on metal ebbs and flows in volume as their dad, Mr. D, flips and turns the strips of meat, whistling a tune he likely made up.

"Hey, honey!" their dad calls over the noise.

"Hey dad," they respond, tossing their book bag on the recliner.

He pokes his head around the corner as his daughter plops onto the sofa and turns on the TV. "Your mother with you?" he asks.

"She had to stay behind and grade papers."

"Ah, shoot. Well, she better be home soon, bacon's gonna get cold!"

"Room temperature isn't 'cold,' dad," Keera says, "It's not going to turn into a block of ice once it's off the stove."

"Yeah, but it's not the same as having it fresh out of the pan!"

Keera rolls their eyes. There is no arguing with this man when it comes to food.

The sizzling dies down, and Mr. D rounds the corner, drying his hands on a washcloth. He is wearing a basic white shirt and sweatpants, and his glasses are all fogged up from the heat he was just cooking over.

"How was school?"

"Mom yelled at me again."

"Because you were daydreaming again?"

Keera nods, not really looking away from the low-budget, locally produced sitcom on at the moment.

"Well, that'll do it," he says. After a moment, he adds, "Where did you go this time?"

"The forest."

"Now, is that the one with or without the fairies?" he asks, as he wanders back into the kitchen.

"Without. The one with the fairies is the garden," Keera responds.

Their father returns from the kitchen again, this time with two plates, each sporting a BLT. Or, well, one BLT and one BL.

"Thanks," Keera says as he hands her the one without tomato.

Their dad nods. The two chow down.

"Been a while since you talked about the garden one. I miss hearing you go on and on about wanting to be friends with all the fairies, and protecting everybody from big scary monsters and all that," Mr. D says between bites.

Keera, with a mouthful, says, "Yeah, that was when I was like five. Before I knew fairies weren't real."

"They might be now for all we know," their dad smirks, waving a floppy sandwich in their direction, "You don't know what's been coming out of The Rift up there these days."

Keera has no response to that. They are pretending to watch TV, but their eyes would betray that as a lie. Really, they are deep in their mind once again. Their dad has a point: no one in Canary Bridge knows what's happened in the outside world for over a hundred years. Their little community dug this pit and sealed all the exits soon after the Second Continental War broke out. And, if the First Continental War was anything to go by... Keera had a worrying intrusive thought creep in the back of their mind.

"Hey dad?" they start.

"Yes, my child?" he responds playfully.

"Do you..." they hesitate. *Is this even worth asking?* The innate human desire to know overwhelms the teenager in the end, however. "Do you think there are still any forests on the surface?"

Their dad's tone shifts to a more serious, peer-to-peer discussion one. This tone is one he takes with his daughter when they ask genuine questions. "What type of answer are you looking for with this question?"

Keera hates it when he does this. They just want there to be *an* answer, not multiple possibilities depending on their mood or preference. That's not how answers work.

"I don't know, dealer's choice, I guess," Keera deflates a bit, knowing they won't be able to rely on what comes next as any kind of fact.

"Alright:" Keera's dad sits forward, hands on his knees, fingers clasped together. He's preparing a rant, Keera knows it.

"My honest answer: I'm not sure. There's no way to know from down here. I like to hope there is. Just seeing the photos from decades ago fills me with peace and calm. They really must have been a sight to see. But my realistic answer is... probably not."

Keera sighs. The teen twists into a dejected fetal position on the couch.

"I'm not sure what you expected of me, Keera," Mr. D responds, "I don't know all the answers. And you're too old for me to lie to like you're a little kid."

"Like you both lied that you were my parents..." Keera mutters into their folded arms.

"So we're doing this again," Mr. D stands, grabbing both plates and moving into the kitchen. He shouts over the running sink as he rinses them off, "We were waiting until you were old enough to understand."

"I was old enough to understand when I went to school and noticed all the other kids looked like their parents," Keera shouts back, "Also, you didn't wait to tell me, you LIED to me. Said you didn't know why I didn't look like you two."

"And we were wrong. Parents make mistakes, too."

"You aren't my parents. MY parents wouldn't lie to their child like that."

Mr. D shuts the water off, "You think so..."

"I KNOW so," Keera snaps, still shouting.

"Oh, you do?"

"Yes, I do."

"How?"

"I—I don't know, I just... feel that they wouldn't lie."

The sink sound stops. Mr. D plods into the dining room, avoiding eye contact, plopping dispassionately in one of the dining room chairs. His eyes are tired and sad, staring through the linoleum.

"Alright."

"Alright?!"

"I'm not fighting with you over this, Keera. Not tonight."

"Why not?!"

"There's nothing more I can say."

"You can give me a straight answer! Stop with this wishy-washy, gray area crap. Who are my parents, where are they, and do you think there are any more fucking forests?!"

He sighs, "I don't know. Also, don't say fuck, please."

Keera's frustration comes to a boil. Like a teapot releasing steam, an exacerbated "UGH!" escapes them as they stomp off down the short hallway to their room. Tears are running down their cheeks. Angry tears. Frustrated tears. Sad tears. They turn in the doorway, and shout into the void before them, "I HATE the way you treat me like a child!"

SLAM of the door.

He'll know by tomorrow. We both will.

I have to find that tree tonight.

Chapter 2

"Hurry up, Keera!" Autumn whispers.

"I didn't hear you volunteering to pick this lock," Keera hisses back, trying to concentrate on the small brass lock they have two paper clips wedged inside of.

"Because you said you could do it," Autumn says.

"I can if you'll just give me a minute!" they respond. They have picked locks like this before. Once or twice, Keera and Bri have snuck out to the overlook above town to shoot the shit and get a little buzzed on cheap beer. Both locations are blocked off to the public. With the overlook, that is said to be because of loose rocks and a lack of structural integrity. And, sure, if dozens of people are making their way up there every day, the cliff-side might buckle and collapse onto a few houses. But for two teens who just need to vent about their day, far from the watchful eyes of parents and authorities? No problems there.

As for the current B&E target, the mine was shut down about eighty years ago. Supposedly, there was a radon leak detected deep in the tunnel, and no amount of filtration systems could clear it out. The site was abandoned, due to nothing of value being found in the upper tunnels, and the inability for them to dig any deeper. Now, a fifteen-foot-wide hole sits a few minutes outside the underground town proper, cordoned off by a secure chain-link fence that extends to the ceiling of the cave mouth. Of course, with any abandoned structure, it is bound to attract certain types of people: partiers, people looking to do illicit things or substances, and teenagers seeking rebellion and adventure.

With a few moments of silent concentration, Keera finally feels the padlock click free in her grasp. They twist it from the latch, place their tools back in their backpack, and open the fence gate, arms wide for showmanship's sake.

"Ladies first," Keera smirks, taking a cheeky bow.

Autumn rolls her eyes, "You're a lady, too, you know."

"Eh, a bit more complicated than that," they respond, still feeling cocky, "Freeloaders who DIDN'T pick the lock first, how's that?"

Autumn scoffs, and scampers in, followed by her friends Tara and Cali, two girls who frequently follow Autumn everywhere she goes. Last, Bri scuttles up to the entrance, "I'm not included in that, am I?"

"Nah. You're too quirky to be basic," Keera gestures in with a wink and a smile. Bri chuckles and heads in, and Keera shuts the gate behind them before catching up with the rest.

The cavern descends at a slight downward angle. So slight, in fact, that one could easily mistake this evenly carved chute to be an unfinished tunnel for an ancient highway. The flashlights Tara and Keera are carrying barely penetrate the pervasive darkness. The smell of wet rock clings to the air down here. Each nervous, shuffling footstep of the girls sends sound waves careening up and down the cavern as they walk deeper and deeper. They are convinced they are far enough away from town, so the teens start to chatter amongst themselves. About twenty minutes of consistent walking later, the party's boisterous conversation is interrupted as they come upon an offshoot to the main tunnel in the left wall.

"Which way do you think?" Cali asks.

The cone of light sweeps left and right, assessing their options.

"It was supposed to be deep in the cave, right?" Bri says.

Autumn remarks, "Yeah, so it's probably not this close."

"I don't know, how deep do you think your brother would go, Autumn?" Tara asks.

"I mean, he is pretty lazy," she concedes. Silence befalls the group. Stumped.

Then, Keera's light catches a reflection at the mouth of the leftmost tunnel. They raise a curious eyebrow and approach the object. Within a few steps, they can make out what it is: a bottle. They kneel beside it, shifting it carefully like a detective at a crime scene.

"What did you find?" Bri asks. The other girls appear beside them. Autumn leans down, snatching the blank bottle from Keera.

She takes a big whiff of the bottles' scant contents, and reels at what her nose finds. "Ugh, gin," she groans, "This was my brother's alright."

"They must've gone down there, then," Keera concludes.

Bri, stepping closer, shines her light forward, then angles it down at an angle. "Are you sure about that?" Bri asks hesitantly.

"Why?" says Autumn.

Bri waves the others over. Together, they peer down the tunnel, which descends vertically downward about twenty feet. "How's your brother with heights?" Bri questions.

"Normally? Pretty bad," Autumn says, "But, when he's drunk, he makes even dumber decisions, so..."

The group stares at the hard floor far below them for a long moment. They aren't sure if it's real or their imagination, but they swear they can feel a rush of cold air blowing up from the tunnel below, like the breath of some frigid, heartless beast exhaling toward them, waiting for the first victim in a long time to venture into its lair.

"Maybe we should leave, you guys," Bri suggests.

"Don't be a pussy, Bri," Tara says.

"I don't see you volunteering to go first, Tara!" Bri spits.

The girl scoffs, "Well, yeah, I can't climb with the flashlight."

"NONE of us can do that, Tara," Autumn chimes in.

There's a pause, as they all consider this. Then Cali says, "What if one of us holds the light while one of us climbs down and that last person tosses down the flashlight?"

"Great idea, Cali," Autumn says, "Alright, let's go."

Silence. Nobody moves.

"Well, someone has to go first," the redhead insists, "What about you, Bri? Aren't you in gymnastics?"

Bri stammers, "Well, yeah. But gymnastics doesn't involve climbing into dark holes in the middle of the night."

"I'll go," Keera says.

Without waiting, Keera steps toward the stony maw, stowing her own light. Bri gets closer and mutters, "I'll hold your light. I don't trust any of them to keep it on you the whole time."

"Thanks, Bri," the white-haired kid places a hand on their friend's shoulder. The two share a trusting look before Bri turns and snatches the light from Tara's hand, ignoring her protests.

Keera slowly begins to lower themself over the edge. The hand holds are rough, unfamiliar, and slick with condensation. Still, Keera has experience in this area. In their spare time, when Bri is busy with schoolwork, and others are off at sporting events or whatever, Keera would climb the cave walls, looking for new spots to sit and overlook the cavern at. Normally, they would do this when the caverns' "sun" was still on. They had a few close calls early on, both with falling and the authorities, but they've managed. And, along the way, they've become pretty good at free climbing.

A few months back, in fact, they got so good at climbing one route that they reached a particularly nice looking ledge they were eyeing for a while. It was higher than the wall they were currently climbing down, maybe closer to thirty or forty feet, so it got a bit nerve-wracking knowing just how far they were going to fall if they fucked up. But it was well worth it: a clear, unobstructed view of Canary Bridge. They could see their apartment complex, the school, the market. They could even see all the way to the other side where the lumber forest and crop fields were planted. All this bathed in unfeeling, clinical, fluorescent-colored sunlamps. It was then Keera had tried to imagine what the town would look like under a REAL sun, a REAL sky, full of clouds during the day and stars at night. They have obviously never seen the actual sun before, but they remember thinking it had to be more comforting than this.

Just then, Keera's foot slips on a rock. They grip tight the slippery handholds as they flash back to reality. No, they can't be somewhere else right now. They need to focus on the dangerous task at hand. Luckily, the light, and Bri's concerned face from above, is enough to help ground them. In no time, they can release the wall and stand on terra firma once again.

"Nice job," Autumn calls from up above, "Okay, Bri, your turn."

Even from far below, Keera can tell she's reluctant. "It's ok, Bri," Keera calls up, "I'm down here, I'll catch you if you fall!"

Bri hesitates, before calling back, "Okay…" She then slowly crouches and begins lowering herself down the wall, "Are you sure you could catch me? You're pretty — ugh! — scrawny," Bri yells through efforts and heavy breathing.

"Well, I'll break your fall, at least!" Keera calls up, grinning. This elicits nervous chuckling from Bri. Keera has faith in her abilities, though, even if Bri doesn't. And sure enough, before long, Bri is beside Keera at the bottom of the hole.

"Okay," Bri says, still catching her breath. She calls back up to the other girls, "Who's next?"

"Oh no, we're not going down there," Autumn laughs.

"WHAT?!" Bri yells.

"Yeah, we're gonna head out," Autumn jeers, "Have fun getting out of there, losers!"

And, with that, the three girls disappear.

Bri flails in the darkness, "UGH! I hate them! See, this, THIS is why I don't get why you hang out with them!"

Keera is still reeling from this sudden turn of events. They've known Autumn since freshman year of high school. And, sure, she can be rude and passive-aggressive. But she was never cruel, and CERTAINLY never did anything like this. "This has to be a joke," Keera finally says, "Give it a few minutes, they'll probably come right back."

A few minutes pass. Nothing.

"They're gone, Keera," Bri says, then growls, "I'm gonna kill 'em. If I get out of this hole, I'm gonna kill 'em."

"Bri, calm down—"

"Calm down?! Keera, they left us alone, in a hole, in the dark!"

"Don't worry," Keera reaches into her backpack and produces her own flashlight, "It's only a little dark, and you're not alone."

With light returned, Keera can now see the mixture of fear and rage on their friend's face. For the most part, Bri is a quiet person. It takes a lot to get her animated, either a lot of poking and prodding, or a lot of booze. A wave of guilt washes over Keera.

Bri sighs, her agitation fading. She turns back to examine the sheer wall behind them. "At least this might help us get out of here," she says.

"Or..." Keera starts.

Bri whips around to face her friend, "No. No, no, we are NOT going down this hole any further."

"Well—"

"'Well' nothing! No one knows we're down here except those three bitches. If something happens, we're dead!"

"Okay, hear me out:" Keera has her hands up, as if trying to soothe a wild predator about to pounce, "What if we keep going? BUT, only until we hit another fork. If we hit another tunnel, we turn around and climb back out of here. That way, either we find the tree, or we know exactly which way we went, and we can't get lost."

Leaning against the cave wall, Bri pinches the bridge of her nose and sighs again. "Why do you still think there's still a tree this far down? Why do you think anything she said was true after what just happened?" she asks.

Keera thinks back to the conversation they had with their father earlier that day. They refused to believe him then. Why were they trusting this random, mean girl more than the man who raised them? It doesn't make sense, but feelings rarely do.

"I'm not sure," Keera finally responds, "I just... want to believe."

Bri stares Keera down. Wheels are clearly turning in her brain, likely deciding whether to chew them out or concede.

Finally, with one last sigh, Bri responds: "You're lucky I like you so much."

"Really?"

"We go until we come to another intersection, OR we are walking for more than one hour," she makes a point by raising one firm finger. She means it. "I'm not about to spend my entire Friday night in a cave."

Keera nods in the affirmative, a well of excitement bubbling up within them. And, with that, the two teenagers, one excited and one begrudging, step confidently into the deep, dark passageway.

***

By forty minutes in, Bri is beginning to get restless. This tunnel is a lot more meandering and inconsistent than the bigger tunnel they traversed to get here. It is clearly still carved, as wooden support beams regularly appear on either side of them. But, the lack of intentionality to the cave is perplexing, to be sure.

"I can't believe you convinced me to do this," she huffs as they take another left turn.

"Right, me neither," Keera muses, "Like, I didn't even have to try that hard."

The brown-haired girl lets out a snort masked by a groan, "Ugh, you're so annoying."

"Then why do you hang out with me?"

"It's easy to be around you. Just, you know, not when you're leading me down a cold dark cave in the middle of the night," she responds, "I like that you're adventurous, just maybe not THIS adventurous."

They both chuckle. It is true, this is probably the most bold thing Keera has done. Even they aren't really sure why they're so persistent in this. It's odd, but ever since they entered the main tunnel, Keera has had this... feeling. It started as a slight tingle on the back of their neck, right at the base of their skull. They thought it was just excitement, or maybe nerves. But the further down they've gone, the more that feeling has persisted. And spread. It's weird, it's foreign, but also... good? Like it feels right to keep feeling it? To keep going? They don't know. All they know for sure is that they need to see this through to the end.

And there it is.

A light at the end of the tunnel.

The duo stands there, frozen. They had only just rounded a corner, just like they've been doing for the past hour. And... there it is.

Something.

They share a glance with each other, one of surprise and wonder. Wordlessly, Keera and Bri creep forward, as if any loud sudden movements might frighten the light away. Eventually, their eyes adjust, and they witness the source.

Standing tall at the center of a dome-shaped cavern is a lone tree. Rooted, somehow stubbornly among the rocks, a solid, powerful trunk cascades upward. As it extends higher, the dark-colored bark gives way to a pure white wood, with specks of brown dotted on its surface, like chocolate chips on a cookie. Erupting from the dappled branches are blooms upon blooms of golden yellow leaves. This creates a plume not unlike that of a large-headed dandelion. All told, the tree is well over eighty feet in height, with its uppermost branches reaching for a hole in the ceiling, almost appearing to evaporate into the warm golden light streaming in.

The two teens are awestruck. They cannot take their eyes away. It's just a tree, but they have never seen a tree like this. Not this tall, not of this type. And not bathed in *actual* sunlight.

Bri is the first to break the silence: "It's... I—I just can't..."

"I knew it was here," Keera says in awe.

Bri shifts her gaze from the tree to Keera, "Maybe I should trust your feelings more often."

Keera meets her gaze. The two smile into each other's eyes. Then, one starts to giggle uncontrollably, which induces the same in the other. Pretty soon, the two are clasping hands and jumping up and down, laughing and elating in a pure moment of excitement.

"Let's go check it out!" Keera exclaims. Bri nods emphatically, and the two sprint to the tree.

Up close, it is clear the trunk is not wide. However, the bark near the base is dark and sturdy, like the leg of an elephant. The verticality of this thing, however, is even more breathtaking up close. Beneath its boughs, it appears to ascend upward toward a golden infinity. The entire spectacle is particularly amazing to Keera, who now can vividly see themselves growing up among a grove of these magnificent beings. A brown to white to gold gradient flowing upward, as far as the eye can see. Wondrous golden sunlight, with ample shadowed ground protecting them and their little family from when the sun gets too hot. Climbing these beasts every day, sometimes to the top, only to be met with a sea of honey-colored treetops.

"Wait, Keera," Bri's voice breaks them out of their daydream, "Look." They turn to see what she is pointing at.

It turns out they were so focused on the major attraction that they had missed a small but miraculous detail: the leaves are falling. Not raining down from the canopy and landing on the cold floor, as normal trees want to do around autumn.

They are *stuck* falling. Suspended in the air.

Keera and Bri approach one of the falling leaves to inspect it, seeing it from every angle. It is small, only about an inch and a half long, thin and linear, appearing like a tiny feather. As they rotate around it, they can see one side is a radiant yellow, while the other is a matte, almost chalk-looking white. It should be noted that, by this point, the tingles in Keera's head have gone from subtle to across their entire scalp. But, they hardly notice, as the sensation only seems to add to the euphoria of the situation.

Carefully, Bri reaches out a hand to touch the leaf. First a poke. It doesn't budge. Then a gentle caressing finger, feeling the slight toothed edge and the plant veins within.

"Wow..." she breathes.

She then reaches out with two fingers, pinching it on either side and giving it a tug. Nothing. She tugs harder. Still unmoveable. It is as if this tiny leaf is rooted in its own invisible trunk, as sturdy as the tree it came from.

"You know what this means, right?" Bri asks, excitement beaming from her eyes.

Keera replies, "What?"

"This tree is timestuck!"

Her companion furrows their brow slightly.

"You know, timestuck? Like frozen in time?"

Keera squints, as if the answer is written in blurry letters across Bri's forehead.

"Do you pay ANY attention in physics class?!" she asks.

"Honestly, when your teacher's your mom, you tend to zone out quite a bit. Especially when it comes to subjects involving math."

Bri rolls her eyes before explaining, "When something becomes timestuck, it is rooted in space and time. It never ages, never moves, just stays right where it was when it was hit by ultra-planck chronologic radiation."

"That's insane..." Keera gasps.

"It IS insane! Especially because, from what Mrs. D says, most things hit with UPC radiation just turn to dust! Something like this has only been rumored to be possible. Never proven to be real."

Glancing up, Keera now notices that *none* of the leaves on the tree are moving. At all. It is as if it was a three-dimensional photo the size of a skyscraper. Their attention then returns to the strange leaf. They cock their head, and curiously reach out their own finger, to give it their own test poke.

It moves.

Keera's instantly terrified. Did they break it? Bri's awestruck eyes are darting back and forth between Keera and the leaf. Wordlessly, the pale-haired teen pokes the leaf again.

It moves again.

"How...?" Bri whispers incredulously.

Gently, slowly, Keera reaches out as Bri did, pinching it between their pointing and middle finger.. And pulls it closer to them.

They are now holding the leaf.

"Keera," Bri breathes, finally shaking off some of the bewilderment, "That's... That's impossible!"

Keera turns the leaf over in their grasp. "What does this... mean?" they wonder.

"I—I don't know!" the girl stammers.

There is a moment of silence, as the two process an impossible situation.

Finally, Bri speaks up, "We have to tell your mom."

"What?! No way!" Keera exclaims, "If I show her this, then we'll have to explain why we were down here. We'll be in SO much trouble. Hell, I'LL be in so much trouble!"

"So you're saying we lie?" Bri asks.

"Only for a little bit. Give ourselves some time to think it over, figure out who we want to tell, and how to explain it."

Bri looks away for a moment, then back to Keera, and nods. "I'll keep your secret," she says.

"*Our* secret," Keera corrects, reaching out and clasping Bri's hands. Bri smiles, and her cheeks turn a shade brighter.

"Thank you for making me come out here," Bri says, "I know I was a bit of a buzzkill today, but I actually do love going on adventures with you."

Keera's smile grows as well, staring into Bri's big, bright, amber-colored eyes. "Me too," they whisper. They don't know why they felt the need to whisper now, but they did. A quiet reciprocation. The tingling feeling in their mind, the adrenaline from this wondrous discovery, and... something else. Something that started creeping into their chest in the past few moments, looking into Bri's eyes — all those things making them want to do something rash, impulsive, and something they've had thoughts about doing for a long, long time... But they hesitate.

Unfortunate, for that was their last chance.

"KEERA D AND BRIANNA FENNINGTON!"

The two teens whirl around to see a sight that makes their blood run cold: Keera's mother, flanked by Autumn, Cali, and Terra. Autumn is trying to play it cool, but a wry smirk can't help but worm its way across her lips. "WHAT are you two doing down here?!" she continues, "This area is off limits, and dangerous!"

"Mom, I can explain—" Keera starts.

"That was a rhetorical question," Mrs. D cuts them off, "because there is NO good reason why I should be woken up in the middle of the night, to your friends telling me that you broke into an abandoned mine, climbed down a cliff IN THE DARK, and are now standing here under this— this what, this tree?!"

"Please, Mom, Bri and I wer—"

"They made us do it!" Bri yells, throwing an accusatory finger at the three other girls, "They made us climb down that hole first, and left us down here."

"We didn't MAKE you do anything, Bri," Autumn retorts, "We told Mrs. D the truth: you both had this idea to break into the old mine and get drunk. Then, you found that hole, and climbed down into it. We were worried you'd die down here or something, so we went looking for help."

"That's not even close to—" Keera protests, before their mom cuts them off again.

"Save it, Keera," she raises a firm hand, "Your father told me about earlier today. How you wouldn't stop going on about trees and forests or whatever."

"It wasn't about the trees!" Keera snaps, "It's about you guys not listening! 'Trees or whatever.' There's proof, right there! You don't care about me, or how I feel. No one does!"

Keera notices Bri flash a look at them. A hurt one. They feel a sharp pang in their chest, where that fluttering had been only a moment ago.

They didn't have the time to process that, however, as their mother hurled another irate barrage at them, "That's it, both of you are coming with me right now. Keera, you're grounded. And Ms. Fennington, your parents will be hearing about this, and will surely do the same. Let's go, girls." The three turn to leave. Keera looks to Bri for some form of solidarity, but is only met with betrayal. Wordlessly, she begins to follow the rest of the group.

Keera is shellshocked. They can't believe it. This magical, surreal moment has been destroyed by crushing, depressing reality: that they're just a kid, Mrs. D is their mother, and they are being dragged back to their home, likely never to see a real tree again.

They look up at the tree, glowing and magnificent. A wondrous find that their mother had disregarded as nothing more than a mere tree in her rage. This sparked something in the snow-haired teen.

"I'm not going back."

Mrs. D slowly turns to face their defiant child, "What did you just say?"

"I'm not. Going. Back."

"You can't just stay down here forever, you know," their mom scolds.

"I'm leaving," Keera points up toward the hole in the ceiling, "I'm going out there."

"AbsoLUTELY not!" she shouts.

"I don't belong down here," Keera says, "I never felt like Canary Bridge was my home. My parents don't respect me," and, with a pointed look at Bri, they say, "And my friends don't support me, either."

Tears begin to well in the girl's eyes. Keera immediately regrets what they just said. They've felt the whole world was against them for the longest time, but Bri was always the exception. Seeing her now, though, standing with three liars and her fake mother... it was as if in that moment, none of the laughs, vulnerable talks, or comforting embraces meant anything to them. They had lashed out in rage, and now... they didn't know what their relationship could be after today.

"That's IT," Mrs. D stomps across the hard floor toward Keera. She grips her daughter's forearm like a rusted vice.

"Hey, let go!" Keera wails. They try to pull, pry themselves free, but they are no match for their mother's hold, "I hate you! I HATE YOU!"

BOOM.

The entire cavern containing Canary Bridge rumbles.

CHAPTER 3

EVERYONE FREEZES, THE SCENE becoming something out of a romanticist painting: two figures, a mother and their child, locked in conflict, while four onlookers stand a few feet away. All of this is under a bright yellow tree, illuminated by the heavens. And every one of them is looking up at the cavernous ceiling.

"What was that?" Autumn finally breaks the silence.

"An earthquake?" adds Cali.

"We've never had an earthquake before," Bri replies.

Another loud BOOM, followed by a crackling rumble, shakes the ground. Everyone steadies themselves, and Keera scrambles free from their mother's grip.

"Come on, everyone, we have to get out, now," Keera's mom orders.

"Wait, where are we going?" Keera protests.

"Back to town," Mrs. D responds, "Now go."

"You want us to go further underground? During an earthquake?!"

"Keera, we don't have time for thi—"

Another echoing BOOM rattles through the space. This one doesn't stop, as a low roar begins to build all around them. Sand and bits of rubble rain down from above.

"There's a way out, to the surface, right there!"

"We are NOT going outside!" Mrs. D snaps, "We are going back the way we came, and back to the town, where it is safe! The walls are fortified there."

Just then, a loud CRACK explodes in the mouth of the cavern. The sand and rocks turn into boulders, the space collapsing in on itself. First to go is the entrance to the cave, as stones the size of sedans cascade in. The way back is gone. More stones are falling, missing some girls by inches. Everyone runs, screaming, toward the tree — the only shelter their panicked brains can process. Everyone, except for Keera: they're running the opposite way.

"KEERA!" their mom calls after them.

They do not hear her. Their instincts are kicking in. They run. Run as hard as they ever have before, dodging falling rocks, and doing their best to keep their footing. They reach the wall and begin scrambling up it. Rocks fall and pelt them in the back and shoulders. They hurt, but they know they can't stop. The teen slips and falls to their knees, skinning them on the unforgiving gravel. Keera lets out a quick gasp, looking down at their legs, seeing bits of stone poking out of their kneecap.

Below, their mother is shouting something now imperceptible to Keera over the roar of the cave-in. They can't even see the girls huddled beneath the tree anymore. They think for a moment that they could turn and run, go back and bury themselves in their mother's arms and be okay. But the rocks keep falling, and they know they have to continue. Turning back to the light, they scramble their way up the treacherous rocky slope. The pain throbs on their back and their knees and their head, but they don't stop, they can't.

However, they are not fast enough. The roar of the collapsing cave rolls over them like a speeding train, boulders pinning them to the ground, only feet from the golden gap in the rocks.

With one solid thunk of their head on the rocky floor, everything goes dark.

The unconscious mind processes time differently than the conscious one does. That's why, as Keera's eyes slowly open, their perception of reality is distorted. They aren't sure how long they've been out, how much of the past few hours were real, or how much was a wild, terrifying dream. But, soon, their faculties returned to them, one of the first being waves upon waves of throbbing pain rolling up their body. They squint their eyes, being met visually with only a blinding white light. *This hurts. Everything about this hurts. Was this death? Was death just pain? I wouldn't be surprised,* Keera supposed. Their eyes eventually adjust to the light, and the first thing they see is a figure standing over them. They're a tall, blurry silhouette.

"M—mom?" Keera calls out. Given she was the last adult she saw, it was the only name their rattled brain could conjure up.

The figure squats down before them, and as more of them come into focus, it becomes clear: This is not their mother. Deep brown eyes set under a stern brow, an angular face, powerful jaw, to a pointed chin. Smooth skin, pale, but not as pale as their hair. Long, white hair cascades well below her shoulders, with bangs parted down the middle, falling to chin-level. The person looks Keera up and down with cold objectivity.

"Good, you're awake," the figure says in a low, feminine voice. They stand again and reach out a black-gloved hand toward the child. Keera hesitates a moment too long, so the figure adds, "Get up. You can't just lie there."

Reluctantly, Keera grabs the stranger's hand, and suddenly they are standing. The aggressive hoist up makes them teeter, the pain throughout their whole body crying out in protest. They double over a bit, thinking they are about to wretch from the stress of it all, but keep their composure.

"Come on," the stern woman orders, "Get a grip. We don't have time for this."

Keera glares up at the person, the rebellious teen impulse almost kicking in, until they realize what the rest of the woman looks like. She is dressed head to toe in black leather: high leather boots, leather pants, leather armored top, and a leather jacket with powerful angled shoulders, fastened at the waist by a leather belt. This is imposing, but the weapons she is wielding make her straight-up intimidating. In one hand, the woman grips a semi-automatic pistol. In the other, they have unsheathed a slender, gleaming-silver katana.

All things considered, Keera decides it's best to do as this woman says.

"Can you move?" she asks.

Keera nods.

"Good. Then get behind that rock over there," the woman gestures to a large boulder about 20 feet away. Using this opportunity to get their bearings, Keera notes the surrounding land; flat, dry, and virtually lifeless. It stretches as far as the eye can see. Only rocks and the occasional dead tree dot the horizon. And the sky, while bright, is just an endless expanse of gray clouds.

And then it hits them. They're outside.

"Wait, where are—" is all they get to say as a bullet whizzes within a foot or so of them. They flinch instinctively, covering their head and ears.

"Go, NOW!" the woman shouts. Keera doesn't need to be told twice. They dash over to the rock and dive for cover.

A few more shots ricochet off the ground back where they were standing. The fire isn't focused on them anymore.Out of some innate sense of human curiosity, Keera pokes their head out from behind the rock to observe the scene.

A few yards away, in the direction the bullets came from, approach three stocky figures. From far enough away, they might be mistaken for bikers with poor posture: hunched over, and wearing all combinations of leather and metal. However, the two key features that betray their true nature are their thick scaled tails that drag and thrash on the ground behind them, and their elongated, reptilian faces, bearing a variety of head spines, scales, and frills. When these entities move, they do so like apes being forced to walk upright. They can not rightly walk on all fours even if they wanted to, however, as all three are carrying automatic rifles. As they near the woman in black, her blade raised in a defensive stance, they let out animalistic hisses and fire another volley.

BRRRAPAPOW! Impacts all around the woman, none hitting her. She slowly walks toward them. BROW, BRRAPOW! Another volley. Reflects off her blade, still none hitting her. The lizards are hesitating now, their form breaking as the woman draws closer. POW, BRR—! Their last attack is cut short, as the woman suddenly dashes forward, and is upon them. With lighting speed, and three loud POPS from her pistol, the three lizard-men collapse to the ground, dead. The entire encounter is over within a few seconds.

Keera can barely wrap their mind around what they just saw. Just a few hours earlier, they were just a normal kid going to school, planning mischievous nighttime escapades at the behest of their mother. And now? They just watched a woman single-handedly take out three heavily armed mutant lizard-men, after having recently survived a cave-in while observing a natural phenomenon that had never been properly observed before. In fact, their entire situation, while theoretically possible, had seemed statistically improbable until it happened. They have no idea what to make of this. They'll unpack it all later. Right now, they need to know where their friends and family are. They didn't see them anywhere among the various rocks and debris scattered around.

"Is it safe to come out?" Keera calls to the woman.

"Not yet," she responds.

"But I need to find my family! And my friends, they're still down there!" they protest.

"Later," she calls back, "Right now, I still need to take care of the—"

As if on cue, the ground erupts a hundred feet away. A colossal, worm-like creature, exploding out of the ground like a living skyscraper, emerges from below, sending dirt and rocks flying in all directions. The woman shields herself from the debris, while Keera ducks behind the rock again, but only for a moment. As the creature lets out an ear-shattering screech, Keera watches in horror as this strange woman does the unthinkable: she runs toward this beast.

Even with no discernable eyes, it immediately clocks the comparatively small person running in their direction. It lets out another threatening hiss, boney plates all across its exterior rippling, and its massive five-jawed maw opening wide. It rears back, and from somewhere deep inside it, a stream of yellow-green liquid fires out in a line, just missing both the woman in black and Keera's hiding spot. The liquid rips apart the earth with an acidic hiss. The monster worm lets out another frustrated bellow. Its adversary is closing in, not skipping a beat. The giant worm cocks its head back again, and this time, with shocking speed, crashes its head into the ground where the woman is standing. Keera gasps as the woman disappears in a cloud of dust and rock, the creature twisting and grinding its head, like someone's foot stamping out a cigarette. As the dust settles, Keera prepares themself to see the splattered remains of this stranger they only just met.

Yet, for the third time today, Keera could not believe what they were seeing: the woman. Holding the weight of this massive creature pressing down on her. Pushing back against a crushing force so strong it had dented the surrounding ground.

Using only her sword.

The creature pushes and grinds. Suddenly, the ground shifts under the woman. Then again. The *ground* is giving way before the woman is. And, sure enough, with explosive force, the massive worm and the woman shoot down into the earth.

The full length of the worm emerges from the first hole, and disappears down the second, revealing the creature to be at least double the length of what was seen above the surface. As the worm disappears into the ground, the holes it leaves behind fill themselves in with loose rock and rubble. The scene goes quiet again. Keera is stunned. The only sound is a faint and ominous wind blowing across the barren battlefield. Their heart is still racing. Blood pumping in their ears. Eyes wide, they dart around, looking for any sign of the worm or the woman. Certainly it must have crushed her, if not with its own weight, then by piles and piles of earth.

KABOOM! The giant tube of meat, muscle, and boney plate explodes once more from the ground, this time within a few dozen feet of Keera. They don't even look. They instinctively hit the deck. The worm blots the sun out, careening overtop of them in an arc. The head of the beast collides once more with the dirt, digging back down. Keera grips the ground, eyes wide, and the arc above them gets lower and lower. They can hear the rock behind them being ground away, sanded down as if by a blacksmith's grindstone. It gets closer and closer. Keera slams their eyes shut, bracing to be shredded into a red smear on the ground under this thing.

Then there is suddenly sunlight again. The creature is back underground. Slowly, Keera opens their eyes again, taking stock of their surroundings. They look behind them to the rock that had been their shield for this entire endeavor so far.

It's now about a foot tall.

The worm burrows out of the ground, causing Keera to flinch. Luckily, it is about sixty feet away now, and moving in the opposite direction. As it veers slightly to the right, Keera could swear they see a small dot attached near the head of the creature. Over the roar of the creature's movements, they hear a familiar but faint POP before it digs back underground in a corkscrew motion. When it emerges again, this time about a hundred feet away, Keera is certain they hear a distinctive POP POP POP of a pistol going off. *There's no way,* they think. As if to affirm their suspicions, the worm rears back and flicks it off, sending the stubborn black-clad tick flying from its form, smacking and bouncing along the dirt. A moment later, the figure stands slowly, propping themself up on their long curved blade. The woman is *still alive.*

Keera dashes closer to the action, hiding behind a different boulder about fifty feet away. This felt like a safe distance, probably. Another jet of acrid liquid fires from the creature's mouth, making Keera second guess their choice to get closer. However, it isn't aiming at them, but rather at the woman, who has recovered enough from being thrown to mount another assault. She is sprinting directly at it. Again. Keera is starting to think that, while this woman is pretty tough, she might not be the brightest. She is fast though, they'll give her that, as she dodges that incoming breath weapon attack. Then another. Then a third, the worm roaring angrily at its inability to zap this little pest. With another mighty bellow, the body of the worm ripples, and the tail end of the worm explodes out from the dust, directly under the woman in black. She is ready for this move, and preemptively leaps in such a way so that she can avoid the brunt of the impact. Instead, she latches onto the tail as it rises to meet the head. Then, using the momentum she gained from the worm's attack, she launches herself toward the roaring, open mouth of the monstrosity.

SNAP.

The five-pointed mouth of the beast slams closed, disappearing the brave woman inside it. *Holy shit,* Keera thinks, *That was... pretty dumb. Badass, but dumb.* Keera is so lost in their mind that they don't notice right away the worm, still erect high above the barren land, is scanning for something. Then it spies its quarry: Keera.

They snap out of it. A low hiss rumbles across the worm's body. Keera's eyes are like saucers. Slowly, they start backing away. The worm advances forward, slithering on the ground. Even at a leisurely pace, the beast is still faster than them. It's closing in. Keera backs up faster. It picks up speed. Keera trips and stumbles. They're now scuttling backward like a crab. The worm is DEFINITELY gaining ground now. As it bears down on her, it opens its mouth wide, ready to swallow yet another tiny morsel down its tubular gullet, when—

POP.

A light flashes from somewhere deep within the worm's throat. This interrupts its approach. Confusion.

POP POP.

The worm begins to struggle and wriggle in pain.

POP POP POP POP!

The worm thrashes desperately, all two hundred feet of it, wriggling in the dirt and dust. Gallons of thick, purple blood begin to leak out from the mouth and from between its plates. While it has ceased its attack, Keera is still unsafe, as its wild flailing still could squash her to bits. The pause gives Keera time to scramble to her feet, and sprint in the opposite direction. They don't dare look back, just run and run away from the cries of pain and the rippling impacts. Suddenly, the ground begins to fall out from under them. *Oh, come on!* They sprint harder, faster than they even thought they could, as the ground below them begins to collapse inward. Feeling themselves falling, they run up the ever-increasing incline. They see the edge, though. The part of the ground at the edge of the sinkhole. A goal. With all their might, they leap forward, arm outstretched.

They impact the ledge with one hand.

They are hanging there now, lungs on fire, arm even more so, as their grip feels like it already may fail them. Keera glances down to see multiple stories, straight down, onto a bed of jagged rubble. Tears well up in their eyes. They didn't want this. They didn't want any of this. All they wanted was to see the world. To be free. To maybe find out where they came from, where they belong. But all that they found was fear, death, and pain. Looking back up to the sky above, one they only just met minutes ago, they are shocked to see a silhouette blocking their view. The silhouette reaches down. A wet, sticky, but familiar leather gloved hand grabs them by the wrist, and yanks them up out of the pit.

Keera stumbles up and collapses to the dirt yet again. They don't like how acquainted they are getting with the floor lately. But, so far, it's been better than the alternatives.

The woman, bloodied, bruised, and covered in purple-black slime, plops down on a nearby rock. They are balancing part of their weight on their blade, wedged into the ground.

Keera just stares at the woman for a moment. Their brain is almost becoming numb to all of this. There are only so many improbable events that can happen to a person in a short period before they break. Luckily, Keera still had the wherewithal to not overthink themself into insanity.

Eventually, they manage to croak out, "Thank you."

The woman makes no eye contact with the child. They merely let out a barely audible "Mhm" of acknowledgement. The woman sheaths their sword and holsters their pistol, then sits with hands clasped, elbows on knees, staring off down into the distance. Her breathing slows to normal. Cold and in control.

Silence. Finally, some silence. Wind echoes across the barren valley. Keera uses this opportunity to relax their own breathing and assess their condition. Lots of aches and pains all over; burning skin abrasions, deep bruised muscles and aching bones, but miraculously nothing that feels unbearable or horribly wrong.

They let out a sigh of relief. The peace gives Keera the opportunity to observe what the woman and the worm had been up to behind them while they were running for their life. Stretching out before them is a massive crater, over a mile long. They are tempted to peer down in and see the mangled corpse of the monster, but they decide they've been curious enough today.

But then, a cold realization hits them: "Canary Bridge! My town, my friends and family, they were down in that cave, too. We have to see if they're alright!"

The woman looks down, her blood-soaked white hair draping over her face.

"Come on, we have to help them!" Keera repeats.

"There's nothing we can do," the woman mutters. She gestures forward.

To the pit.

Keera's heart sinks. No. No, it couldn't...

They step toward the hole. Slowly, carefully, as if that will change anything, they step to the edge and peer down. Far below, they see the bloody, serpentine form of the giant worm. It is motionless, dead. And, surrounding the body of the dead worm, is a sight that sends tears rolling down Keera's dirt-covered cheeks.

Canary Bridge. Their hometown.

Reduced to rubble.

Chapter 4

"No..." Keera breathes, "They're all..."

Behind them, the woman in black speaks, "The fight weakened the structure of the dome. There's likely nothing left."

"NO!" Keera's voice echoes out across the vast expanse of the collapsed cavern. The sheer weight of the revelation sends them to their knees. The tears are flowing like rivers now, sorrowful sobs convulsing their thin frame. Immeasurable loss, impossible to comprehend all at once, rolls over the teenager like hungry, storm-birthed waves.

The snow-haired woman stands, grabs a nearby bag that had been stashed behind a boulder, and turns to leave. Over her shoulder, she mutters, "I'm sorry."

Keera hears this and whirls around. "Wait, you're leaving?!" they exclaim.

"There's nothing else to be done," she says, not turning around or stopping, "I suggest you find some shelter before it gets dark."

Keera is still inconsolable, "You can't just... go without doing anything!"

"I said there's nothing else to be done."

Keera sits there, sobbing. That sadness turns to rage in an instant, and it explodes out of them, "YOU DID THIS! It's YOUR fault, and YOU need to fix this!"

The woman stops.

Swiftly, she stomps back to the crying child, stopping virtually on top of them. Her eyes are no longer pitying, like they were a moment ago. They are sharp, like daggers.

"This is NOT my fault," she says firmly, "Your town was attacked by the lizard-men. They used that worm to break through your defenses. I chose to stop them and save you. Don't you DARE put their blood on MY hands!"

Keera, eyes wide, is no longer crying. Fear has suppressed their urge to cry.

"Got it?!" the woman barks.

Keera nods swiftly. Satisfied, the woman turns to leave once again. As her piercing gaze leaves the teen, Keera lets their shoulders drop. They hadn't realized they were tense until then.

Letting out a quivering sigh, their predicament is now setting in. Everything they knew and cared about, for their entire life... Every person, place, or thing that held their memories... Gone. They couldn't depend on their parents, or their friends, or the town as an institution. They had no one to rely on except themselves in this brand new world that they know nothing about. And, based on what they've seen of this world so far, their prospects look bleak.

Unless...

They stand.

"Take me with you," Keera demands. Tears are still trickling down their cheek, but they are trying to appear commanding. Brow is furrowed, lips pursed, fists tightened.

The woman stops again. She glances over her shoulder for what feels like an eternity.

"No," and she keeps walking.

Keera's composure shatters. "Wait, no!" they sprint to catch up with the stranger, "Please—"

"No," she repeats.

"But I have no one! Everyone I know is..." they trail off. It's still too soon to state the truth aloud.

"You will need to figure it out yourself," the woman says.

"I've never seen the surface until, like, ten minutes ago!" Keera retorts, "How am I supposed to figure out living in a place I've never been to before?"

"You survived all that just now," she says coldly.

"That's not—" Keera stops themself with sounds of frustration and exacerbation.

This is pointless. This woman is a brick wall. Pretty soon, she's going to leave, and they will be here alone. A wave of powerless anxiety crashes into them, snatching their breath away. The tears begin to flow again, the fear and angst clenching their jaw shut.

Despite that, Keera tries one last time with a desperate, squeaking plea: "Please, I... I don't want to be alone..."

For a third time, the woman stops. Keera doesn't know if they're about to be scolded or just ignored. But instead, the woman lets out a deep, full-body sigh before saying, "Fine. I will take you—"

"Really?!" Keera perks up and darts back to the woman's side.

"Let me finish," she says, "I will take you to someone who can keep you safe."

"Other people like you?" Keera asks, "Like, I just saw you take down all those—those—"

"Lizard-men," the woman finishes.

"Yeah, lizard-men, and that—that big—"

"Wrathworm."

"Yeah! Who else could be more qualified to teach me how to survive than you?"

"Trust me, kid," the woman says, "you're in more danger with me than you would be on your own."

The way this woman calls them "kid" really pisses them off. It feels condescending. And, after going through what they just went through, they are not in the mood to be talked down to.

"My name's Keera, if you want to call me something other than 'kid,'" they protest.

"I didn't want to know that," the woman growls.

"Why not?" Keera asks.

"Didn't want to get attached," she says, "Names hold weight. If you're coming with me, you're cargo, not a friend."

Keera rolls their eyes a bit and mutters, "Damn, sorry miss dark-and-brooding."

"Radley," the woman says, "Name's Radley."

I dIdN't WaNt To KnOw ThAt, Keera thinks to themself. They almost say it, but are aware how tenuous their situation is right now. Instead, they follow Radley in silence.

Awkwardly, the two pale-haired figures walk across the flat dirt ground. The silence gives Keera time to process things in relative safety. Well, as safe as they presume they'll be for the foreseeable future. Part of them regrets leaving the ruins of their town so readily. They didn't even try to search for survivors. It's an enormous cavern. Some people might have survived, hidden in some of the sturdier buildings, like the school or the warehouses. But, even if they had stayed, what would they have been able to do? They couldn't move rubble. They couldn't dig, not through that much debris. This woman, Radley, might have been able, but she seems convinced it would be a lost cause.

Then, a dark thought creeps over Keera's mind. They hoped, for a brief moment, that there were no survivors. That they all just passed quickly and as painlessly as possible. They could only imagine what it would be like to survive, trapped in a basement or something, only to never be found. To slowly starve to death, or bleed out from a wound, waiting for help that was never coming...

Keera shook that thought from their head. Some people had to have survived. And, if a woman like Radley just *happened* across them like she claims, then there must be plenty of people like her up here, only with more hope or time or whatever, to save them.

Mom... Dad... Bri...

Keera's head drops. Their thoughts dwell on those they lost as they walk with Radley through a dead land of dust and wind.

A somber precession. A wake only they can imagine.

It is then that they feel something in their hoodie pocket. Pulling it out, they realize what it is: the leaf from the timestopped tree. It's amazing that it survived everything. But, there it was, pristine as when they had plucked it from the air out of curiosity. Keera thinks to themself, *If something as fragile as this can survive, then so can I.* A silly thought, but they need any motivation they can get to keep going. Where they are going, they're not sure. But they know they will see it through. They will survive. For their friends. For their parents. For those they've left behind.

CHAPTER 5

T HE NEXT WEEK FEELS like a lifetime to Keera. They have never done as much walking in their life. Hell, they haven't had this much space to walk this much before, either. However, the ambiance of the new world is not any more interesting than a sunless cave. In fact, for the first couple of days, it is mostly the same: dirt. Just flat, hot, boring dirt. Radley can always find places for them to spend the night, away from the bone-piercing winds that rip across the planes. That doesn't help with the ambient cold, though. They only have the bare minimum of supplies they had brought with them into the cave on that fateful night: the flashlight, a reusable bottle of water, a granola bar, and some random school supplies they had left in their backpack from school the day before. Helpful, but not a survival kit by any means. Their hoodie does little to retain heat out in the elements. Radley, for understandable reasons, is more prepared, and luckily can share a blanket with the child. Still, the cold hard floor keeps their sleep restless. They miss their bed.

The days are even worse. Their guide insists they move toward these mountains in the far distance. According to her, the sooner they cross those, the sooner they'll be away from the harsh sun. And what a harsh sun it is. Keera was not new to UV radiation, as the architects of Canary Bridge had thought about that ahead of time. The simulated daylight not only served to keep the town's circadian rhythm consistent but also to help raise crops, and provide the townspeople with as many benefits of sunlight that can be produced artificially. That being said, Keera still arrived in this new world pallid, something the *actual* sun seemed to take umbrage with. Even after wrapping their hoodie around their head during the day, and attempting to hide in Radley's shadow to avoid direct sunlight, the teenager *still* winds up burning by the end of day one. And day two isn't much better. Sunburn, along with most things they're experiencing for the first time on the surface, sucks.

Reaching the mountains switches things up a bit, but not in a wholly positive way. As they near the natural superstructures, Keera is in awe. They, of course, have read about mountains in books in the town library, but even the most high-resolution photos and detailed descriptions can't do the real things justice. Towering spines of stone rising high, with caps of snow that appear like a passing cloud painted them white. And, according to Radley, these aren't even the *biggest* mountains out there! They can't fathom the idea and wish they could see *those* mountains. But, as the duo begins their ascent, Keera quickly becomes thankful these mountains are on the smaller side. They are pretty at a distance, sure, but walking their way along the narrow paths and through claustrophobic crevices just makes it apparent to Keera that mountains are just deserts with more verticality and more treacherous falls. For the first few days, it didn't even feel like they were climbing that high. It just felt like a really big hill. But, around day five, they come across a thin ledge, requiring them to practically hug the wall for what feels like too long. Keera then makes the mistake of looking down, seeing the drop, well over a hundred feet. Way higher than any ledge Keera had traversed in Canary. From then on, even though the trail had widened, the awareness of how high up they were never left Keera's mind.

Around day seven, the duo comes across yet another environment: wedged in a valley between the peaks, a verdant forest blooms. The trees are of a variety Keera has not seen before. It's unlike the forest they had dreamed of the week prior, but that's because it is unlike anything they could've imagined. And, even better, they're finally headed downhill! The elation of this discovery is almost too much for the overtired teen to handle. And so, the duo descends.

The trees don't disappoint: much like the mountains and the giant worm, the true scale of these conifers doesn't hit them until they are up close and personal. Dwarfing even the timestop tree, but not nearly as voluminous, the tall rods of bark and needle radiate out in all directions. Looking horizontally instead of vertically, rolling and uneven terrain, as well as dense patches of ferns, chokes the horizon. A layer of moss on all surfaces. With a great deal of the sunlight obscured by the fronds above, the temperature in this valley is considerably lower. The humidity is higher, though, and a perpetual mist persists, glittering dew bedazzling leaves. Stepping down into this forested valley feels like stepping into yet another alien world for Keera.

Radley mentions that there should be a stream nearby. Soon enough, they come across a small clearing with a babbling brook wandering through it. The two dismount their packs, and get to refilling their respective water containers, and bellies, with crisp mountain spring water. For the entire journey so far, the conversation has remained rather sparse. Keera could tell Radley wasn't much of a socializer.

So, Keera decides this was their moment to try to break the ice: "So, you seem to know a lot about this... survival stuff."

Silence. The woman is re-filling her water bottle.

Keera clears their throat awkwardly, fidgeting as they respond, "Because, like, you knew there was water here before we saw it."

"Could smell it on the air," she responds.

Keera was not expecting an answer. Seizing the opportunity for a conversation, they respond with another question: "So, have you been doing this for a while, then?"

"Doing what? Surviving?"

Keera, feeling sheepish, concedes, "Actually, yeah, that's a good point." Awkward silence claims the space. Keera, determined to learn though, breaks it once more, "What exactly do you DO? Apart from surviving."

No response. Keera presses some more, "Because, like, someone just surviving doesn't need all the weapons you have, right? Like, a gun *and* a sword?"

Radley pauses, actually glancing at Keera over their shoulder, before returning to clean some supplies. "I'm a mercenary," they mutter.

This term is a new one to Keera. They ask, "What do mercenaries do?"

"I fight other people's battles for them," she responds, "Get my hands dirty, so they don't have to."

"Is that why you were at my town, then?"

"No," she says, "I've been headed somewhere for a while now. Saw the lizard-men digging for something in the dirt. Figured they were up to no good."

"How did you know that?"

"They usually are. Greedy, violent bullies who sack small communities like yours for resources; Food, weapons, goods they can sell off." She pauses, then adds with disdain, "Slaves."

Keera shifts a bit. They knew Canary hadn't had much in the way of goods. They had some food, some basic gadgets and creature-comforts, but that's it. That being said, they were a large community... They shudder.

"Well, for what it's worth, I'm glad you came along when you did," they say finally, "That worm was no joke."

"Yeah..." Radley trails off.

Keera senses the hesitation. "What is it?" they ask.

"Lizard-men don't usually deploy such a powerful resource like a wrathworm just to sack a community."

"What could that mean?"

"I'm not sure," Radley says, "They're dead, so it doesn't really matter, though."

"Oh, it certainly does matter to someone, my dear," a deep, humming voice emanates from the tree line.

Radley springs to attention, a hand on both the pistol and katana at her hips. "Who's there?" she growls.

Keera freezes. The voice is coming from a figure lying casually on a low branch in a nearby oak tree. The shade from the tree is obscuring their face, but their silhouette is long, slender, and masculine.

As they are addressed, the figure slowly rises to a sitting position. A raven, perched on a branch close to them, departs with a caw. "Someone representing the interests of people who don't like what you've done," they respond to Radley. They then hop down from the branch, causing the mercenary to draw her weapons, "You pissed off some pretty powerful people, Radley of The Wastes."

Keera can swear she sees their eyes glowing yellow from the shadows. Those flecks of gold suddenly flick to Keera, sending a chill throughout the child's entire body. "Interesting," they muse, their voice low and smooth, "No one said anything about a child being involved."

"She has nothing to do with this," Radley bites back, "Leave her out of it."

"I shall, unless she tries to intervene," he says. It is then that the figure strides into the light, revealing his features: straight black hair that barely reaches his shoulders, skin like that of rugged porcelain, and a chiseled, stubble-clad chin. He is wearing an open black leather duster with a popped asymmetrical collar. Underneath, he has no shirt, and instead is showing off toned pecs and a smooth six-pack. To round it out, he's wearing black jeans and pointed black cowboy boots. Two sheathed weapons sit on his hips, his hands resting on each.

Radley turns to Keera. "Go," she growls.

This snaps Keera out of it. Their wide eyes dart around the clearing behind them, searching for a place to take cover. Spying a good sized pine tree, they opt for that, and book it.

"Yes, run along, little lamb," the man calls after them. Then, addressing Radley again, they declare, "This is grown-up business."

Keera reaches the tree before spinning back around to see two warriors holding their ground. Radley is visibly ready for a fight. Nevertheless, the stranger is keeping their cool. They clearly feel they are in control of the situation, and offer, "I would advise you to lay down your arms. I would like to take you in alive, but your bounty does also allow for death."

"Who posted the hit, the lizards?" Radley demands, clearly unphased by this man's nonchalance.

"Heh," he chuckles, "Those scaly skinned thugs wouldn't have the scratch to post bounties *I'd* be after. No, the ones who hired the lizards also requested my services."

"Now I know you're full of shit," Radley retorts, "Lizard-men gangs don't work for anyone but themselves."

"You clearly haven't met Vertex, then. That enterprising iguana is always looking for a new benefactor to help him get a leg up over the other gangs," the man says.

Radley pauses, before spitting back, "I don't care who you work for. I have places to be. Find a different bounty to chase, or this will be your last gig."

The man chuckles again at her threat, then unsheathes his two curved guardless sabers. "I'd love to see you try and kill me."

In an instant, the man is upon Radley, the creek between them barely rippling as he dashes over it. Blades clash and flash in the sunlight. He pushes in, but her blade blocks, holding strong, and she unloads a shot from her pistol into his gut. This sends him stumbling back, but he remains standing, blood oozing from the wound.

"You're fast," he breathes, pushing back some hair from his face, "This'll be interesting."

He lunges forward again, his dual bladed technique requiring Radley to block and dodge at the same time. She tries to fire off a couple more rounds, but his proximity causes the shots to go wide. The barrage is unrelenting, forcing Radley back toward the tree line. Realizing this, the mercenary attempts to pivot to keep the fight in the clearing, blocking and twisting his blade to the side. This works, but at a cost; the man's second blade catches her in the flank. She winces, but holds her composure.

"Not fast enough," the man taunts. Then, in a fluid motion, he raises the bloodied blade to his lips, and swipes his tongue across it, licking the blood. He smiles and says, "Now that I have a taste, I'm not stopping until I have the rest."

The man lunges again, this time with more ferocity. The woman doesn't have time to shift to the offensive. Keera knows Radley is strong, but this man is giving her trouble. They're not sure if it's the fresh deep wound, or if this man is just really that powerful, but they can see her buckling under the weight of his blows.

The fight is now headed Keera's way. Before they can react, a careless wide swing from the man sends one of his blades slicing toward them. They dive out of the way; the sword cleaving halfway through the wood. While leaving Keera exposed, this gives Radley an opening: BAM BAM BAM! Three shots fired into the man's arm that was attempting to retrieve his blade. He reels, groaning in pain, three new bloody holes in his arm. He looks to his wounds, then to Radley, a new wild rage in his eyes.

"You BITCH!" he shouts, and rips his blade free from the tree, slashing at her again. The man's wounds barely seem to slow him down, as more and more of his attacks are landing now. Cut after nick after slice connects, and the man laps up more and more of Radley's blood from his blades. Slash, lick, cut, lick. It's fluid, seamless, and ferocious. With each cut, it seems like his animalistic assault is growing more and more powerful. Certainly, he could end the fight at any point now. It's almost as if he's intentionally drawing this out. Enjoying the fight. Savoring it.

Radley is stumbling back toward Keera again, becoming visibly weaker from all the slashes. The teen scampers out of the way to avoid being tripped over. As they do, though, they see a small golden object go tumbling out of their pocket. It's the leaf. Instinctively, Keera dives to save it. This move, however, doesn't remove them from the path of the duel. Radley stumbles over Keera's boot, sending her crashing to the ground. Clutching the stupid little trinket, Keera whirls around, fear and shame flooding over them all at once.

The man looms over the two of them. He glances at Keera. This close, Keera can tell that his appearance has changed since the start of the fight: cat-like pupils flash hungrily, and his hair has turned from black to a deep crimson. With a wide smile, he says to Keera, "Thanks for the help, kid. Maybe I'll make your death quick. Unlike hers..."

He then plunges his two blades into Radley's shoulders. The swordswoman lets out a scream of agony.

Keera shuts their eyes, unable to bear seeing the carnage. They grip the leaf in their hand so tight; they swear they feel it drawing blood.

Opening their eyes again, Keera sees the bloodthirsty man lean in close to Radley's face, the woman gritting her teeth through the pain. "It really is a shame," he muses, "You were worth more alive."

He stands off balance for a brief moment, as if exhausted or perhaps inebriated. Whatever all this blood is doing to him, he seems more unhinged than when he first appeared. Radley is too defeated at the moment to react. He yanks one of his blades from her, inducing another scream. "But, now at least this way..." he says, raising the blade back in a swinging motion, aiming for her neck, "I can drink my fill."

Keera squeezes their eyes shut.

His blade comes down.

Keera's eyes open.

They look around, confused. Something just happened, like the world skipped a bit. They look back to the confrontation happening a few feet from them. The man was once again crouched over Radley. Thinking he was true to his promise and was drinking the rest of her blood, Keera has to do a double-take when they see the woman still moving.

She's still alive.

Then, they hear the man utter those words again, "It really is a shame. You were worth more alive."

This isn't possible. Keera just saw this. They just heard him say that. They just saw him—

No time to think.

As the man groggily stands, they shout, "RADLEY, HIT HIM, NOW!"

Radley's eyes shoot to the teen, then the man's left leg, then BAM!

The man, caught unawares, is sent tumbling to his knees. Before he can react, Radley rips his blade from her own shoulder, and smashes him in the temple with the pommel. He falls flat on his back in a daze. Radley tries to move, but the second blade is sticking her firmly in place.

Keera knows he won't stay down for long, not from how well he's taken gunshot wounds so far. *Think, think.* They search their surroundings, trying to find anything that would help.

The tree! The tree that was virtually chopped in half. It was the best shot they had. Quickly, Keera stumbles to their feet and sprints behind the trunk. They position it between them and the man. Peeking around, they try to gauge what angle to push it from. Their head is buzzing like mad. *Snap out of it!* they think, but it doesn't help. Their vision is blurry, almost like they're seeing double.

Wait. They *are* seeing double. Of the tree. One they feel with their fingertips, while the other, almost spectral in appearance, is falling toward the man. A perfect shot. Only Radley is in the way, too. They don't understand, but at the moment, can't question it.

They can't risk it. "Move, Radley!" the teen cries.

Radley doubles her efforts, the man next to her beginning to stir. With a wild cry of pain and determination, the woman yanks the man's second blade from her body and, in a fluid motion, dives out of the way.

Keera shoves the tree with all their might.

And it falls.

CRASH!

The assailant lets out a searing yell, the pine landing squarely across his abdomen. The man wriggles and writhes, desperately trying to move the heavy column of wood, to no avail. Radley and Keera, both out of breath, take a moment and glance at each other across the clearing. Neither can believe what just happened, but their looks convey an unspoken agreement of "we'll talk about this later." For now, the two make their way over to the bounty hunter.

Radley levels her gun at his head. "Who set the bounty," she commands.

Through gritted teeth, he responds, "Manhattan Gate!"

This sends a brief wave of confusion and fear across Radley's face. "Why?" she barks, "What do they want with me?"

"I have no idea," he responds, "I just take bounties, don't ask questions."

Radley mutters to herself, "Attacking some random town? Sending lizard-men instead of their own troops? None of this makes sense..."

"Well, you better figure it out soon," the man retorts, seeming to have given up struggling, as blood drips from his mouth, "Because they're not going to stop. And neither am I. I'll get your bounty, Radley of the Wastes. And you," He looks to Keera, "You're... something else. Keep this up, little fox, and it's only a matter of time before your bounty comes my way, too."

"Yeah, we'll see about that." Radley says. Then fires.

Moments before the bullet makes contact, a flurry of black and feathers explodes from the man's prone body. Keera and Radley flinch, shielding their eyes from beaks and talons, as a swarm of ravens flies past them, up into the sky. Uncovering their eyes, the two realize the man is gone, without a trace, only a small pool of blood where he once lied.

"Fucking daywalkers," Radley spits, kicking the fallen tree, only to send herself wincing in pain at her wounds.

"What?" Keera questions.

"Daywalkers. They're lesser vampires that are active during the day, hurt by moonlight." Radley explains as she hobbles over to her bag by the creek again.

"Huh," Keera nods, processing the new info. Then they do a mental double-take. "Wait, vampires are *real* up here?!" they exclaim.

"Have been for a while," Radley says. She has produced medical supplies from her pack and is treating her wounds. She continues, "Came through in one of the breaches."

Keera slumps down against the fallen tree, knees to their chest, head in their hands. "What the fuck..." they whisper to themself. They instinctively tense up a bit after they swear, but after there is no reaction from their guardian, they remember where they are, and return to ruminating.

They look over at the woman. Even from this far away, they can see that the fresh bandages are already soaked with blood. They ask, "Are you going to be ok?"

"I'll be fine," Radley says, focusing on her work, "I heal better than most."

"Alright," they nod. Then, tentatively, they ask, "Are you, like... a daywalker too, or something?"

Radley scoffs, "No. It's complicated."

"Okay," Keera says. They let it go for now. Besides, there are more relevant questions they need to ask. Like: "What's 'Manhattan Gate?'"

"Bad people," she responds.

"Okay, but what do they want with you, or Canary Bridge?" Keera responds, "They destroyed my home, came after you, and I'm with you, so I'm *clearly* in danger, too, so—"

"That's why I said you need to get away from me. As soon as possible," Radley interrupts, "It's for your own good."

Keera is fuming inside. They have felt this feeling before; of not necessarily being lied to, but of information being withheld from them. "For their own good." They hated that. That frustration finally boils over.

"I'm not some helpless kid, okay?" they assert, "Just because I'm new out here, doesn't mean I can't contribute. I can help you if you let me. Hell, if it wasn't for me, you would be dead and sucked dry right now!"

"Yeah, about that: how did you know when he was vulnerable like that?" she says, shifting the conversation, "You warned me almost before it happened. How did you do that?"

"I..." Keera is surprised, "I don't know. It was like... I saw you. Saw *him* kill you. But then, it's like... my mind snapped back in time, and I was able to warn you."

"Same thing with the tree?" she asks. Her gaze is locked on Keera intently for the first time in a week.

"More or less," Keera shrugs a bit.

"Hm…" Radley turns back around. She's still for a moment, before she starts packing her bag up again. "We have to keep moving," she says, "That daywalker was hurt pretty bad, but he'll recover. We don't want to be in the same place when he does."

"I've never done anything like that before, *seen* anything like that. What happened to me?" Keera persists.

Radley shrugs, "No idea. You know as much as I do." And she starts walking.

That sentiment almost scares Keera more than anything they've experienced in the last week. They faced death twice already, but at least they had an idea what that meant. But these… visions they just had… Not even the grizzled veteran of the surface world has an idea what they just witnessed. As they continue on, Keera's mind stays with these events. What could this mean? Hopefully, they can find someone with answers, the sooner the better.

Chapter 6

Keera is restless. Even though conditions have been objectively more comfortable lately, they still find themselves unable to sleep. It's not for fear of being jumped by the daywalker again, either. Radley assured them that they would not come for them in their sleep. The new moon wasn't for another week, so they still had a sliver of moonlight protecting them from being caught unawares. No, it's not a fear of any external horror they've experienced within this short period.

Every time they close their eyes, they're worried about what they will see when they open them again. They're worried that all of this has been just one big dream. Or premonition? Whatever it was they had experienced during the fight with the bounty hunter. What if they open their eyes, and they're in their bed a few weeks ago... What then? Sure, they would be home safe and sound again, and their family and friends would all be okay. But, does that mean everything that they saw *will* come to pass, and only they alone know it? Would it be up to them to prevent this horrible future from happening? How are they supposed to trust that anything they experience is real anymore, after an experience like that? It's all worse than any nightmare.

While these thoughts keep them up at night, during the day, their mind races with curiosity and determination. Much like how a scary film is less scary in the light, so too are their current circumstances. They want to understand things, to master things, and to learn how it works, so that it will not seem so scary when night takes hold again. If Keera's mother taught her anything, it was that knowledge is power. And, right now, Keera is starting to feel sick of being powerless.

While walking through the dense forest, mist hanging low and thick like bathhouse steam, Keera decides it is time. Perhaps they have committed to exactly what they wanted to say, having rehearsed it so many times. Or perhaps it was simply the plethora of thoughts clogging their mind that demanded a release. Either way, today is the day:

"Radley," they begin carefully, "I want to learn how to fight like you."

"No."

Shot down, immediately. By now, Keera *should* be used to their guide's bluntness. But, somehow, it almost always takes them by surprise. So, it takes them a moment to recover from the harsh rejection, before they build up the courage to press the issue.

"Please?"

"No."

Now why would that have worked? they think to themself.

"If you're going to be dumping me off in the middle of nowhere here at some point, shouldn't I at least be taught the basics to keep myself safe?"

"What I do isn't just basic self defense," Radley explains, "And besides, you aren't being left in the middle of nowhere. You're being left with someone I trust."

This was news to them. Regardless, they can't let up now. "Yeah, but *I* don't know them," Keera continues, "Are they as strong as you?"

"Not strong, but—"

"So, what if the lizard-men come back? Or that other guy?"

Radley sighs and stops. "If I teach you something, will that shut you up?" she asks.

"Yes," they reply emphatically, "I don't want to always have to run and hide whenever something tries to kill me."

Radley drops her pack and turns to face the teen. "First technique:" she says, "Run. Second: Hide." Keera groans and rolls their eyes. "I'm serious," Radley continues, "The best way to stay safe out here is to run. Run wherever, however far you have to in order to escape. And, if that isn't an option, then hide. You're small, you can fit places most things trying to kill you can't. Be quiet, be fast, avoid sightlines, and blend in with the environment whenever you can."

"Okay, but what if none of that works?" Keera questions.

"Then," Radley says, unloading the magazine from her gun and popping the round from the chamber. She then levels the gun at the child's head, continuing, "You fight."

"How do I—"

Radley pulls the trigger. *Click.* "You're dead," she says.

"Okay, but you didn't—"

Click. "Dead again."

"You haven't taught me what to—"

Click. "You better figure it out, or I'll just keep killing you."

With frustration building, Keera moves to punch Radley in the face. But, before they even get close to connecting, they hear the telltale *click* from the gun.

"Too big of movements, and too obvious. You need to come at them from an angle they don't expect," the mercenary explains, "Think, what is your goal in this fight?"

"Beat the other guy?" Keera replies.

"No, your goal is to not get shot. So, go after the gun, not me."

Keera thinks about this for a moment. This isn't what they had in mind, but if they play along, maybe they'll get to learn some *real* fighting moves once this is over.

This time, the teen swipes at the gun from the side, gripping the barrel. They grip tight, and try to pull it from Radley's grip.

Click.

They look down, and the gun is pointed directly at their chest.

"You'll never win a tug of war," Radley instructs, "Not with your scrawny arms."

"Hey!" Keera reacts, releasing the gun and getting back in position.

"Get out of the way of the gun, or get the gun pointed away from you."

Keera furrows their brow. This would be so much simpler if she just told them what to do. They huff and inspect their mock assailant's pose. Pulling doesn't help. Maybe...

They rush in, sweep from the side, but this time shove the gun to the left, pointing it away from them.

"Good, both hands," Radley instructs. Keera slaps their other hand near the rear sight, toward the back of the gun. To their surprise, they feel Radley's control over the weapon waning. "Now, keep twisting away, get it out of my hand," Radley continues.

Keera keeps twisting until suddenly *they* are the one holding the weapon. They follow through on the motion, spinning to a pace away, and level the gun at their teacher.

Click. "You're dead," they say, a smirk on their face.

"Good start," she responds. She goes for her bag and starts putting it back on.

"That's it?" Keera exclaims.

"For now," Radley says, "You picked that up quick, though. Maybe you'll be able to take that gun from me while I'm actually using some of my strength."

Keera sighs. "At least let me like, try shooting this thing or something, do some target practice," Keera says, aiming down the sights, pretending to be lining up a shot at imaginary targets. Radley snatches the gun from their hands. "Hey!" they protest.

"Too loud, would draw too much attention." She loads and holsters the weapon again on her belt. "Besides," she continues, "If she takes you in, Lady Adley will make sure you know how to fire a weapon."

"Is that who you plan on dumping me with?" Keera responds, a hint of attitude left in their voice.

Radley, clearly done entertaining this, simply nods and starts walking again.

Keera, realizing they're finally close to some more answers, shifts their tone to be less hostile and asks, "Is she like you? A mercenary, I mean."

"No."

"Then what is she?"

"A hotel manager."

Keera reels at this. "Why would a hotel manager teach me how to shoot a gun?" they ask.

"Because she's not just a hotel manager," she responds.

Strategy failed. Their attitude comes back, "You know, you're *really* hard to hold a conversation with."

"This feels more like an interrogation than a conversation."

"Well, that's because it is!" Keera explodes, "Like, I don't know anything! I don't know how to fight, how to survive, who a 'Lady Adley' is, what a 'Manhattan Gate' is, nothing! And it would sure be nice if you would just explain these things to me, instead of giving me these cryptic fucking one-liners!"

Radley whirls around, finger jammed in Keera's face, intensity in her eyes. "Look, kid," she hisses, "I don't know what you think I am. But I'm not your mom, I'm not your teacher, I'm not you chaperone. I'm just here to make sure you don't die long enough so that I can hand you off to someone who has the time and patience to put up with your endless fucking questions. So, please, do us both a favor: be quiet, do what I say, and without any more questions. Got it?"

Keera is shellshocked. They cannot respond. Just stare deep into the woman's dark, furious eyes. Taking that as an understanding, Radley turns and continues on walking.

The rest of the trek through the forest between the mountains is silent.

Chapter 7

Pretty soon, the wide, verdant valley begins to narrow, until plants have little room to grow, and the forest gives way to gravel and stone yet again. Breaking from the horizon-choking foliage, they are once again approaching another mountain. As Keera realizes this, every ache in their muscles and bones intensifies tenfold. They feel the weight of their exhaustion press on them like a ton of bricks. They can't help but let out a groan. *I am so done with mountains.*

This noise is the first one they've made in a few days, so they were fully expecting Radley to whirl on them again and chew them out for it. But the stoic warrior continues her march toward some unknown destination. This seems like a good sign. Maybe she's calmed down from their little spat the other day, and might be amicable to more questions, or perhaps even training. Keera knew better now, though, than to just waste their guide's precious patience on fleeting musings or minor things. They need to think about this, consider what is most vital they learn from this miraculous stranger, before their time with her is cut short.

By the time the two begin their ascent toward the first of many cliff faces, the sun has already set, and the sky has become a slowly fading canvas of reds, oranges, and pinks. That is something Keera hasn't quite gotten over yet, just how beautiful the sky is. Underground, the manufactured sun didn't produce anything nearly as interesting when it was setting. Rather, it just slowly faded from on to off. No artistry, no theatrics, just dimming into nothingness. So, early mornings and late evenings have become Keera's favorite times to look up at the sky and try to clear their head. Oftentimes, there are clouds present — they seem to hang like a perpetual shroud over the sky up here — which only serves to enhance and refract the warm light into an even more exquisite tapestry.

Unfortunately, today, Keera's mind is too preoccupied with their own thoughts to appreciate the light show nature has for them today. Their eyes are instead focused on something through the floor, as they are going over what is most important for them to know going forward. Should they ask more about Radley? They doubt she'd give up any more information, would be a wasted effort. Maybe ask for some more training? They may not learn to use a gun from her, but maybe she would teach them to use a sword? Probably not. At best, they'd get a few more self defense lessons in. Who Manhattan Gate is might be important. But, no, if they're splitting up, they may never have to worry about that organization again. Hopefully. This process continues as they begin the setting up camp ritual they've done for over a week now. It's becoming muscle memory at this point: taking off their pack, checking supplies, finding a place to bed down, helping Radley find kindling. They are so in their head that they almost miss the yawning cave mouth in the rock face a few yards away. Almost.

Their attention is suddenly drawn to the black shape in the corner of their eye. They are used to that being Radley, but this one was quite a bit bigger. The mouth is roughly the size of a three-story townhouse, wider than the last cave Keera encountered. It is similar to said previous cavern as well, though; the precise curve of the cave's arch, as well as solid geometric shapes that can be seen just within the entrance, indicate it was probably man made. That fact, coupled with how far away it is from any other sign of civilization, gives Keera goosebumps.

The curiosity once again gets the better of them. "Are we sleeping in there tonight?" Keera asks, gesturing to the cave.

"No," Radley responds, with what at this point feels like her catchphrase, "That tunnel runs under the mountain. Too much risk of being attacked from both sides."

"Oh," Keera responds, "Are we going in there tomorrow?"

"No," she says again, "Too risky. We'll go up and over. Brezio City is just on the other side."

Keera presumes that is where this Lady Adley is, and doesn't bother asking for clarification. They do ask, however, "How long will that take?"

"About two or three days, if the weather holds."

"Wait, a few days?! Isn't the new moon supposed to be sooner than that?"

Radley doesn't respond.

"Come on, it has to be faster than three days if we go through there," Keera insists.

"Like I said, too risky. Out here, we can see things coming in all directions. In there, we are a lot more limited. If that daywalker comes, I'd rather do it out here," she reasons.

"But you won't HAVE to fight him at all if we take a quicker route," Keera persists.

Radley shoots a glance at Keera. "What did I say about doing what you're told?" she growls.

That was it. They burned up all of her patience by asking about a stupid fucking tunnel. *Nice job, idiot,* Keera thinks to themself. In a huff, Keera plops onto their blanket. Feeling drained and defeated, they arrange their pack as a pillow, crawl under the covers, and lie facing away from Radley and the fire. They stare into the ominous tunnel. *This is stupid,* they think. Trying to talk to this woman feels like talking to one of these damned cliffs. She was being a bit more forthright with information, which was nice. But she still refuses to seriously consider any of Keera's ideas. Yeah, Keera is new to all this, but if they were going to be in this together, it needed to be an equal partnership. Feeling unheard and unvalued like this causes some sort of angry fire in their gut to flare up, just like it did with their father days ago.

As the purples in the sky fade to black — the only lights are from the faint crescent of the moon above, and the dancing firelight from their campfire — Keera can feel that inner fire continues to burn. They can't take their eyes from the hole in the rock. A cold night wind blows from the maw of the tunnel, but this does little to deter Keera's focus. They don't know if they both can survive another encounter with that vampire. Radley thinks so, but Keera remembers just how close she came, how close they *both* came, to being bled dry. Certainly, nothing in that tunnel could be more deadly than him, right? They hated this feeling of being trapped by someone else's decisions.

Unless... Keera's mind feels itself working toward a solution. *She's going to abandon me, anyway. She clearly doesn't want me or need me around. And, I'm my own person, I can make my own decisions. So... What if I make everyone's life easier, and go through the tunnel on my own?* This feels right. This way, they can get to this city faster, they can avoid seeing that vampire again, and Radley doesn't have to cross the mountains at all. She doesn't have to worry about them anymore. Besides, they have to learn to defend themself at some point, anyway. What better time than now?

All these reasons and justifications begin to solidify in the child's mind. Whether they are sound or not, they have made up their mind. They are taking that tunnel. Tonight.

***

A few hours pass. They aren't sure exactly when Radley falls asleep on a given night, as they are usually out well before her. So, they do their best to monitor the sounds coming from behind them, all the while the dancing lights of the fire on the rock wall threaten to lull them to sleep. Keera is determined, though, and keeps focused on their singular goal, one that drove them to explore the abandoned mine: independence.

Over the past few days, they've gotten to appreciate Radley. She can be cold and stoic, but there is a level of confidence that exudes from her as well. Plus, it certainly does make Keera feel safer knowing they're with a woman who can take down a colossal death-worm with just a sword and a pistol. All that said, they know their time together is up. They can't stay here, beholden to someone else's decision making anymore. They need to be free. There is an entire world to explore. The time is now.

Peering back over their shoulder, they see the warrior leaned up against a tree stump. Vigilant, even in sleep. The teen watches her for a while, making sure her breathing is slow and calm. Then, when they are confident she's not just resting her eyes, they slowly, quietly stand, and collect their belongings. Even though their shifting and lifting causes a few noises, eliciting terrifying shifts from the lady in question, Radley does not wake. Almost home free, Keera slowly steps away from the campsite, toward the beckoning tunnel. They've had some practice at this, sneaking out multiple nights to hang out with Bri, but never in this environment. Nonetheless, it works; they are successfully far enough away from the camp where they can let their guard down.

Standing at the mouth of the tunnel, a familiar unease rolls over them. This scenario seems entirely too familiar. Remembering just what the previous one led to, they can't help but give one last look over their shoulder at the camp. What if they are being foolish? What if they make a mistake again and get themselves, or worse, someone else hurt in the process? Maybe they should go back... *No,* they think. That fire in their belly flares up again, and they shrug off the anxiety. They can't keep living a life based on what others think is best. Not anymore.

"Thanks for the help, Radley," Keera whispers, "I've got this from here."

And, with that, the teen enters the dark tunnel, a chilly wind blowing. Calling them into its depths.

***

It is uncanny to Keera just how similar this tunnel feels to the abandoned mine. A long, straight, carved tube of rock, stretching on further than their flashlight beam can reach. The only sound, apart from their footsteps, is the occasional drip of some water somewhere down the tunnel. The hollow wind cutting through them is the only difference. That is a good sign, at least. From what they understand, airflow means an exit. Which is better than the mine, where they had no inkling of the outside world until they reached the tree.

The thought of the tree causes them to shove their hand in their pocket, and grip the leaf tight. Its rigidity and consistent tactility have made it something of a fetish object to the teen. A familiar shape, one that reminds them of home, while still grounding them in the here and now, they fear the thought of ever losing it. Then, they would have nothing sentimental left from Canary Bridge except their memories, which are impermanent and could fade in time.

Keera shakes their head. Focus. Radley said this path was dangerous. And, just because *they* think it is less dangerous than taking the high road, doesn't mean they should let their guard down.

They march on, deeper and deeper into the tunnel, until they are well enough in where they can no longer see the entrance from which they came. *Better not get turned around,* they thought. Would be frustrating and a waste of time to find themselves back at the campsite, face-to-face with a pissed-off Radley. It should be pretty hard to get turned around in a two-way tunnel, though, they reason.

This walking continues for miles. Keera has a feeling it's been a few hours, but there is really no way to know for sure. Every so often, they pass the skeleton of an abandoned car, betraying this as once being a traffic tunnel. This must have been a while ago, as the entrance Keera had used to get here clearly was not attached to any road. Of course, these vehicles were nowhere near functional, with windows missing, tires long disintegrated, and everything covered in scaly red rust. Some seats inside still looked mildly comfortable, and it is then that their body reminds them that they are missing sleep for this rebellion. The fatigue of walking all day prior, with only a few hours of rest and no sleep, all begin to pile up on them, until they are less confidently marching to the beat of their own drum. It's more like a tired shuffle. Their eyes are getting heavy, and with the darkness all around, broken only by their solitary flashlight, they could easily fall asleep if they were to stop and rest now.

The thing is, they aren't sure how far they are going to be walking. They knew it would be less than two days, but that means it could still be as long as a full day. This thought had not crossed Keera's mind until now. And that thought brought back that unease once again. Keera is certainly used to being underground for long stretches of time. But alone? In the dark? Maybe they should turn back...

It's then that they hear a noise. It sounds like it was from up ahead, but it is hard to tell with how the sound echoes here. All they know is it was a distinct, wet *plop*, like something heavy falling into a puddle. They freeze, unsure of what to do. Hesitantly, the teen advances forward. Then, they hear several lighter, but equally wet, *slap slap slap*ping sounds. Keera is certain they are coming from up ahead now. Their body is shaking, partially from exhaustion, and partially from fear and anticipation of what could be down here with them. Pretty soon, a couple shapes fade into view on the fringe of their flashlight beam. The bigger of the two is another wrecked car, up against the left wall of the tunnel. The other object, about three feet high, is a round, amorphous mass in the center of the road. Neither are moving.

Assuming the car is like every other the teen has passed, they focus their attention on the blob. As they approach with caution, it becomes clear the object is a deep green, like an unwell grape or a ripe booger. Its surface appears wet in the light, and some of said light can penetrate the object, revealing it to be translucent. As they enter within a few feet, a strong sour odor hits Keera in the nose. They plug their nose in disgust. *What the hell...* They dare not get closer, but they continue inspecting the object from a distance. With the light penetrating the mass like it is, Keera is just able to make out a round, basketball-size object near its center-mass. They can't make out any more details without getting closer, and they have no desire to do that with the smell. Whatever it is, it's wet, it's gross, smells like vomit, and is...

Moving?

They swear they just saw it quiver a bit. Like gelatin being given a light tap. Curiosity is starting to overpower caution again.

"What the...?" they murmur. They lean in, trying desperately to see what that thing inside could be...

And then it turns.

A blood red eye, with a pupil the size for their fist, looks back at them.

The shock of the sudden movement sends Keera shooting backward, tripping over their own feet. They fall flat on their ass, barely stopping themself from smacking their head on the pavement. Wincing from the pain, they look down the length of their body to see the gelatinous mass sliding toward them. Eyes wide with panic, the teen scrambles backward frantically. They are just barely faster than this thing while crawling; they could get away if they just had a moment to stand.

Suddenly, the green glob shoots a part of its form as a projectile. An orange-sized piece of green goop arcs through the air and lands directly on the teen's ankle. It burns like hell. Letting out a shout of surprise and pain, the teen attempts to kick the glob off, but it's adhered like molten metal. Instead, they can feel this ball of burning snot anchor itself to the cement ground. They are stuck, helpless, as the rest of this blob monster slowly slides its way closer to them. Even worse, *they* seem to be moving closer to *it*. The snot ball on their ankle begins scraping them across the wet pavement. Keera scrapes and claws at the ground in desperation, trying to find anything to stop them from being dragged closer to this monster. But there's nothing. Screaming and crying, the child's ankle is pulled into the rest of the gelatinous mass that is now on top of them. The searing pain and sizzle sounds intensify, their leg being sucked further and further into this creature.

They cry out, tears flowing down their cheeks. It all went so wrong, so fast. How were they supposed to be prepared for a living blob-monster made of acid? Radley could have told them, could've been more clear. But no, no, they got themselves into this. The flame inside Keera burns hotter and brighter than ever before. It has found an alternative fuel source; instead of being fueled by angst and rebellion, it is now fueled by rage. Rage, and the instinct to survive.

The cries of agony turn to cries of anger as they look down at this thing slowly consuming their leg. It was almost to their knee now. They have a precious few seconds to react. Think, think! They instinctively jam a hand in their pocket to grasp the leaf, stimulating their sense of touch and their mind. Suddenly, in the dark, their vision begins to double again. They watch their foot as it slides deeper into the blob, just barely brushing the eye at its center. They see the blob react sharply, shifting the eye to another spot in its goopy form before continuing to engulf their leg.

That's it. The eye.

Just as the blob shifts its grip on their leg so that it can pull them in deeper, Keera jerks their leg upward, impacting the spongy eye. It recoils stronger than it had in their vision and loosens its grip on their leg. Without hesitating, Keera yanks their leg free, and scrambles away as the thing recovers. Keera struggles to their feet, but their freshly freed leg buckles under their weight. They wince; they won't be able to run away with a limp, especially since it can hurl parts of itself at them again, slowing them down even further. Unable to run, unable to hide in a wide open tunnel when they are only feet from their assailant. Keera has only one option left.

It's time to fight.

But how? All they know how to deal with is a person with a gun, and this fucking snot ball wasn't packing. They had to think: what would Radley do? They think back to the lesson at the core of what she had taught them: the goal in a fight shouldn't be to just win. Have a specific goal. And, while they don't know much about green slime monsters, they just learned one thing: they don't like being hit in their glowing red eye.

The creature, by this point, has fully recovered from the minor prodding and is advancing on them again. Keera needs a weapon. They aren't about to reach their hand in there to try to punch it. They need something long enough to reach. As it inches closer, they whirl around their surroundings, looking for anything that could do the job.

They spy a windshield wiper on the derelict car. If they could pry that off, it could be long and sturdy enough to knock the eye clean out. Hobbling to the car, they're still faster than this monster. But it has the advantage of ranged attacks; they hear a wet *slap* from their right, and turn just in time to see an orb of goo come hurtling toward them. Ducking, the projectile just misses their head. They keep moving. Another *slap*. This time, it's anticipating their movement, trying to hit where they will be. How smart are these things? Apparently, not smart enough, as Keera slows their pace and does a pained hop over its failed attack.

Reaching the car, Keera falls onto the hood, catching their breath. The pain in their leg has not subsided, and it's taking everything in them to not collapse from it right now. Despite this, they manage to shimmy along the hood until they're at the wipers. They've never owned a car. They have no idea how to properly remove a wiper. All they know is that they're long and pointy. The plan is to just yank and see what happens.

Unfortunately, as they're reaching for the closest wiper arm, a ball of goo slaps their other hand to the car, firmly plastering it in place, and burning it to all hell. They let out another scream of surprise and excruciating pain. This only makes them more determined, however, and they yank at the wiper arm with all their might. Luckily, the rusty decay on the hinge has made it quite breakable. One good tug, and it's free. They quickly slap at the goo with their new implement, breaking apart the integrity of the blob enough to remove their now chemically burned left hand.

In doing so, they realize the wiper blade itself flops around unwieldy. So, they remove it, leaving them with the wiper arm, a two foot long poking implement. In doing so, they realize the tingling in their burned hand has rendered it virtually useless for fine motor control at the moment. So, they shove it in their pocket, and grip the leaf with it for emotional support. They whirl around to face their amorphous assailant. It has closed quite a lot of distance because of the struggle. It's only a few feet away.

They need to end this soon, their body can't take much more punishment. Moving as swiftly as one working leg will let them, they dart toward the blob. It quivers, and Keera sees an afterimage of some slime arching toward their left shoulder. They duck just in time. Then again, this time the right. Same move, dodge. They're within striking distance. It quivers again, reaching out a pseudopod, trying to grab them. But Keera is faster.

SQUELCH.

The wiper arm pierces the blob's massive eye.

The creature wiggles and jiggles in pain. It tries to move and turn the eye away from Keera with surprising force, but Keera holds firm. They grip the pole with both hands, gritting their teeth. This thing wasn't getting away. With all their force, they push down, down with the arm, slicing a bloody gash down the creature's eye. Blood and eye fluid begin pouring out from the punctured organ, changing the vibrant green slime to a cloudy brown. With a final yank, Keera retracts the arm from the creature. It jiggles and wiggles helplessly for a few more moments, before deflating onto the pavement, its noxious smelling fluids leaking out of its membranous skin.

Keera huffs, their body drained from the entire ordeal. *I killed it,* they think to themself, *I killed it!* Either from the thrill of the victory, over-exhaustion, or both, the teen can't help but chuckle. A chuckle that turns into a laugh. A laugh that turns into all-out cheering. "WOOOOOHOO!" they shout, fist pumping the wiper arm into the air, "Take that, you stupid slimy piece of shit!"

Their elation is cut short by a familiar *plop*ping sound from a couple of yards away. Their head shoots in that direction, and their blood runs cold, as they see another green pile of goo rising from the pavement.

Then another *plop.*

And another.

And another.

Oh no...

Keera manages to grapple for their flashlight just before another *plop* sounds just a few feet from them. This time, they see why they are appearing with this sound.

Slowly, they raise their light to the ceiling, and gasp in horror, as dozens of green masses dangle above them. Keera lets out a gasp and backs up, bumping into the car behind them. Back on the ground, a hoard of these things is sliding slowly toward them, each with large, crimson eyes staring hungrily at them. They wave their wiper arm in front of them in a panic. It won't be enough to keep them all at bay, but they have no other option. "Stay back!" Keera shouts, "Stay the fuck back!"

They don't listen. And as they inch closer, the acidic smell almost overwhelming, Keera regrets everything. They should have seen this coming. Radley told them it was dangerous, but for the second time in two weeks, they ignored the warnings and entered a deadly cave. This time, it would be them who paid the price for it, at least. Their reckless actions would hurt no one else. Maybe this is fate, or karma, or something, they don't know. All they know is that they are going to take as many of these things out with them as they can. They turn to the nearest slime, that determined rage furrowing their brow. Holding the metal stick with both hands, they prepare to stab the blob, when:

BLAM!

The creature's eye explodes in a shower of goo, coating Keera in the backsplash. They flinch, expecting it to be a new type of attack. But no, they see the creature deflate, ooze pouring onto the ground. They look to another, and BLAM! Its eye explodes, too. BLAM, BLAM, BLAM! One after another, eyes are popping like balloons hitting hot lightbulbs. One slime nearby, clearly unphased by its comrades' deaths, jiggles and fires off a ball of goo at Keera.

Just then, a flash of white, and the airborne orb is cut in twain, both halves falling to either side of Keera. A familiar figure now stands in front of them. All they can see in the relative dark is a long mane of white hair flowing to just below waist level.

"Radley!" Keera cries out.

Their excitement is cut short, as the merc throws over their shoulder, "Don't. We're going to have a talk after this."

They slash again and fire off another shot, killing another slime. "Can you run?" she asks coldly.

Keera puts a little weight on their burned leg to test it. Keera winces. It still hurts too much..

That is enough of an answer for Radley. "Grab on to me," she orders. Keera does as commanded, grabbing her around the waist. Suddenly, their legs are no longer on the ground as Radley cradles them in their arms. In a flash, the two are speeding down the tunnel, faster than Keera could've run if their leg wasn't injured.

"Wait, why are we running? Those things are super slow," Keera shouts over the rushing wind.

"Not when they get together," Radley responds.

Keera, confused, hears a loud, rapid *slap slap slap slap* behind them. Looking back over Radley's shoulder with their flashlight, Keera's blood runs cold for the second time tonight, as the entire tunnel behind them is filled with an undulating mass of green, acrid slime. Scattered within it, like the world's grossest gelatin dessert, are dozens and dozens of angry, blood-red eyes, moving and sloshing, yet trained on the two of them.

"Oh my god, run faster!" Keera shouts.

"NOW do you see why I didn't want to go in this tunnel?!" Radley scolds. The slapping behind them is getting louder.

"Yes, okay, I do!" Keera says, "I am sorry, I'm so so so sorry, but can we go a little faster, please?!"

"Don't you even START!" Radley shouts.

It is then that Keera notices what's in front of them: light. They're close to the exit. They turn back behind to see the slimes nearly on top of them, pulling and sliding themselves at astonishing speed. This is going to be close.

"HOLD TIGHT!" Radley shouts.

Keera grips Radley with a white-knuckled grip, buries their head into her chest, shuts their eyes tight, and screams. The rushing wind, pounding footsteps, menacing *slap slap slap SLAP SLAP SLAP—*

Then, the two are airborne.

Keera opens their eyes. It's as if time has slowed. Before them, a fresh golden sunrise kisses the landscape. Wide, rocky terrain inter-cut by a shimmering river. Along the river, spires of shining metal and glass reflect the heavenly light of a new dawn. If this was what the Old Faiths called heaven, Keera would not be surprised if they died in that tunnel.

But no, they are certainly still alive. As, pretty soon, gravity kicks in, and the two crash onto the rocky slope, tumbling down and down, rocks slamming into them, bruising and cutting and rolling and falling. Eventually, the two come to a stop. Up the hill, the writhing mass of slimes screams at the touch of warm, angelic sunlight. Slowly, it burbles back into its hole, angry and unsatisfied by today's hunt.

Radley releases Keera from her grasp, and the two lie face-up, out of breath, staring up at the sweet, orange, cloud-dappled sky.

Fuck caves.

CHAPTER 8

"You could have gotten yourself KILLED!" Radley scolds, "Hell, you could've gotten us BOTH killed!"

The two are resting on some rocks near where they landed after ejecting from the tunnel. They have assessed and dressed wounds, and Radley clearly has decided Keera is in good enough shape to be chewed out for disobeying.

"I said I'm sorry, okay?" Keera says. They are still exhausted, and they can tell this isn't going to be a short conversation.

"Sorry isn't good enough," Radley continues, "Why? Why did you do it?"

"I thought it was a good idea, so—"

"But I TOLD you it wasn't!" Radley snaps back at them, "You've said it yourself; you don't know anything about the world out here. What makes you think you know enough to run off on your own?"

Keera grits their teeth, "I don't know anything because *you* won't tell me! I'm sick of being left in the dark, being dragged along, not knowing what is going on. I want to know, to be in control of my own life. You're not my mom! You can't just order me around like you are!"

"You're right," Radley responds, "I'm not your mother. But I'm the best chance you have at surviving out here right now, or at least for the next few hours. Then, I'm leaving your disobedient ass with Adley, so I suggest you learn to swallow your pride, and do as you're told for just a little." She continues packing her bag.

"Why do you refuse to admit you care about me?" they state.

The warrior pauses. "What?" she questions.

"You heard me," Keera asserts, "Why are you pretending to not care about me? There are a bunch of times you could've let me die, or left me to fend for myself."

"I..." Radley starts, but Keera steamrolls over her meek response.

"You didn't have to come looking for me in the tunnel. You could've just kept on going. But you didn't. You keep coming back. You say you're going to leave me with this Adley person, you threaten to leave all the time, are pissed off at me, tell me nothing. But you keep. Coming. Back. And, I just don't get why—"

"YOU REMIND ME OF MYSELF, OKAY?" Radley bellows.

There's a pause. Keera didn't know what they expected her explanation to be for their rambling questions, but it sure as hell wasn't that. Radley's words hang in the air, echoing across the rocky mountain scape.

Finally, Radley says, "And I don't just mean because of the hair."

Keera says, "I figured tha—"

Radley interrupts, "Please. You want answers, right?"

Keera nods.

"Then, please, just... let me finish," she says. Keera shuts their mouth and listens. *Finally.*

The mercenary sighs a deep, nervous sigh before explaining, "I lost my home when I was young, too. Younger than you were, even. I was about eleven. People came and attacked. Someone I cared about died. And my home was destroyed. Just like you. But *I* didn't have anyone come along and save me. Nobody taught me how to survive, not for a while at least. I was alone, scared, tired, starving... So, when I saw you, half buried in rubble, but still breathing, I... I couldn't leave you there. But, I'm also not a good person to stay with for an extended period of time..."

"Why not?" Keera asks, "You're strong, skilled. You know how to get by pretty well up here, I feel like."

Radley looks down, the gentle desert wind pushing her hair in front of her face, blocking it from view. "People around me die, Keera," she says, "No matter what I do, they die. It just seems like... death follows me wherever I go. I'm just... not worth the risk. There are plenty of others out there who can help you get by.

My road is only leading to one place. And, it's best that I walk it alone..."

Keera gazes at the sorrowful woman. Even without seeing her face, they can feel the pain they carry. Their eyes then drift away, and the two sit in silence.

Keera is conflicted. On one hand, they disagree with Radley's assessment of herself. Even though she projects this cold, callus, death-emanating persona, they can tell she is more than that. They just have a feeling. She cared enough to save Keera multiple times. She saw herself in the poor, broken child lying in the wreckage of their home. They know, through the sadness in her voice, that she wants to be more. To be better than she thinks she is.

But on the other hand... Keera doesn't know if it is their place to decide these things for her. They've only known her for a few days. Maybe she's right, maybe she *is* some monster for whom death has an affinity. Moreover... they don't know if they can trust their intuition anymore. They don't know who they are, where they are. They aren't sure who or what they want to be anymore. Before, their only goal was to see the surface, and now that they have, they have no idea where to go from here. So, if they don't know themselves well enough to decide what's best for them right now, what makes them think they know well enough to tell someone else who they think they are?...

"Alright," Keera finally speaks. No more explanation needed. Radley looks to the child, who gives her a resigned nod in return.

Radley takes a deep breath and grabs her bag. "We should get going if we want to reach Brezio by nightfall," she states.

Keera nods, stands, and follows Radley toward the spires of steel and glass.

***

The journey to Brezio City is deceptively long. Having become used to only seeing things a few dozen feet away in the forest, or even less in the dark tunnel, Keera has forgotten just how tricky perspective can be, especially when looking at buildings that are immensely taller than any they've seen before. Dawn turns to day, day turns to dusk, and pretty soon, the sun is already setting again below the horizon. Keera is exhausted, with only the image of a nice, soft, hotel bed keeping them moving. That, and the half-worn highway they are now walking on is slightly easier than natural terrain.

The walk has been quiet, even more than usual. This is because of a strange feeling between the two. Not tension, but more of a mutual understanding. A melancholy awareness that any sort of bonding or small talk would be wasted, seeing as, within a few hours, they likely would not see each other again. But, also... it is something else, for Keera at least. For them, they feel as though they do not need to pester this stranger for answers anymore. They feel they know enough now to understand where she's coming from. That heaviness they've carried ever since they left the crater now feels like a shared burden. They know they walk beside another who shares a similar burden. Two pallbearers, trudging down the road together. Not a word shared, but they both know the grief the other carries with them. That is enough.

As the two get within about a mile of the first small building signifying the informal edge of Brezio City, a wondrous miracle occurs that stops at least Keera in their tracks: All across the city, as the sky begins its transition from purples to black, lights of all different kinds blink into existence; a window light here, a street light there, signs and billboards, everything begins to come alive.

"Wow..." they breathe. Another wonder of the surface world.

"Welcome to Brezio City," Radley says. Keera doesn't register it until later, but there is a new gentleness to Radley's voice.

After the awe has worn off, the pair continues down the highway, headed toward the center-mass of the city. Only a few blocks in, and Keera is already walking past buildings taller than any they've seen back home. They are used to three or maybe four stories, but these are easily reaching seven or more. And these buildings are still *dwarfed* by ones they can see in the downtown area. Keera can't help but stare up in wonder at each one they pass.

How long must it have taken to build these? Were these new, or had they somehow survived the wars?

Their wonder is cut short, as a gentle elbow to the ribs brings their eyes back to ground-level. "Don't do that," Radley scolds, "You stand out."

"I was just looking," Keera protests.

"People from Brezio don't look. They're used to it. Act like you're from here," Radley's eyes dart across the street, "See? You're already drawing attention."

Keera follows Radley's gaze over to two hooded figures on the opposite street corner. At first glance, they seem like they're loitering outside a nearby shop. But, as Keera watches them, they notice the two repeatedly glance in their direction. Anxiety immediately bubbles up inside them, and they avert their eyes, locking them straight ahead.

"Just keep your head down until we reach The D'acier. Once you have the Lady's blessing, idiots like them won't bother you."

Keera nods. *Lady Adley must be a big deal here*, they think, *If your average criminal knows not to fuck with her*. Keera is starting to feel a bit better about being left in the care of this person.

***

It doesn't take long for Keera to break their promise to not look up. Above them, the illuminated edifices of glass, steel, and concrete reach heights greater than even the massive pine trees they had just recently experienced. They almost cannot comprehend that within each one of those buildings, each one of those tiny windows, there is a person or people doing something. Living a life of their own. The thought is oddly alluring.

So whimsical are their thoughts that they are almost run over by a speeding car as they absentmindedly begin crossing a street. Luckily, Radley grabs them by the arm and yanks them back just as it passes. VrrrrrOOOOOOOOmmmm! The driver lays on their horn as they thunder off down the road. The car in question appears cobbled together, with an exposed chassis possessing the wildly large shocks of a dune buggy. It entirely clashes with the sleek, clean architecture of the downtown area.

"You need to watch where you're going," Radley hisses, still gripping their arm tight, "What did I say about looking up?"

"Okay, okay, ow! Sorry!" Keera whines, yanking their arm free. With their eyes back to ground level, they observe hoards of people moving every which way, both by car and on foot. They've never seen this many people in their life, let alone in one place. It's fascinating, but terrifying at the same time. Not knowing a single face, who is just passing by, and who could take a harmful interest in them.

Keera has to stop their mind from spiraling into paranoia. So, they focus on the task at hand, "Are we almost there? I could really use a nice bed soon." They yawn.

Radley wordlessly points about two blocks down the street. There, Keera sees a massive building, one of the biggest in the city, they wager, standing at a five-way intersection. Above the skyscraper's gargantuan set of double doors, in large, fancy-script lettering, is the phrase "The D'acier" in glowing golden light.

Alright, Keera thinks, taking a deep breath, *This is it.*

CHAPTER 9

K EERA ISN'T SURE WHAT they were expecting, but nothing they've experienced in their sixteen years of life could have prepared them for what lies beyond the doors of The D'acier. The first thing that jumps out at them are the colors: brilliant reds, accented by lush green plants, shimmering glass and crystal chandeliers. And, above all, the *gold*. Shimmering yellow metal, either real or imitation, is everywhere: trimming every wall, running along every banister, swirling in elegant patterns through every carpet and on every curtain. Just wall-to-wall opulence that leaves Keera in shock.

Keera's eyes follow up the grand staircase that diverges up to the left and right, meeting a u-shaped balcony surrounding the ground floor. At the base of the u, another set of impossibly large doors takes up a majority of the back wall, forcing the ceiling to be at least forty feet high. On the ceiling, wonderful murals of beautiful, powerful, semi-nude figures engage in many activities; from fighting to frolicking to fucking, they are doing it all.

"Come on," Radley says, making her way toward the stairs, "The Lady will be in the next room." Keera follows, still gazing around what is apparently just the lobby. Seeing all this — the building, the wealth on display, and the fear that this woman strikes in the citizens of this city — Keera is starting to put it together why Radley feels safe handing them off to her. She clearly does more than just "own a hotel."

Reaching the landing at the base of two more immense doors, two muscular, well-dressed men impede their progress. Keera can make out rhythmic thumping noises coming from the other side.

As they approach, one of the men pointedly steps in front of Radley. He is taller than her, but given what Keera has seen this woman accomplish, his action is a bit comical. "Move," Radley orders.

"Do you have an invitation?" the man responds sternly, barely as a question.

Radley responds, side-eying him, "My name is Radley, and I have business with The Lady. That's my invitation." She makes a move toward the door, only to meet more resistance.

"The Lady isn't conducting business right now," he says, "Come back tomorrow."

Radley's gaze slowly turns to the stubborn man. She is right in his face now. "Move, or The D'acier is going to have a new job opening," she orders.

Her hand rests on her gun in the holster. The man, seeing this, begins reaching for the semi-auto rifle strapped to his back.

Just then, the second bouncer puts a hand on the first's shoulder. "Don't," he says to his colleague. Then, noticing how much he is projecting, clears his throat and assumes a more professional expression, "She's been waiting for this one."

The two men share a look, nod, and the first takes a step back, reaching for the door handle. With a hefty tug, he pulls the door open just a crack, enough for Radley and Keera to enter. The rhythmic thumping Keera could hear gets exponentially louder, revealing it to be the bassy beat of club music. Through the crack, Keera sees forms shifting in a colorful, dimly lit space.

"Go on," the first guard instructs.

Radley gives the man one last death stare, before turning back to Keera. "Stay close," she says. Keera does as the pair files into the room, the doors shutting behind them.

Keera didn't think the music could get any louder. But, being in the space, they feel like they are being assaulted by it. It almost hurts their ears, and the base feels like it's beating their heart for them. On top of the auditory assault, the two are forced to contend with a wall of people. Each one is dressed in an outfit that is simultaneously too tight and showing a lot of skin, in various ways. Amid the flashing lights and a low haze, Keera can see flashes of shimmering jewelry; golds, silvers, and a rainbow of colored gems, represented in earrings, necklaces, bangles, and many more forms of jewelry. All these fancy, glimmering items are being flung around aggressively by the people wearing them, as they're jumping and gyrating and grinding up against people near them. There are so many warm, moving bodies that the room's temperature is considerably warmer than outside, even though it is a good deal larger.

As Radley begins to push through the crowd, Keera instinctively reaches out and grasps her hand tight. For a moment, they are worried Radley is going to react negatively, leaving Keera stranded in the sea of bodies. But she doesn't and leads the teen through the heart of the throng.

Wading through the crowd, Keera is horribly uneasy and out of their element. They haven't seen this many people packed in one space before. Every so often, they catch a person glancing at them as they pass by. Given how they were being looked at by those men in the street earlier that day, Keera is worried with every person they barge past that one will get angry and attack them, or try to grab them and escape into the crowd.

To distract themself from worrying thoughts, they call out to Radley, "HOW ARE WE GOING TO FIND HER WITH ALL THESE PEOPLE?"

"SHE'S HARD TO MISS," Radley responds, and gestures ahead of them. Keera has no idea what *that's* supposed to mean.

And then they look up.

Seated in a massive marble throne, on a dais above the rave, is an impossibly large woman. Scale is a tricky thing in a place like this, but even seated, Keera can tell this woman is over double the height of the men on either side of her. Her skin is a burnt umber, and she sports a voluminous black afro atop her head. She is wearing a red pantsuit, with a black handkerchief in her breast pocket, and a pair of red and black stiletto pumps. Keera wonders why a woman *this* tall still feels the need to wear heels. It must be purely for the aesthetic. As she sits, legs spread wide, her expression is stoic as she scans the crowd before her.

"I TAKE IT THAT'S ADLEY?" Keera shouts.

Radley nods, "THIS WAY," and continues leading the way closer to the giant woman.

Keera just can't take their eyes off her. Unlike most of the partygoers, Lady Adley is dressed rather conservatively. Sure, she has on some jewelry, and she looks put together, but it's a more subtle display of status. Though, it makes sense, Keera reasons; given the fact this is *her* place, they wager she doesn't have much to prove once partygoers see the lobby.

So lost in their thoughts is Keera that they almost don't notice that the colossal woman is staring right at them.

"STOP THE MUSIC!" the titanic woman bellows, and in an instant, the obnoxiously loud music cuts to an even more deafening silence. The crowd around them looks around in confusion. The Lady raises a menacing finger toward Radley and Keera. "You two," she says, her speaking voice still echoing in the cavernous dancehall, "with the white hair. Step forward." She emphasizes that last point by flicking a "come hither" gesture at them.

The surrounding crowd has taken several steps back. As the duo does as instructed, the people part like fields of grain, expressions ranging from fear and confusion to anger on their faces. The lighting in the place has shifted as well: spotlights that were previously flailing wildly in a myriad of flashing colors are now all trained on The Lady and a small space before her below the dais, right where Radley stops them. Keera stares up at the woman, more nervous than she's been in a while. Facing down mindless monsters and lone bounty hunters is one thing. But, being in a room, front and center, with over a hundred people staring them down, one of them being a giant woman who is looking down her nose in disdain at those who just crashed her party... they feel they unlocked a new fear they didn't know they had.

"Radley of The Wastes," The Lady declares, her voice made punchy by her strange accent, and deep booming undertones, "And, what is this small creature you bring with you?"

"Her name is Keera," she responds. They realize they never told Radley what they like to be referred to as. They figure now isn't the time, though. Besides, they're fine with her as well as they. Instead, they give an awkward nod up to the tall woman. Radley continues, "Adley, I request tha—"

"That is Lady D'acier to you," she corrects, pounding a heavy fist on her throne for emphasis, "And you are in no place to make requests of ME. Did you forget that you are a deserter?"

Keera's head shoots to Radley, eyes wide. The woman doesn't betray any indication that this is a lie. *Oh, you have to be joking,* they think.

"Do you recall," the massive woman says, standing and slowly pacing toward the duo, her height and power on full display — afro, heels, the works, "That you were at one point indebted to me? After I scraped you off of the desert floor, taking pity on you, and saved your miserable little life. You owed me your service, and you betrayed me!"

"Lady D'acier, I—"

"DON'T interrupt me again, or I will stomp you FLAT!" she booms. The entire crowd shudders, Keera included.

Regaining composure, Lady D'acier slowly paces across the stage toward her throne, each click of her heels reverberating the ground. She continues, "As I was saying, you abandoned your squad. Your city. You abandoned me." She sits down as she finishes her statement, "How can you possibly think you are in ANY position to ask a favor of the queen you betrayed?" she finishes.

Radley takes a moment, clearly waiting to see if it's really okay for her to respond now. Then, she says, "I know what I did was wrong. I betrayed the trust of my unit, and of you, and for that, I am sorry. That being said, the favor I ask isn't for me. It's for her." She gestures to Keera. "I found this one in the wreckage of a bunker town. She is young, but a quick learner. I believe she will be both safer under your care, and a good addition to your militia."

Keera is appalled at the suggestion Radley just made. They aren't looking to join a militia! If they would've known *this* was her plan, they would have stayed back at the crater.

The queen seems to ponder this suggestion, stroking her chin. Keera could feel her eyes looking them up and down, appraising a new weapon she was planning to add to her arsenal. Finally, she says, "This is a tempting offer." She strokes her chin, considering something, before continuing, "Let us discuss this proposal of yours back in my chambers. I do not wish to hold up the party any longer." She gestures wide with her arms, and the crowd erupts with cheers and applause. She then stands, declaring, "Come, Radley of the Wastes. We will decide the fate of you and your little... peace offering." She strides around her throne, flanked on either side by the two regular sized guards, toward yet another set of giant double doors at the back of the space. Radley and Keera follow, as the lights once again dim and start flashing, and the wild music surges to life around them. The crowd returns to dancing, as if nothing had just happened.

Reaching the doors, the woman pulls them open like they are nothing, and says to the two guards, "Stay out here. No one else disturbs us." The man nods, and they take up positions on either side of the double doors. Keera follows Radley into this next space, their eyes not leaving the back of her head. They can't believe she would do something like this. No, that's not true. They should have expected this from her. She's never shown genuine care for Keera. This whole time, she only wanted them as a living bargaining chip to settle a debt with her former employer. It all makes sense now. And they can't believe it took them until now to see this side of her.

The private quarters of The Lady are about what Keera expects at this point: Lavish, gold and red furniture, beautiful artwork on every wall, as well as a mirrored ceiling, and an elegant, curtained, four-post bed. And, of course, everything is over double the size it should be. It is a bit unorganized and disheveled, with tables stacked high with paperwork and trash. The floor is riddled with shoes and clothes, laying in organized, but haphazard piles. These details and their perspective of the space give them flashbacks to walking into their mom's room as a young child. She'd ask young Keera to find something of hers while she was busy getting ready to leave the house. The directions were never clear enough, though, and Keera usually ended up digging through the wrong pile, only to have their mom come in a few minutes later and just grab it herself. If she was just going to find it herself, what was the point of asking your child to do it for you? Those interactions were always aggravating to Keera. But, now, they'd give anything to be back in those mundanely frustrating situations again.

A loud BAM, SLAM brings Keera back, as The Lady has kicked off her heels, sending them clattering into the others like bowling balls into pins. She mumbles, "Ugh, these damn things are killing me!" She flops back onto her bed with an exhausted sigh.

Without moving, the giant woman groans from her bed, "What are you doing back here, Radley?"

"I told you," Radley says, sitting in a chair that is comically large for her. Keera wearily does the same, but they have to shimmy onto it like a tall barstool. Radley continues, "I need you to take care of the kid."

The queen rotates and flips over on her bed so that she is facing the two of them, her chin resting in her hand. Her stoic, regal persona is gone, replaced by informality and deep tiredness. "I'm not running a bloody daycare here," she protests, "Like, for fuck's sake, has the girl even shot a gun before?"

"No," Radley says, "But you can teach her. She killed a slime—"

"Oh, killed a slime, has she?" the queen says, almost mockingly, "Was it one of the reasonable sized ones at least, or was it one of those little fucks, barely bigger than my big toe?"

"It was a reasonable size for her. Plus, she helped me survive being jumped by a daywalker," Radley adds.

"You were jumped by a daywalker?" Lady D'acier asks. She makes a *tsk tsk tsk* sound as she shakes her head, "Really gotten soft out in the wastes, haven't we?" At this, she stands, wanders over to a nightstand with a few large bottles on it, and begins pouring drinks.

"He was a bounty hunter," Radley states.

"Oh? I thought you wanted to leave my employ to avoid people like bounty hunters coming after you," D'acier says. She walks toward them, carrying two normal-sized glasses and one massive one.

She hands one to the mercenary and attempts to hand the other to Keera. They shake their head cautiously, "N—no thanks. I don't drink."

The giant woman shrugs, "Eh, suit yourself." And she downs the entire glass like a shot. She then pulls up another chair and sits in it backwards, leaning her arms on the headrest. "So, who did you piss off this time?" the queen asks, sipping her drink.

"Stopped the guys attacking her town," Radley says, referring to Keera, and taking a sip of her drink as well, "Who were apparently working with Manhattan Gate."

The Lady's eyes go wide, and she coughs like her drink went down the wrong pipe. "Manhattan Gate?!" the queen gags, clearing her throat, "I thought you shook them years ago."

"I wasn't looking. They just found me. Or, rather, found her," she responds.

"Right, that's how it always is, init? Trouble always finds *you*, not the other way around," D'acier says, raising a suspicious eyebrow.

"It was bound to happen eventually, anyway," Radley adds, ignoring that jabbing comment.

"I suppose," The Lady takes a sip, "Wait, you didn't lead those cunts back to me, did you?"

"No, there were no survivors," Radley says.

"Alright, good," the tall woman nods, "Because I just got the windows redone."

The trio sit in silence. There is no tension here, unlike in the main hall. This disorients Keera.

With this break in the conversation, they figure it's as good a time as any to speak up: "Um, Lady D'acier..."

"Please," The Lady waves dismissively at them, "Adley's just fine back here."

Another conflicting bit of information. Okay. "Alright, uh, Lady Adley," they start, "Can I ask a potentially dumb question?"

"Go for it," she responds, sipping.

"What..." Keera collects themself, before blurting out, "What the fuck is going on?"

Now this seems to catch both women off guard.

"Sorry," they say, "But, like... a few minutes ago you were talking about deserters and owing debts, and stuff. But now, you're like... shooting the shit over drinks? Like what— Aren't you mad at her? Am I really getting drafted or— I'm just really confused..."

A shared smirk between the two women turns into hearty laughter from the queen. "Oh, sweetheart," she finally says, "That was all just theatrics!"

"Wait, really?" Keera looks between the two of them, "So you're not mad at Radley?"

"Oh no, I'm still pretty bloody pissed off," she says, "I gave her the perfect cover to get out of my employ, keeping both of our reputations intact, and what does SHE do? Walks right back in, as if nothing had happened. Like I hadn't publicly declared her a traitor to our fair city."

Radley says, "I had no other option."

"You could've at least waited until I wasn't throwing a bit of a fucking do."

"You're always throwing parties," she responds, then adds, "Besides, I don't have time to wait."

"The bounty hunter wouldn't attack us in the city like this, with so many people around, would he?" Keera chimes in.

Radley looks at Keera. "I'm not talking about the bounty hunter," she says, then to Adley, "It exists."

The queen cocks an eyebrow for a moment, ready to ask a question. But then, her face shifts to understanding. "You're not serious," she says.

Radley nods.

Keera looks frantically between the two women's faces, trying desperately to understand what cryptic thing they were talking about. Nothing. Frustrated, they blurt out, "Okay, enough of this cryptic bullshit! What are we talking about? Why were we in such a hurry these past few days?"

Adley asks Radley, "You didn't tell her?"

"NO!" Keera responds for her, "No, she hasn't told me anything! All she's done is tell me I'm being left here with you. Not where this was, who you were, that I would be drafted into some private militia, which is something I would *not* have agreed to if I knew that was the plan. Nothing, she told me NOTHING!"

"Radley, you have to talk with her," Adley says.

"She's just a kid," Radley retorts.

"She stopped being a kid the moment she lost everything," replies Adley, "Just like you did. If she's as smart as you say she is, she needs to know what's going on, so she can make an informed decision for herself, for her own future."

Keera tries to read Radley's expression, but the woman is intentionally avoiding her gaze.

"Besides," continues Adley, "I don't need any more reluctant recruits in my company. She'll just run off in a few years like you did!"

Unphased by the giant's attempted humorous turn to the conversation, Radley hops down from the chair and walks toward the door. Keera hops down, too, but Radley says, "Don't follow me."

Keera stops dead. They're frustrated with her right now, but they can't help but feel a pang of hurt from her rejection. She stands silently watching her go, like a sad puppy being left home while their owner heads out into the world. The door creaks open a bit, then shuts with a thunderous echo.

"Such a drama queen, that one," Adley jokes. She gets up and begins collecting the various glasses, returning them to their proper places.

"Was she always like this?" Keera asks as the giant woman tidies up.

"Yep, as long as I've known her," she responds.

"Why?" Keera asks, "What made her... so cold like that?"

The queen scoffs, "Now that is a loaded question."

"Please, I just want answers," Keera says, "You clearly know more about her than I do."

The woman strides back to Keera, saying, "It's not my place to tell."

Keera lets out a frustrated grunt.

"Listen, I get it," Lady Adley says, kneeling down to Keera's eye level. They hate how this act, while well intentioned, also makes them feel like a little kid again, in a world of grown-ups. She continues, "I hate being left out of the loop, too. It makes me feel like other people are making decisions for me. Like they're... taking away my autonomy."

"Right, exactly!" Keera exclaims.

"And it sucks arse," she says, "But some people, like Radley, are stubborn. They think they know what's best for everyone. They don't listen when people talk. So, it's up to you to *make* them listen." She jams a finger into Keera's chest, just hard enough to get her point across.

"How? I've tried asking so many times, so many different ways," Keera protests.

"Well, for starters, it helps to know what you want."

"I want her to tell me what's going on!"

Adley shakes her head, "No, too vague. Too immediate. No: What do you, Keera, WANT? Like, more than anything?"

"I—" they start, but then stop. This same question has been rattling around in their head since the very beginning. Until a few weeks ago, all they wanted was to be free from their sunless hometown. They were a flower trapped underground. Dormant, unchanging, boring, but surrounded by other flowers like them. Still, they yearned to see the sky, and be more. They couldn't blossom from where they were, trapped in the dirt. But, now, they're free. They emerged into a vast, open world, one with plenty of sun and rain and space for them to bloom. But they still feel... empty. Unfulfilled. Alone. They're out in the world, but what does that matter? What is the point of a blooming flower if no one is around to admire it?

And then it hits them.

"I want to find the people I belong with," they say. They weren't aware, but tears had started rolling down their cheeks.

"Do you think you belong here?" Adley asks, "Or with her?"

Keera looks at the door where Radley had exited from. They remember the conversation the two had recently, on that rocky hillside. Bonding over a similar loss. In that moment, Keera had felt closer to her than they had to anyone in their life. They felt like they shared a trauma few others have experienced. But, despite carrying that weight, that pain with her, as Keera does, she still manages to be a good person. She saves lives. She protects the weak. She does what she thinks is best for people she cares for, in her own cold, calculating way. And, for a brief moment, Keera feels a desire to be like her, to be like Radley, someday.

"I want to be with Radley," they say finally.

"Then let her know that!" Adley says, standing to full height and throwing her arms in the air, "I mean, for fuck's sake, girl, show some backbone!"

Keera chuckles, wiping tears from their eyes. Then their brow furrows. "But how will I find her? She could be anywhere by now."

The giant queen smirks down at the little white-haired teen, "Oh, I know exactly where she is right now."

Chapter 10

Cherry blossoms float gently through the night air, landing with elegance onto an invisible, rippling surface. Pink neon lights illuminate the pond on which the petals float. This being the highest point in Brezio City, there is nothing breaking the horizon for miles. Only a few stars dapple the black sky. Leaning against a railing, Radley gazes at the cherry tree, bathed in fuchsia fluorescence.

From the roof-access doorway, Keera peers at the woman, who herself is also bathed in pink. It is hard to tell from this distance, but she doesn't appear angry. Well, any more pissed off than usual, anyway. Instead, the mercenary looks contemplative. This makes sense, as Lady Adley had reassured them that this was the place Radley would go to when she needed to be alone and think. Keera can understand why; the aesthetic of this space — especially at night, with the only light being from the "D'acier" sign atop the tower — is calming. A simple rock garden, some bamboo in one corner, and the cherry tree surrounded by still water as the centerpiece. Another eccentricity of her majesty, surely, but one Keera actually finds appealing.

Cautiously, Keera creeps out from the doorway. They figure Radley already knows they're there, given her skill-set. But the teen still feels the tension from their last encounter and decides to move with caution. Reaching the railing, Keera leans on it, mirroring Radley, a foot or two away.

Keera clears their throat preparing to speak. They need to know what they want to say and say it right. They are just about to gather the courage, when, "I take it she told you I would be up here," Radley says.

Keera, already on the back foot, responds shakily, "Yeah. She said you used to come up here a lot before missions."

"Hm," Radley grunts.

A pause. Then, Keera adds, "It seems like she really knows you. How long did you work for her?"

Silence.

Keera sighs. They should've known it wouldn't be that easy. But this at least gives them an opportunity to start the discussion how *they* want to. So, they start, "Look, I know why you don't want me around. I'm... just a kid. A kid who doesn't know how to fight, how to walk around in a city without looking like a tourist. I don't know a lot of stuff up here. And you clearly have important things going on. You don't have time to look after me while also doing whatever you have to do. I get all that. But... I don't want to leave you."

"Ever since our talk this morning, I've felt... connected to you. We've both lost so much, and we are both still carrying that. Don't you feel that, too, at least a little bit?" Keera asks.

"So, what, because both of us lost everything we ever loved, we should hang out together?" Radley snipes.

"No, it's..." Keera contends, "It's more than that. Like... My whole life, I've always felt alone. Like no one understands me, or what I've been through, anything. I didn't lose my parents when Canary Bridge collapsed. I never knew them to begin with. I was adopted, and every day down there, I was reminded of that. I never felt at home. There was no one there that felt like they got me, and I *knew* I had to get out of there someday. I needed to find... find where I belonged. So, no, it's not just that we're trauma bonded. It's more than that. I feel like... you might be my people. Maybe, if you would just let me."

Radley is still staring straight ahead at the tree, as if it were the one talking to her and not Keera. Then, finally, she murmurs, "I'm no one's people. I don't belong here."

Keera cocks their head a bit, "Why do you say that?"

"It's—" Radley starts.

But, Keera cuts her off, "And DON'T say 'it's a long story.' I have time, and you've run out of places to run to."

Radley gives the demanding teen an annoyed glare. Keera doesn't flinch an inch. They know what they want, and they're not backing down anymore.

The mercenary seems to notice this, and explains, "I'm not from here."

"Like, what, from this area? I know you're from The Wastes down south."

"No," Radley says, "I'm not from this universe."

It takes a moment for the implications of that statement to hit Keera.

But, when they do, they exclaim, "Wait SERIOUSLY? You're from another dimension?! Like the vampires and the giants and stuff?" Radley nods. Keera can't believe it. They have to know more. "So then are you, like... some type of weird monster, too?" they ask, "Like, do you have magic powers? Or, like, animal parts, like wings under your jacket or something like that?"

Radley gives Keera a disbelieving look. "Do I look like I have a secret pair of wings?" she retorts.

"I don't know. I've seen weirder so far," Keera shrugs. Radley rolls her eyes and lets out a snort, a slight smile curing her lips. *Progress*, Keera thinks. Then, they say, "But, seriously, do you have powers or something?"

Radley waffles her head a bit side-to-side, "I guess it is a type of power, yeah."

"WAIT REALLY?!" Keera explodes, "Holy shit, you HAVE to tell me! Can you fly? Can you shoot lasers from your eyes? I mean, I already know you're super strong and super fast — wait, that's not it, is it?"

"The strength is all natural, actually," Radley says, "I trained with an order of gnumans; a hybrid race of goat-men. Their diet, training, and fighting style, the reason has... interesting effects on the human body, if practiced properly. Wildly increases muscle mass and bone density, as well as helps the body rapidly heal itself."

"Okay, now I KNOW you're fucking with me," Keera says, "No diet or exercising is ever going to make me stop a giant worm's tail from squishing me like a bug."

"You never know," Radley retorts, "But it is a hard and painful process. Plus, it probably helps that I wa—" She stops herself, seeming to realize she was rambling more than intended.

"Helps that you were what?" Keera pushes.

"Nothing," Radley says.

Well, that was still solid progress, Keera thinks. "It's ok," they say, "You can tell me another time."

"What makes you think there will be another time?" Radley posits.

Keera shrugs, "I don't know, you seemed to like opening up just now. And I don't plan on going anywhere, so..."

"You still want to be around me?" she asks, "Even after finding out I'm an EUE?"

"I don't even know what that is," Keera says.

"It's an Extra-Universal Entity. Lots of folks from up here have problems with people like me," she says.

Keera shrugs again, "Well, good thing I'm not from around here." They give Radley a little smirk, who promptly returns it with another eye roll.

There is silence once again, only the sound of the city far below echoing up to meet them. It's peaceful. Keera is enjoying this peace for the first time in a while.

Eventually, Radley murmurs, as if not wanting the silence to end, either; "We'll see in the morning."

Keera's heart skips in their chest. They honestly weren't sure they had made that much impact here tonight. But they did, and they're elated. Tired, but elated. Smiling, they turn to watch the bright pink tree with Radley, a head full of hopes for tomorrow. For the first time they can remember, Keera has something to look forward to.

Chapter 11

K EERA'S EYES SHOOT OPEN. They didn't think anything could wake them from sleeping tonight. After being set up by Lady Adley in a luxurious suite, equipped with the most comfortable bed they've ever laid in, they were out like a light. They desperately need this sleep, but the pounding at the door has other plans.

At first, they think it's Radley. She was given the room right next to theirs, after all. But, no, Radley would have said something by now. Plus, the banging sounds less like a knock, and more like a body slam. Repeatedly.

Someone is trying to break in.

Quickly, or as quickly as they can in their groggy, sleep-deprived state, they assess the room. There's the door. Clearly a bad idea. Only other egress is the window, but it's hard to open. The intruder would be on them before they even make it budge.

Okay, running isn't an option. Then they need to hide. There's under the bed, but that's too obvious. The bathroom? If they can knock in the front door, they can knock that in too. Then it hits them: the armoire. It's big, with plenty of clothes to hide behind. It will have to do. They dart out of bed, throw open the armoire doors, and shut them tight just as the door to the hotel room explodes open.

Silence. Then, a subtle hissing sound. Heavy footsteps, followed by more hissing. Keera cracks the door just enough to peek with one eyeball. It is then they spy a shape similar to some they saw a few days ago: a scaly, hunched-over lizard-man, clad in leather and metal, slinks through the space, tail and head swaying methodically back and forth.

"Come out, come out, little one," they hiss, "Don't be afraid. We won't hurt you. We just want your friend with the sword."

It lifts up the bed skirt, peering under. Not finding what it was hoping for, it drops it angrily, and growls, "The longer it takes to find you, the more hungry I'll get. And, while Vertex said we can't eat on the job... you don't need *all* your fingers to be the bait..."

Keera is shaking. They have their hand over their mouth to stifle their own involuntary noises. Tears begin to well in their eyes as the lizard wanders closer and closer to their hiding spot. Any moment now, these doors will fly open and they'll be done for.

Suddenly, thumping can be heard from the room next door. The lizard-man hears it too and turns its attention to the far wall. Muffled thumps and thuds, then a louder *bang bang*. Silence.

Then, the opposite wall bursts open, and a darkly dressed figure flies through the space at the lizard-man. The lizard fires off a shot of his shotgun, only to have it go in the ceiling as the figure forces the gun away. They rip the gun from the lizard's grasp. The figure then fires a shot, BANG, right into the lizard's side. It stumbles, then hoists the bed at the attacker, flipping it over in an attempt to crush the new intruder. But, the figure in black is too fast, and splits the bed in twain with something almost unseen in the dark. The hotel room is now in disarray. Wounded, the lizard grips his already gushing flank. It stares down its assailant; a figure dressed in black, from head to toe, with long white hair falling to her waist. In one hand, she holds a pistol, and in the other, a shimmer of metal in the dark.

***

After a harrowing escape from the hotel, Keera hides, rattled and terrified, behind Radley. They are surrounded. But, true to herself, Radley is unphased.

"This is your last warning:" Radley states, "Leave now, and don't look back."

The lizards seem unshaken by this display of bravado. Another loud laugh bellows from the boss lizard, "You still think you're in a position to negotiate, huh?! Well, unfortunately for you... I like to let my Boombox do the talking."

The lizard levels the massive shotgun toward the two.

He fires.

With a slash of her blade, Radley deflects the buckshot.

Errant pellets deflect into some lizards around them, sending them crumpling to the ground. The big lizard-man seems shocked that his point-blank shot didn't work. That surprise quickly turns to rage, and he snarls to the surrounding pack, "GET HER!"

Lizard-men charge, and shots ring out. Radley shouts, "DUCK!" to Keera. They do so without question, getting low and covering their head. All around them, a barrage of bullets rain in on them. With every BANG and POP, POP, POP, Keera flinches, ready for that to be the last thing they hear. But shot after shot misses. They peak up, only to see Radley rotating around them, deflecting incoming bullet after bullet like a baton twirler doing an intense routine. It would be mesmerizing if Keera wasn't so terrified.

The lizard-men with melee weapons charge. Before they can get close enough, however, they all are hit by a shot from Radley's gun or a deflected bullet from one of their comrades, and fall to the ground dead.

Except the big one.

He also charges, but even though Radley reflects a bullet straight into his torso, he's barely phased, and is on top of her. She raises her blade just in time to block a sweeping claw attack headed right for her abdomen.

The attack, however, causes the two to slam into Keera, sending them stumbling a few feet. As they recover, Keera sees that Radley is now in close combat with the behemoth, and cowering near her would only make them a tripping hazard yet again. They are out in the open, a sitting duck that any enterprising lizard-man left standing could snatch up no problem. Luckily, for Keera at least, most of the attention is on Radley, who can hold her own.

Unluckily, however, one thug notices this and decides to seize the opportunity. He is stocky, and a bit short as far as lizard-men go, sporting a white tank top, black leather pants and boots, the latter with metal spikes protruding from the toe, and a chain wrapped around his waist. He glares at the vulnerable teen with his one good eye, a triple-scar where the other eye should be. An evil grin crosses his scaly lips, and he charges.

Keera, wide-eyed, scrambles to their feet, running in the opposite direction from the lizard, who has now started cackling maniacally. "Why are you running, little girl?" he wails, "I just want to give you a hug!" Suddenly, Keera feels something cold wrap around their neck. It's tight, and they gasp reflexively. They reach up to grab for it, feeling metal links that start to tighten around their neck, and pull them backward. They manage to turn around, only to see the wild lizard-man holding the other end of the chain. His long forked tongue whips around wildly as he laughs maniacally, pulling them in closer. Keera digs their heels in, trying to stop moving, but this only makes the chain tighter. They tug and pull with all their might, but they only feel themselves getting weaker as the chain chokes off their air. There's nowhere to go. They can't run, they can't hide, they can't fight. All they can think to do is—

The leaf.

Without a second thought, they jam their hand in their pocket and shut their eyes. They grit their teeth, trying desperately to make something, *anything*, happen. But, when they open them again, nothing's changed. The chain is still constricting their windpipe, their assailant still pulling them closer, a hungry mania in his eye. Bullets fly between them, just missing Keera. As they duck, they glance over to see Radley still engaged with the big lizard. The shots from the other gangsters land this time, and she staggers a bit, giving an opening for the boss lizard to punch her as well. She's hurt, but still fighting. Which is more than can be said for Keera.

Dodging the bullets puts Keera off balance, and they fall to the ground on their back. Now with less resistance, the lizard has them pulled right to his feet in seconds. He grins down at them, their face thoroughly blue now, as their vision begins to blur.

"Hello there, delicious," he hisses, then pulls them up by the chain. They kick and squirm, being hung up like a freshly caught trout.

"Hey, feisty bitch!" he calls over to Radley, "Look what I've got here!"

Keera can just make out Radley as she notices Keera. Her shocked hesitation is all the big lizard needs: from behind, the boss, with jaws open wide, clamps down on Radley's neck. All they hear is a sickening *crunch.*

"R—Radley..." is all they manage to croak out before darkness overwhelms their vision.

Then Keera opens their eyes again.

They are being strangled, their heels dug into the pavement, the one-eyed lizard-man reeling them in again. They look around frantically. Radley. She's still alive, fighting the big lizard. They did it again! But how?

Not the time, as the barrage of bullets from the side starts again. Keera is ready this time, though, and instead of ducking away, they stand tall and pull the chain taught, right into the line of fire.

Chik!

The bullet meant for Radley instead impacts the chain, exploding the link, and severing them from their would-be captor. Keera falls back on their ass, while the lizard-man staggers in surprise. Seeing his prey unrestrained, he snarls and runs toward the prone teen. Thinking fast, the teen unwinds the chain from their neck and begins flailing it wildly. It gives the lizard pause, enough for Keera to get to their feet.

"Come on, little one," the lizard jeers, "Let's see what you've got." With that, he whips at them with the other half of the chain. Keera barely dodges. *Alright, magic leaf, I need you again,* they think, gripping the sharp little leaf in their pocket. Sure enough, they see a superimposed image of the chain coming down right where they're standing. They duck to the side. Miss. They see it happen again. Dodge. Miss. The lizard is getting more frustrated, his attacks coming faster and faster, making it harder for Keera to dodge. A couple knick them, leaving gashes from the broken ring at the end of his improvised whip. But, most attacks still miss, and soon the two have backed up near the edge, or what used to be the edge, of the lizard circle.

The lizard stops to collect himself for half a second, which gives Keera time to strike. They see the angle of attack a moment before they strike, allowing them to hit the lizard straight across the face with their own sharpened chain-whip. He is surprised, and even more enraged. He begins his next assault. But, Keera changes the pattern: attack, dodge, miss, strike. Attack, dodge, miss, strike. Blow after blow, cuts begin forming across the lizard's body, over half a dozen bleeding gashes. It's wearing him down. Keera has the upper hand.

Until they reach the curb.

Upon stepping back to avoid yet another attack, their footing doesn't account for a sudden sidewalk behind them. This sends them clattering to the ground, slamming their back into the curb. Pain shoots through their shoulders. They wince in pain, and before they can react, they feel a new, heavier pressure on their throat. The thug's boot is crushing their neck against the curb. Looking up, they see the now bloodied lizard gangster grinning down at them. Keera flails their arms around, searching for the whip. It's too far. They try to throw their hand in their pocket again in desperation, only for said arm to be painfully stomped into the pavement as well. Their bones begin to groan under the pressure. They try to scream. Nothing comes out. The figure leans down as close as it can. Keera can clearly see the wild look in the figure's reptilian eye.

"You know, before, you were only going to be a distraction, so my boss could finish off the merc lady," he hisses, "But now, with us being so far away... I don't think she can even see you. So... how about I have a little snack for all my troubles...?" He leans in close, hot, rancid breath wafting over Keera's face. A long, snake-like tongue slithers out toward them. A circle of serrated teeth inch closer, and closer, until...

Keera feels a drip on their face. Not saliva, it's darker. Red. The lizard freezes.

Then, suddenly, the gangster's head falls at them, bouncing away yo the side, and they feel his muscles that were pushing Keera into the cement slacken. Confused and horrified, Keera quickly scrambles out from under the now lifeless, but still heavy corpse. They back up a few steps and look in horror and confusion. The menacing head of the lizard-man is cut clean off.

And that's when she notices the figure standing next to them. Tall, dressed in dark clothes and a black jacket, with an asymmetrical collar. Brandishing two curved blades.

The bounty hunter.

Keera scrambles a foot or so back.

"Easy, little snow fox," he says.

"Don't touch me!" Keera shouts.

"I don't have any business with you... yet," he reassures, "I'm still after her." He points back to the front of the hotel, where the fight between Radley and the lizards is still going on.

Keera growls, "I won't let you hurt her, either!"

"Then maybe convince her to come peacefully," he says. Just then, sounds of roaring engines peel past them, toward the fight. Four massive vehicles, covered in rusted metal and bones, roll up to the scene, out of which dozens more lizard-men come scrambling out.

"Neither of us will get our way if those arseholes get to her first," he says, "What do you say? Temporary truce?" He holds out a hand, offering one of his two blades to Keera. They eye it, then him. Behind them, the shouting and sounds of combat intensify. *I don't trust this prick,* they think, *but dammit...* Gritting their teeth, they grab the daywalker's strange curved blade. He chuckles, "Let's bring them hell, snow fox."

Chapter 12

K EERA CHARGES TOWARD THE lizard-men circle. The bounty hunter is faster, and by the time Keera gets there, the first few foes are already in pieces, run through, or decapitated. While they don't like working with a man who tried to kill them a few days ago, they do appreciate how efficient he's making this process so far. Even just holding it, Keera can tell this sword is unwieldy for them. With no training, they think they'll be lucky if they even kill one lizard-man. It's all they've got, so they'll have to make do.

Meanwhile, the daywalker has made quick work of quite a few gangsters. Reaching the outer circle, Keera beholds a bloodbath: lizard-man bodies are strewn everywhere, blood glistening on the pavement. At the center, Radley is looking cut up, panting, but still fighting. The big lizard, on the other hand, seems in relatively good condition. A bit winded, but unscratched.

Keera follows close behind the bounty hunter, eyeing the crowd of jeering lizards who are eyeing them back. As they approach, the big lizard rushes in for another grab at Radley, only for her to juke spin around him, firing a few shots into his chest. The bullets merely bounce off.

The lizard cackles. "Stupid girl," he taunts, "Haven't you realized by now, my scales are hard as steel! Punny little bullets like yours won't leave a scratch."

"Wonder what a blade will do to you, then, Vertex," the bounty hunter says, as the two approach the lizard boss from behind. He spins around in shock. Shock that slides back into a cocky grin.

"Well, well, well," the big lizard known as Vertex laughs, "If it isn't Jack Cressfield! Come to help me clean up this little mess?"

The bounty hunter, Jack, waffles his head back and forth, as if contemplating, while effortlessly twirling his blade. "Oh, I'll clean up this mess. But I won't be splitting a bounty."

Vertex growls, "What are you trying to suggest?"

"I'm suggesting you step aside before this gets ugly," he says.

"Careful what you're saying, boy," Vertex retorts, "I'm not just another lowlife hunting a bounty like you. I'm *with* Manhattan Gate. A private contractor! So, if you get in my way, you can kiss your money goodbye."

This gives Jack pause for a moment, making Keera tense up. He then glances around the crowd of armed thugs, to Keera, then back to Vertex. "Well then," he says, cracking his neck and raising his blade, "I guess I just can't leave any witnesses, can I?"

Vertex growls, before ordering his troops, "GET HIM! AND THE CHILD, TOO!"

Dozens of heads swivel toward the two intruders. Jack gets in a ready stance, Keera attempts the same.

Jack says, "Stay close, stay low, and most importantly, stay out of my way."

Keera jams their hand in their pocket, grips the leaf tight, ready to face the hoard. For Radley.

There's a brief moment of stillness.

Then, they charge.

Three or four rush in at a time. A flurry of blades, metal, and blood. Then another three or four. Keera stays low, as instructed, dodging attacks with the help of blurry foreshadowing visions. Dodge, block. They attempt to strike, but their intuition is proven correct, and the blade is too hard to wield. Instead, they keep to blocking strikes with it. Above them, the vampire is laying into any incoming lizard. They are cut through like a hot knife through paper. With each strike that draws blood, he runs his tongue along the blade. Up close, it gives Keera horrible flashbacks to the attack in the woods. They shake off the memories, though, and remain focused on the task: survive, and pull attention from Radley.

Their plan seems to be working. With less heat on her, Radley presses the attack more on Vertex. He's still receiving little to no damage from the bullets, though. Keera knows Radley realizes this. She's just keeping up the pressure. She's smart, she will figure out something, if they just give her time.

A lizard-man with a heavy wooden club dashes forward, screaming, ready to overhand smash Keera into the ground. However, they see the move coming, and dodge backward just in time. Then, from the side, Jack swoops in and slashes his throat, crumpling him to the pavement. He then turns to Keera after lapping up the blood. "He was wide open. What were you doing?" he shouts, blocking another incoming attack.

"Your weird sword is too heavy!" Keera clarifies, dodging under another attack.

Jack slashes another foe to the ground, then snatches a small dagger from their hands.

"Need something lighter?" he asks. He tosses the knife, which they barely catch without cutting themselves. It's way lighter, but VERY small.

"What am I supposed to do with this?!" they protest.

"You seem like a bright kid. You'll figure it out," he says, before his attention is drawn to two lizard-men trying to interfere with Radley and Vertex's duel.

Keera grips the tiny knife tight. They don't like how close this means they have to get to these monster men. They don't seem to have any qualms with getting close to Keera, though, as another rushes in close, blade drawn. Keera, instead of dodging away from the foreshadowed attack, dodges closer and lower. They slice a point they know is weak; the Achilles tendon. Immediately, the lizard buckles down to their height, giving them a chance to stab the lizard-man in the neck. It lands, and they watch the shock and rage fade from their face as their consciousness fades. Keera has to take a moment to process: this is a humanoid creature they just killed. Not an instinct-driven slime, but a *humanoid man*. That introspection has to wait, though, as an idea springs to mind: The boss lizard. If Keera could get in close, slash the man to the ground, that might give Radley an opening to finish this once and for all.

Whipping around wildly, they find the dueling pair. Radley is aiming for another shot, but Vertex rushes in and smacks the pistol from her weakened grip. Keera needed to act, now. Rushing forward, they see an image of them attempting to run by, but it misses. Then they see a leaping attack, where they grab the lizard's shoulders, attempting a neck stab. They get thrown off, no effect. So, instead, they rush forward, slide under the man's crocodilian tail, and once again slash for that tendon. It does prove to be a bit tougher to cut, and they only manage to make a small slice. But, it's enough to get his attention. Vertex whirls around and growls at Keera, "You little BRAT! How DARE you make me bleed! I'll gut you, devour you, wear your skin as a belt!" He levels his massive shotgun at them, its barrel now chipped and worn from being in close melee with Radley. Keera Instantly regrets their decision, holding their breath, as they stare down the barrel of the largest gun they've ever seen.

The giant doors to the hotel fly open, a red and black heel kicking it through. Stepping out, flanked by at least a dozen armed suit-wearing security, is Lady Adley. She is also armed, with the *new* biggest gun Keera's ever seen: a mini-gun. Because of her size and strength, she wields it like a smaller person would wield a tommy gun.

Fury engulfs her expression, as she shouts, "Hey arseholes, you weren't invited! So, let me and Antoinette show you how we deal with party crashers."

With that, she levels her gun and unleashes a stream of high-caliber rounds into the fray. The bullets shred through bodies and vehicles alike. This breaks Vertex's resolve, and he shouts to his comrades, "RETREAT!" As he hobbles past, he hisses at Keera "We aren't finished yet, you and I." He then dives into one of the nearby transport trucks that peels away down the street. The rest of the vehicles explode as the barrage continues, the queen yelling with rage, assailants being splattered into a fine paste across the cement. Finally, the fire ceases, and all but Radley, Keera, and Jack are decimated.

Silence falls over the battlefield. Keera, who hit the deck when the lady began firing, looks around at the carnage. They've never seen so much blood in their life. Slowly, they and Radley stand, the latter much laboriously. They look at the Lady as she stomps down toward them.

"I thought you said you didn't leave anyone alive," she says.

Radley is about to respond, when from behind her, Jack calls out, "Sorry to disappoint, miss, but there might be one loose end they didn't tie up."

Keera, Radley, and Adley all ready their weapons at him, Adley's mini-gun whirring to the ready.

"And who the fuck are you?" Adley asks.

He goes to respond, but this time, Radley cuts him off, "The bounty hunter..."

Adley glares. "Should I waste him?" she asks coldly, the readied weapon aimed.

Just then, Jack sheathes both of his swords and raises his hands into the air, "Now hold on. I no longer have a quarrel with either of you."

"You tried to kill us less than a week ago!" Keera corrects, "And you JUST told me you'd try and collect Radley's bounty once we dealt with the lizards."

Radley, hearing this, throws back to Adley, "Yeah, waste him."

The mini-gun whirs even louder.

"WAIT WAIT WAIT!" the man pleads, "I know, I know what I said before. But, I just made myself an enemy of those posting your bounty. And the scaly bastard was right. I won't be getting a payout if I take you in now. Odds are, my head will be mounted right next to hers."

"So, we're just supposed to forgive and forget you trying to kill us?" Keera exclaims.

"I don't expect anything," he says, "I only ask that you recognize I was a man doing a job. And that job is no longer viable, so I will leave you alone if you let me live."

Keera doesn't trust him one bit. They've seen first-hand that he has a ferality inside him. Something he struggles to control. Plus, if another bounty *is* put out on either of them, they feel like there is a good chance they'll have to deal with him again. Keera figures they should deal with him here and now while he's vulnerable.

"Let him go," Radley says.

Keera whips around to her in dismay. "Are you serious?" they say, "After everything he did, we're just going to let him go?!"

"I've heard of a bounty hunter named Jack before," she explains, "Didn't know what he looked like, and certainly didn't know he was a daywalker. But what I do know is that Jack Cressfield is a professional though-and-through." She then looks at Jack before continuing, "Leave. And don't let me see you coming after either of us ever again."

"No promises, but..." he gives a slight bow, and starts to back away from the scene.

"Hold on a tick," Lady Adley suddenly calls from behind them. The man stops. "You said you were a merc for hire?"

"Yes madam," he responds.

"And how much was the bounty on these two, exactly?" she asks.

"It was only on the mercenary, but," he ponders for a moment, remembering, then says, "Thirty million credits."

Without hesitation, Lady Adley says, "Triple that. If you bring me the head of that gator that fucked up my hotel."

"Well, that sounds—"

"AND," she bellows, "If you help these two get where they need to go."

Both Keera and Radley whip around at this suggestion. "Wait WHAT?!" Keera exclaims.

Radley adds, "Adley, that is a lot of money."

"Eh, would cost close to that to repair this place. At least this way I'll get some nice croc leather boots out of the deal," the Lady adds, "I know you're going into something dangerous, Radley. The least I can do is to put my money behind something, or someone, to keep you safe."

"But why—"

"Stop questioning it," she says, stern, but quiet, like a caring mother, "You ran off on your own last time. Let me help this time, you and the kid. One that I've taken quite a liking to, to be frank." She gives Keera a small wink.

"Okay, but what if we don't WANT him with us?" Keera protests. Radley shoots them a "quiet down" look.

Adley responds, "Think of it this way: He can't stab you in the back if he's at your side."

Keera isn't sure that's a very logical thought process. But, based on Radley's disposition, it doesn't seem like they will have much say in the matter.

"Alright," Radley eventually says, "Thanks, Adley."

"It's nothing," she says. Then, to the vampire: "And how about you? Taking the contract?"

"Ninety million is more than tempting," he says, "However, my mistress doesn't usually take kindly to me traveling with others, *especially* other women."

"Would she really care if you came home with ninety million scratch?" Adley rebuffs.

He rubs his chin. Finally, he says, "Alright, you have a deal."

Keera huffs indignantly. This is not a good idea.

"Just know, we'll need to travel in daylight, and be in cover by the time the moon rises."

"What a coincidence, that was already the plan for tomorrow," Radley responds sarcastically.

Jack snickers, before turning around, saying over his shoulder, "I'll meet you both out here at sunrise. I'll get us a ride in the meantime." And, with that, he once again explodes into a flock of ravens that disappear into the moonless night.

Keera is still reeling from recent revelations. The confirmation this leaf is giving them powers, their first time killing a person, and now they're going to be traveling *with* a man who just tried to murder them a week ago? They feel like they are losing their grip on reality at this point. Plus, still not getting a good night's rest isn't helping either.

As if reading their thoughts, Adley says, "Apologies for your rooms getting wrecked. I'll get you an upgrade. On the house, of course."

"Thanks Adley," Radley says, "For everything."

"No problem," she says, "But, you owe me that lizard-man! I'm serious. I'm gonna start finding me a seamstress that can make him into a nice leather skirt once you come back."

The two chuckle before everyone makes their way back inside to retire for the rest of the night.

On their way up the stairs leading to their new room, Keera mutters to Radley, "Hey, um, so... you didn't correct Adley before when she said I'd be coming with you. Does that mean...?"

"Don't make a big thing out of it," she responds sharply, not looking at the child.

"Oh, okay," Keera says. They are holding in so much excitement. They aren't sure why, but knowing they will be sticking with this stranger they only met a few days ago is making them all giddy. Then, a thought dawns on Keera: "Well, if that's the case, then we should probably talk about something before we head out tomorrow."

"What is it?" Radley asks.

"I..." Keera doesn't know where to begin or how to start explaining it, so they just say what's been on their mind for a while now, "I think I might have powers, too."

Chapter 13

"So, just to make sure I'm understanding this," Radley says, "You see visions of the future whenever you grab this leaf?"

"Yeah, kinda," Keera responds, "It's more like... visions of *possible* futures. Sometimes, they're very vivid, and sometimes they're just like transparent ghosty-things on top of reality. I don't know, it's hard to explain."

Radley hums, thumbing the hilt of her blade in the sheathe she removed from her belt. The two are sitting on the floor of their new suite, even more lavish than the last. This one has a balcony view of the city, but neither of them couldn't care less about that right now. They are both staring at the small golden leaf lying between them on the beautifully ornate rug.

Keera breaks the contemplative silence, "So, is this... normal?"

"No," Radley says, not removing her eyes from the leaf.

"That's it? No insight from a seasoned traveler of the surface world?" Keera pushes.

Radley shakes her head slightly, saying, "All I know about timestuck objects is that they're just that: stuck." She goes to pick it up, only to struggle, like someone trying to pick up a penny glued to the sidewalk. Giving up, she says, "I've never heard anything about them giving anyone special abilities."

"Well, I'm guessing not many other people can do this, either," they say as they pick up the leaf, just as one would a normal leaf.

The mercenary's face can't mask her amazement. "Right," Radley says.

"So, what does this mean?" Keera asks again.

"Like I said, I don't know," Radley asserts.

"Do you know anyone who *might* know, then?"

"No, I—" she cuts herself off.

Keera can tell she is considering something. They press, "What? What is it?"

"I... *did* know someone that knows quite a bit about time and EUEs..." she trails off.

"That's perfect!" Keera exclaims, "Who are they? Where can we find them?"

"It's... complicated," Radley hesitates.

"I thought we were in this together, Radley," Keera presses more, "If I want to be a more competent fighter, I need to understand what's happening to me. Help me out here."

Radley sighs. This information she is holding onto clearly has a lot of weight to it. Finally, she asks, "You remember I'm from another universe, right?"

Keera nods.

"Well," Radley states, "My mentor in that other universe was an expert on things with time. He had to be, partially because it was his job within his order, but also because... I have abilities relating to time as well."

Keera's jaw nearly hits the floor. "You're kidding!" they exclaim.

Radley shakes her head.

"So wait, can you see the future and stuff too?! Is that why you're so fast?" they ask.

"Not quite," she responds, "I don't see the future, but instead slow down time around myself. To other people, it looks like I speed up, when in reality, they're the ones slowing down to me. It's because of relativity or something, that's what my old master used to say."

"That is... SO cool!" Keera shouts, "Like, what are the odds we BOTH have powers involving time?!"

Radley doesn't respond, looking off into the middle distance. Keera isn't going to let her angst bring them down, though.

"Well, then we have to go see this person," Keera says, before sudden disappointment hits them, "But... you said this person was in another universe, right?"

"Right," Radley says, "I mean... there is a chance that he will still be in this universe, just like all the organizations and locations here I'm familiar with." Keera hadn't thought of that; she had said she was from a different universe, yet she was aware of all these places and people. She clearly has been here for a while, given how close she is with Adley, but that still wouldn't account for *all* the information she possesses. Keera can only imagine how confusing that all must be.

"We could still give it a try? Do you know where he would be?" they ask.

"Not really. He could be anywhere, realistically."

"But you remember where he was in the other universe, right?"

"Yeah, but—"

"Then that's where we should go," Keera declares. Radley glares at them. "Come on, Radley, we have to try! I don't want to be the helpless tag-along kid forever."

There is a pregnant pause, before Radley once again sighs, "Fine."

"YES!" Keera throws their fists in the air, their body exploding with excitement.

"Let me finish," Radley growls, "Fine, if we have time, we can make a slight... detour."

"Is this person close to where you're headed?" Keera asks, simmered down a bit from the clarification.

"Last I knew, from a completely different causal universe, yes," with that, Radley stands, and heads toward one of the two beautiful beds, "But, please, enough questions for now. We need as much sleep as we can get. Early morning tomorrow."

At first, Keera is frustrated at being shut down again. They still had so much to ask. Every question seems to lead to a million more. But, they catch themself, remembering that they no longer have limited time with Radley. They can ask these questions tomorrow, or the next day, or next week. That feeling of certainty lifts a slight weight from the child's shoulders. Satisfied for now, they crawl into bed as well and fall almost immediately asleep. This time, it is an uninterrupted few hours of comfortable sleep. The most comfortable night they've had in a long, long time.

*****

This wonderful sleep is short-lived, as they are awoken by Radley a mere three hours later. Keera almost breaks down in tears, knowing that they may never have another chance to sleep like this again. Instead, they merely groan, groggily gather their supplies, and head down to the disheveled hotel lobby behind Radley. In the daylight, the havoc caused by the night's combat appears less intense, and strangely macabre. By now, the bodies of the lizards and the unfortunate party goers are disposed of, leaving behind only red stains that a few unfortunate service workers are currently trying to clean up. The harder-to-fix messes, like shattered windows and bullet holes in wood and stone, are easy to miss if one isn't specifically searching for them. Something told Keera that The Lady would have this place up and running again by nightfall.

Outside, the carnage is a bit more obvious: more blood, more bodies remaining, and a couple of burned-out husks of cars the queen's mini-gun had left in its wake. However, given the state of some parts of the rest of the world Keera has seen, these sorts of sights might not be the most deterring to determined clientele of The D'acier.

Parked nearby is a car with a flatbed, a dark-haired figure leaning against it. Well, it should be said, it *used* to be a car. At some point in its life, its owners seem to have brought it upon themselves to raise it a few feet with a massive suspension, equally huge tires, and some unartistically applied corrugated sheets, barbed wire, and sharp scraps of metal. What once was a nice car with some nice utility, has been transformed into a rusted, dusted, all-terrain vehicle of survival and a misanthropic worldview.

Jack is looking out at the sunrise when the two arrive. "Good morning, early birds," he says, as they draw his attention.

Radley immediately side eyes the vehicle. "Where did you get this?" she asks flatly.

"Found it," he shrugs.

"Well, I hope its previous owners don't come looking for it," she says, "I can't imagine this souped-up fossil is all that quiet."

"I wouldn't worry about them," he says, which makes Keera shiver with unease. The bounty hunter must have noticed this, as he adds, "I didn't kill them. I bought it off them. I'm not a monster."

"Vampires were always monsters in the stories I've read," Keera mutters.

"Well, the real world is a bit more complicated than stories, little fox," he says.

"My name is Keera," they assert.

"Noted," he says, clearly not particularly interested, "Now, can we get going? We're burning daylight." He rounds the car and climbs in the driver's seat.

Radley pops open the other door, then pauses. "You couldn't have found a vehicle with enough seats for all of us?" she criticizes.

"There is enough," he says, pointing as he explains, "I'll drive. You get in the passenger, and the kid can ride in the bed."

"They are not going in the back," Radley asserts.

"Alright, fine, you in the back, and the kid can ride shotgun with me," he concedes.

Keera chimes in, "Wait, no, I don't want to ride in there with him!"

Radley looks to Keera, then the man. Jack then adds to her, "Unless you know how to drive?"

Radley considers this, before turning back to Keera. "Ride up front."

"But Radley!" they whine.

"I'll be right behind you if he tries anything," she says, placing a comforting hand on their shoulder before hopping up into the flatbed. On one hand, Keera isn't jazzed about riding shotgun with this man. On the other, though, Keera did appreciate the nuance of Radley not simply shutting them down. If this was the new norm, Keera will take it. Reassurance, this is nice.

What is less nice is sitting close to Jack. Right away, the smell of copper hits Keera's nose. He doesn't look visibly bloody, so they aren't sure why he smells so much of it. But, knowing his... diet last night, they have a guess. Probably some kind of vampire thing. Keera is glad this car has no windows. Until he turns the key in the ignition, and the vehicle roars to life, filling the cabin with the smell of ripe exhaust.

Over the roar, Jack calls back to the merc, "Alright, where to, white wolf?"

"My name's Radley," she asserts, "And Summit Station."

This causes the bounty hunter to twist toward her in his seat, as if to make sure he heard that right. He states, "I thought that was just a myth." Radley reaches a hand through the open back window, handing him a small scrap of paper. Jack studies it for a moment before whistling in amazement, "Well, at least I'm getting paid for this." He types a set of random numbers into a small device on the center console before shifting into gear. A holographic display appears in front of the device, showing a small arrow near the bottom, and an arrow somewhere near the top right. To almost no one, he says, "Buckle up." The vehicle lurches forward and away, down the streets of Brezio City.

The wind buffets Keera, blowing away any unpleasant smell, but making it ridiculously hard to hear anything. As such, they shout, "Wait, what's the deal with Summit Station?"

"Your friend here must be on a suicide mission," Jack says, "It's said to be one of the most highly secretive and heavily guarded Manhattan Gate research facilities this side of The Wastes."

Keera furrows their brow, processing this new information. Now they understand her comment about going up against Manhattan Gate, eventually. They just couldn't imagine why she would be looking for a research facility, of all things. Is there something there that would help them somehow? Maybe to get home to their universe? They're sure it'll be a bit before they can get to those answers. For now, they'll focus on the journey ahead. They look to the image that they've deduced as a map, and ask Jack, "How far is it to this Summit Station?"

He looks at the map again. "If these coordinates are to be believed, we're about three days out by car," he says, "Although, I personally think we aren't going to find anything there except a patch of dirt."

"What makes you say that?" Keera says, a hint of defensiveness for Radley in their tone.

Jack waffles his head flippantly, "I don't know. Call me a pessimist, but information like this is hard to come by. And, the odds you got this *without* Manhattan killing you first is—"

"It's there," Radley shuts him down, "Trust me. Now, shut up and drive."

Jack raises an amused eyebrow. "Yes ma'am," he says. The next few hours of driving are awkwardly silent as the monster car speeds down a highway, leaving the gleaming city of Brezio shrinking behind them. Keera isn't sure what to say to this strange man, or even if they should speak with him. Keera sighs, and looks out the window at the gray landscape. Even though they're nervous about their new travel companion, they can't help but to be excited about the journey they're embarking on. This is it, this is what they always dreamed of. An adventure. And, while they aren't sure what lies ahead, they know at least one person up here has their back.

CHAPTER 14

JOURNEYING WITH THREE PEOPLE is weird. When it was just Keera and Radley, there was turbulent, yet comfortable silence. This silence, between three people, one of whom doesn't know much of anything about the other two, is more uncomfortably unbalanced. The two adult professionals don't show any interest in talking. Keera can't really talk to Radley in their current seating arrangement, and they don't really have a desire to speak with the man next to them. This all makes for a quiet first day of driving, then stopping at some abandoned roadside building for the night. Same thing with day two.

Until nightfall. The trio have set up a campfire underneath a rocky outcropping a little way off the highway. It's far enough away from the road as to not attract attention, and hidden from the slight sliver of a moon that was just starting to become visible again as the new moon passes. Radley has elected to keep watch, while Keera and Jack stay back by the fire, having a meal before they bed down. Jack eating intrigues Keera: he's having food like a normal person. He has roasted the ever living hell out of the sausage ration they had acquired from Adley's stores.

Eventually, curiosity overwhelms their social anxiety, and they ask, "I thought vampires only drank blood?"

Still with a mouthful, Jack responds, "Once again, the stories are a lot different than reality, kid."

"First, don't call me kid," they protest, "And second, wanna tell me what's different between you and the monsters in the books, then?"

"Sure, I love educating the youth," he says, finishing his first hotdog. He grabs another from the sack, skewers it, and begins roasting it over the crackling flame as he goes on to explain, "So, I do still drink blood. But I don't need it to survive. It just gives me an... energy boost. The more I get, the stronger I am, for a time."

"Like back when you first fought Radley," they clarify.

His expression dims a little. "That time I had a little too much. The more I get, the more I want, and the more I... lose myself in wanting to get it," he says, "I'm not proud that happened. Try to limit my intake, but it's a delicate balance. I wasn't expecting that protector of yours to be so... resilient. I got cocky."

"Not proud?!" Keera scoffs, "You nearly KILLED us!"

He looks back at them, the charismatic smile returning to his eyes. "Well, it's a good thing you and your sharp thinking were there to shut me down before I did," he says matter-of-factly.

Not a fan of that answer, Keera kept the conversation going: "So, what else? What else is different? I saw you turn into ravens, not bats. Is that one of them?"

"That's more of a difference between daywalkers and true vampires," he responds, "Real vampires still turn into bats, are burned by sunlight, killed only by piercing the heart, etcetera, etcetera."

"But you turn into birds and are hurt by the moon," Keera reiterates.

"Exactly," he says, munching the now burnt to a crisp hotdog, "And we're a lot less durable. Still harder to kill than your average Simon or Lacey, but it doesn't have to be as specific as a sharp thing through the heart. In case you were wondering."

"Good to know," Keera says. They intended to sound a bit threatening with that statement, but he didn't seem to notice.

Silence befalls the camp again. Only the campfire snaps and pops permeate the space.

Then, just as Keera realizes they left the space for it to happen, Jack asks them, "So, where are you from, snow fox?"

They still really don't like that nickname. Was it the hair? So dumb. They have half a mind to shut that moniker down right now. But they decide to shrug it off. *Whatever,* Keera thinks, *It's better than "kid," I guess.* They respond instead with, "Why do you care?"

"If I recall correctly," he says, "My job is to get *both* of you to Summit Station alive. And, well, while money is one hell of an incentive, having a personal connection to your client is a good way to become more invested, as it were."

Keera doesn't like it, doesn't fully grasp it... but also figures there wasn't any harm in telling him *some* of the truth. It isn't like their home is something he could use against them if that time came. Couldn't threaten friends and family or anything. Still, specifics feel a bit too personal right now, so they decide to respond with, "I'm from a bunker town."

"Ahhhh, that explains it," he nods.

"Explains what?" they ask, feeling the indignity rising.

"Why you're so skittish all the time," he says, "Like a young kit making her way out of the den for her first spring. Everything is new, I would imagine. From the smell of the air, to the feeling of wind on your skin."

The way he talks about it, Keera can tell this is deeper than just a good educated guess. "How would you know what that feels like?" they ask.

"That's a... a long story," he says, staring off a bit into the distance, "But, just know, I get what it's like, to have to learn all about a new world, and a new way of life." He pauses, and then says, "If you ever have any questions, feel free to ask. I would hope either Radley or I can answer to the best of our ability."

This openness surprises Keera. Maybe they are just so used to Radley's icy demeanor from before, but it feels odd not having to fight for every scrap of information they wanted. But now, with the promise of not one, but TWO adult figures in their life willing to be open and honest? This feels almost too good to be true.

"But," Jack says, yawning, "I think that's enough for tonight. Ask me tomorrow, and I'll give you the story, alright, snow fox?"

Keera resolutely nods, "Alright."

With that, Jack picks himself up, wanders a bit away, and curls up in his sleeping bag for the night. Keera stays and watches the fire for a bit longer. Maybe they had misjudged this man. Sure, he is a killer, but so is Radley. And, she was right, Jack Cressfield does seem like a consummate professional. The bit of blood turning him feral is slightly concerning, and Keera hopes that is something he really *does* have under control, and not something he just said to make them not worry. Either way, they figure Radley seems to be staying up for a while tonight, off on a rock, staring into the night sky. If anything happens, they know she'll protect them. That is enough comfort for Keera to grab their own things and get some shuteye. According to Jack's estimate, they should be reaching Summit Station in a bit over a day. They need all the sleep they can get.

***

Come day three, the trip hits an unexpected and sizable speed bump.

"Well, shit," Jack says. He is standing beside the other two, hands on his hips, surveying the problem ahead.

"This wasn't on your map?" Radley asks.

"Must've happened within the last year or so," he explains, "Satellites haven't updated in this area yet."

Before them is yet another city. Compact, and in way worse shape than Brezio, the towering skyscrapers look more like dead, rotted swamp trees than gleaming pillars of human ingenuity. Adding to the bog-like aesthetic of the city — and the main reason it has stopped the group dead — is the fact that the entire city is sunken in a flooded crater-like lake. The water levels are high enough to reach, on average, the third or fourth floor of said buildings. The tallest of these skyscrapers, a monolith that Keera had seen from miles away earlier that day, stands at the heart of the flooded basin, bearing a massive array of radar dishes at the top. It would be another peculiar, striking scene, if not for its implications for their journey.

The crater itself is a bit traumatizing to Keera specifically, flashing them back to the wreckage of Canary. They try to push that thought away, but it keeps creeping up, as if a ghostly hand is squeezing their heart.

Only Radley's voice pulls them away, "Keera, come on." They turn their head to see the two hopping back in the car.

"Wait, what are we going to do?" they call back to them.

"Go around," Jack calls back, "Should only add another day and a half to the trip."

Keera sighs. They're impatient to see this person Radley thinks can help them with their new abilities. And, while it is only a bit over a day riding in a car instead of walking, the disappointment is still there. Begrudgingly, Keera returns to the car, and the group speeds off clockwise around the rim of the crater. This is unfortunate, because no matter what direction they look, the sunken city is in some part of Keera's view, which draws their mind back. Eventually, they give in, and let themselves be taken with the admittedly beautiful view of the ruins. Their mind wanders back to home, and just how far they've come in such a short period. How much they've learned, how much they've felt since the last time they saw a crater like this. The loss is still fresh, however, and they catch themselves tearing up a bit about nothing in particular. Just the memories. They wipe them away, though. There will be time for that later, they're sure of it. For now, they are going to try to enjoy the view.

As they gaze out at the dilapidated city, the setting sun bounces off the surface of the crater lake, creating a glittering blade of silver across the water's surface. Higher up, however, another glitter catches Keera's eye. Well past the waterline, near the top of the tall tower at the center of the city, something is flashing intermittently. The teen squints their eyes. It could be a reflection from one of the rare remaining windows. But no, something about the way it flashes...

KA-POW!

A crack echoes through the crater. The front right of the car nose dives into the dirt, sending the whole thing flipping ass over teakettle. It flips and rolls and tumbles down, down the embankment of the crater, landing with an abrupt splash in the hungry black water below.

Chapter 15

Keera's ears are ringing. Darkness fades into vague shapes, into the image of Jack and Radley crouched over them, backlit by a beam of light. All they can feel is soreness and a burning in their lungs. As the ringing dissipates, it becomes clear both adults are trying to say something to them. They have been this whole time.

"Keera! Keera!" Radley exclaims, "Thank fuck."

Keera is confused. Why is she so worried? Where are they? They can't remember. They just feel cold all over, a realization that all at once sends them into a full-body shiver. Radley and Jack slowly help them up, a warm and dry something being wrapped around them. But they barely realize, as their mind is still trying to remember what just happened. The last thing they remember is the gleaming waters of the half-sunken city, a gleam high in one tower, and then the car—

Their eyes go wide. "Radley, the car—" is as far as they can get before spiraling into a coughing fit. They feel soaking wet and frigid to the bone as the retching rattles their thin frame.

"It's alright, little fox, take it slow," Jack soothes, "You've just been through the wringer."

Eventually, as the coughing subsides, Keera can croak out, "What happened?"

"We were ambushed," Radley says, "Someone shot out our tire, and we fell into the crater. Jack saved you from drowning."

"Not all credit is mine. Radley here pulled you out of that wreck and dragged you to shore here. I merely administered CPR," Jack adds.

"Still, thank you," Radley says. There is what sounds like genuine thanks to her voice.

Looking at Jack, they notice a darker spot on the shoulder of his jacket. He must've seen them glance at it, and he says, "This? Our sniper friend managed to literally wing me in my raven form," he explains, "Don't worry about it. Just won't be flying for a while. We all got really lucky."

"I don't know if luck has anything to do with it," Radley insists, "That person hit a car's tire moving at over seventy miles per hour, and a bird mid-flight. We're dealing with one really good sharpshooter."

Jack stands and walks a few steps away with Radley to have a slightly more private talk. As private as one can have in a space like this; Keera observes the dark, barren room, with stark-white walls and gray concrete floor. The aforementioned beam of fading orange light is coming from a few windows about ten feet up, all missing their glass. To their left, Keera sees the floor crumbled away into a dark pool of undulating water. Where they must have come ashore.

Just then, Radley's voice explodes in the silence, "We can't stay here! Pretty soon, that sniper's reinforcements will be on top of us, and we'll have nowhere to run!"

"We don't know where they are," Jack retorts, "If we step one foot outside this building — hell, one TOE — we're liable to get it blasted off. I say we wait them out."

"You don't seem to get it," Radley says, gritting her teeth, "Snipers don't work alone, they work in pairs. Also, they likely have had time to make sure they have supplies for the long haul. This feels like a trap."

"You don't know ANY of that!" Jack exclaims, "For all we know, this is another bounty hunting asshole who just happened to spot us through their scope!"

Radley gets up in Cressfields' face, "I don't believe in luck." With that, she storms off toward the stairs, in a corner of the vacant space.

"Where are you going?" Jack calls after her, like a parent talking to a petulant teenager.

"Figuring out how to take out this sniper," she replies without turning around, "Stay with Keera."

"Again, you don't know where they are! You could step out right into their crosshairs!" Jack argues.

It's then that Keera croaks in, "Tow-er."

Both warriors stop and turn to the child. They continue, through coughs, "I saw... a light... in the tower..."

"Show me," Radley says.

***

"There," Keera points a weak and cautious finger up at the massive central tower. The trio had to climb several flights of stairs to reach a window with a reasonable vantage point. It was a struggle for Keera, who was still aching. Jack had helped them carry on, though, and by the top, they were feeling a bit better. They were a bit hurt that Radley was being so demanding of them in a time like this, but they understand she is a woman on a mission right now.

"Hm," Radley responds, "Well, that certainly is a good sniper's nest. Good view of the entire area, open sight lines near it to prevent people from trying to get in close. Yeah, we're dealing with a pro here."

All three duck back behind the cover of the wall.

"That settles things," Jack says, "There is no getting near this person to take them out. We need to wait them out, figure out how to sneak out of this crater without them noticing."

Radley sighs frustratedly, "Crater walls are too steep for all three of us to climb it in time."

"You're working off only assumptions,"

"And so are you," Radley retorts, "But I, for one, would much rather go down fighting than wait to get cornered or starve to death."

A silence falls over the room. Neither of the options are ideal. Keera doesn't like their odds either way. There are too many unknowns, and so little room for error. Sure, Radley and Jack are tough and fast, but even one bullet could end it all.

Then, a thought occurs to them. "What about going at night?" they ask, "They shouldn't be able to see us then."

"Odds are, they will have some form of night vision setup," Radley says, "But, even with that, it would still limit their visibility a bit. Hm..."

"We still couldn't stay outside long, though," Jack adds, "Or I'd burn up."

That's right, Keera forgot about Jack's weakness to the moon. Damn him for being an ass-backwards vampire. Still, Keera thinks this is the best plan. Stay close, move in the cover of night. But is there a way to keep Jack out of direct moonlight for most of the trip? Keera thinks, staring out the window at the brick building next door, with its window framed within theirs. And then it clicks.

That's it!

"We go building to building!" they exclaim.

"What?" Jack responds.

"We jump from building to building to get closer," they explain, "It's a lot faster and less risky than swimming down below, and the cover from the buildings will keep us hidden from both the sniper and the moon!"

"Some of these buildings are pretty close to each other," Jack contemplates, rubbing his five o'clock chin, "This could work, at least up until we reach the area around the tower."

"What do you think, Radley?" Keera asks.

The stoic mercenary is deep in thought about this as well. "I don't know..." they mutter, trailing off.

"I mean, you're right, Radley, we can't stay put. This way, we're trying both of your ideas, at least partially. Hide for a while until it's safer to move. Then we get a bit closer, so we can figure out how we're going to get up to that asshole."

There's a pause from Radley. "Alright. Seems it's the best plan we have for now," she finally responds, "Give it a few hours, get some rest. Stay away from windows. Around midnight, we'll move out." Keera feels a bit of warm pride wash over their still shivering body. They actually came up with a plan Radley seems to agree with. Maybe they're getting ahold of this surface survival stuff after all. The three congregate near the center of the room, laying up for a brief nap, as the last of the red sunlight sets somewhere outside. The room grows darker and darker, until it is eventually pitch black, only hints of light from the moon and the stars outside illuminating the barren room, as Keera slowly drifts off to sleep.

***

Keera isn't sure what woke them. As they fade back to consciousness, they can hear a faint buzzing sound. It's a sound not dissimilar from the one they heard ringing in their ears after the car wreck earlier. However, this one is quieter, with more of a humming tone than a ringing one. Blurry-eyed, they try to blink through the darkness to see what could be making such a strange noise. They can't see anything. Looking to the other two, both Radley and Jack are still asleep beside them. The events of that day must've taken their toll on both of them, as well. As Keera's eyes are now slowly adjusting to the darkness, the teen sits up a bit, squinting in the direction the sound is coming from. It is coming from a *direction*, which is promising; it's not just in their head.

Then they see movement. It looks to be about sixty feet away. *That doesn't make sense,* Keera thinks. The room itself is not that large from where they're posted up in the middle of it. Then they see the figure dart to the right, and as it does so, it passes behind something. Then it hits Keera: that something it passed behind and has now appeared on the other side of is the outer wall of the room. It's outside. Outside a six or seven story window. It's flying.

A drone.

They've been made.

Not looking away from the drone, Keera slowly reaches an arm back, and when it hits one of her companions, she shakes them frantically. The figure snorts awake. It's Jack.

"Huh, wha—" he mumbles.

Keera silences him with a, "Shhh!" They then point toward the drone. It is still hovering there, menacingly peering in. Jack's eyes go wide. He reaches over and does the same to Radley. She wakes with an abrupt start, reaching for a weapon. Jack stops her and silently gestures to the drone as well.

"Oh, shit," she whispers.

"What are you doing? Shoot it!" Keera hisses.

"We don't know if it's spotted us yet," Jack responds. The gun would give away their position for sure.

The three watch in silence for a moment, neither them nor the drone moving. Seconds feel like minutes. Neither budges.

"Keera," Radley suddenly whispers, "Do the thing."

"What?" Keera is confused.

"The thing, you know... the thing that lets you see the future," she clarifies.

"Wait, you can see the future?" Jack responds, almost a bit too loud, "Well, that explains how you were able to best me."

Keera shoots him a stern glare. *Time and place, dude,* they think. Then, heeding Radley's advice, they grip the leaf in their pocket and try to concentrate, still afraid to drop eye contact on the drone. Nothing. They try harder, gritting their teeth and trying to urge the power to happen. Still nothing. They then realize they haven't been breathing and release the pent-up air.

"I don't think it worked," they report.

Radley snaps back, "Wait, you don't *know* when it works and when it doesn't?"

"I guess we'll see in a little bit. If something bad happens, and time rewinds," Keera says, unsure what else to say.

"That doesn't sound very helpful," Jack chimes in.

KA-POW!

A shot crackles from somewhere. There's an impact on one windowsill, and suddenly Radley cries out in pain. The other two spin to her, seeing her clutching her left arm.

"WE'VE BEEN SPOTTED!" she shouts, "RUN!"

Instantly, the three are on their feet, sprinting as one. They go to the nearest window. Radley goes first, then Jack. Keera hesitates. The jump is only a few feet, but they make the mistake of looking down and see inky black water fifty feet down.

"Jump, now!" Jack orders, holding out an arm toward the teen. Another KA-POW shatters the night, and concrete from the wall next to Keera explodes into their face, the bullet just missing them. No hesitation.

They jump and land in the other building, Jack steadying them on the dismount.

"Come on, keep going!" Radley calls, motioning for the group to keep running. They do so, as another KA-POW sends a bullet impacting somewhere near them.

The three dodge and weave through the unused space, once an office building, as they dip and weave through abandoned cubicles and desk setups. Intermittent sniper shots explode nearby plywood furnishing, or scatter stacks of rotted paper into the air, feet from the group. Even with the cover of night, being inside a building, and being three fast moving targets, this sniper is still getting unnervingly close.

They reach another window. The building on the other side is further away than the last. But, with built up speed and adrenaline, the three leap, tumbling into it, one after another.

This one's an apartment. Keera trips over a knocked-over lamp that they don't notice, sending them careening to the floor. Catching themself, a couch near them explodes, another KA-POW. They fall into a reflexive fetal position. They tremble there for a moment, before a familiar whirring noise makes them peek up cautiously. It's the drone, watching from outside a now shattered window. A bit closer now, they can see its large, six-foot wingspan, with two spinning rotors on either wing, and the subtle gleam of a camera eyeing them from its belly.

Just then, a hand grabs their arm and yanks them to their feet. "Come on, keep up," Jack orders.

Keera complies, and the two catch up to Radley, who is about to jump to the next building. They do so, but not before glancing to their left to confirm their suspicion. Sure enough, the drone is beside them, keeping pace.

They jump to the next building, a hotel. As they duck through the room they just landed in, Keera shouts from the back of the pack, "It's the drone! It's following us!"

"Radley," Jack shouts up the chain, "Take it out!"

Without hesitation, the mercenary whips out her pistol and fires a few shots at the pursuing entity. Unfortunately, the drone dips up above the windowsill, dodging shots. "Damnit," Radley curses, "I'll never get a clean shot like this!"

"So keep running, then?" Keera clarifies. Just then, another KA-POW detonates the wall next to Jack's head. Inches.

"Those shots are getting too close," Jack disagrees, "We have to take out that drone if we want to get anywhere close to the tower!"

As the trio busts through the door of another hotel room, Jack whips his head to the right. A long hallway extends ahead, turning right into darkness. He shouts, "This way!" Keera follows, and Radley doubles back to follow Keera.

"Where are you going?!" Radley questions.

"Somewhere with no windows," he responds, "Trust me!"

No time to argue now. Keera and Radley follow Jack through the snaking hallway, turning left, then right, then left again. It reminds Keera of the last hotel they had to make a daring escape from. Only, this one is pitch black, and they are using the vague outline of Jack's back to guide them.

Eventually, Jack halts, hugging a corner. He motions for the others to get around it as well. Radley and Keera crouch down, while Jack hugs the wall, peeking the corner. All three of them panting. Keera's heartbeat is echoing in their ears, not showing any signs of slowing down.

For a handful of long, drawn-out minutes, it is silent.

Then, echoing from somewhere down the hallway, a quiet and ever-growing buzz can be heard. At that, Jack gestures for everyone to get back. He whispers, "Okay, I'll pin it in place. Radley, light it up when I give the signal. Keera, stay back, and stay safe."

For a moment, Keera wants to protest, but the desire to be done with this thing overrides their desire to be the hero. So, they move down to the other end of the hallway, and duck in the threshold of a room, still crouched. The other two do the same, Jack near the corner they were all crouched behind, and Radley about half way.

They wait again. The buzzing grows louder and louder. Eventually, the sound becomes so loud, its piercing tone almost makes Keera wince.

Soon, the wide, flat silhouette of the hovering drone slowly curves around the corner. The thing's wingspan nearly clips the walls as it moves, just barely fitting in this space. They see the machine rotate toward a doorway, pause for a moment, then continue. It moves to another doorway and does the same. It's checking every nook and cranny. Keera's heart beats faster. It will find Jack before he has time to spring the trap. They don't know if this thing has weapons too, but they don't want to risk Jack to find out. Keera thinks fast. They can only think of one option...

Just as the drone is about to turn toward Jack, Keera summons the courage, and leaps up from their crouched position, arms wide and waving. "HEY, YOU PIECE OF SHIT!" they shout.

The drone instantly swivels their way, the gleaming black camera eye focused on the teen.

Jack sees the opportunity. He springs out from his hiding spot, blades in hand, and drives them through near where the propellers meet the body of this thing. He holds on tight, the drone twitching and wriggling in response. "RADLEY, NOW!" he shouts.

Radley pops out and fires an entire magazine into the body of this thing. It flinches and sparks; the bullets ripping through the metal components. In the flashes from the gun, Keera can clearly see this thing reeling from the assault. One shot seems to hit it straight in its camera, glass and components flying everywhere. It is damaged, but still hovering.

As Radley goes to reload, the drone suddenly rolls from side to side, a three-sixty counterclockwise spin mid air. This is too much for Jack, as he winces from his shoulder wound. The blades break free, sending Jack flying into the hallway wall. No sooner is it free from its unwanted passenger, does it turn around and buzz away, slamming into walls as it maneuvers back down the hall from where it came. The sounds of it banging and smashing into walls follow that of buzzing rotor blades, growing fainter and fainter, until the hallway is quiet once more.

Jack slowly gets off the floor, adjusting his shoulder, groaning.

"Should we go after it?" Keera asks.

"No," Radley responds, "I got its camera. It won't be able to help spot us anymore. We should be safe for the rest of the night."

"Still, we should keep moving," Jack adds, "We have them on their back foot. We should get as close as we can before we bed down again."

Radley nods, and so does Keera internally. Together, the three take the time to navigate a different route to the edge of the hotel. After orienting themselves by locating the tower, the group hops a few more buildings, trying to move low and quickly. Eventually, they run out of buildings to hop to, finding themselves in another hotel, looking out at the courtyard that surrounds the infamous skyscraper. A wide circle of water surrounds it, what would have been three or four lanes wide if the road were still visible. The three linger on the scene for a while, each studying it, trying to figure some angle of attack. But, because of exhaustion, and a lack of true visibility, they decide it is best they take what's left of their night and rest up. It has been an unexpectedly stressful day. And tomorrow, they will be storming the tower.

CHAPTER 16

DAWN BREAKS, AND THE crew wake from a restless sleep. Keera, at least, could not stay asleep, periodically waking up in a panic, thinking they heard that drone's terror-inducing buzz. But, it never was never the case, and they had a restless night on an old, broken hotel mattress for nothing.

By the time they awake, Jack and Radley are already up and about. Jack is nowhere to be seen, while Radley is standing, arms crossed near a window, staring out at the plaza. Keera grabs a bit of food from their pack and decides to join her.

"Anything yet?" Keera asks, chewing on jerky.

"No," Radley replies flatly. Her eyes haven't moved from the skyscraper. Keera looks out at it, too. In the day, the sight is not much different: too much water and open sky between them and its base.

"Where's Jack?" Keera asks.

"He's scouting out the rest of the hotel," she responds, "Trying to see if there's anything here that can help us."

Keera nods, still munching. An odd calm pervades this moment. Only the gentle lapping of waves down below and a gentle breeze interrupt the stillness. If Keera didn't know any better, they would assume the sniper had left in the night, and the three were just taking a well-needed, quiet rest before moving on. But they did know better, and Radley's pensive stare was evidence, if it was needed.

"Wish we could just build a bridge," Keera muses, munching.

"Too little cover," Radley adds. Keera hadn't intended that to be a serious suggestion, just wishful thinking. But, if they are *actually* spit balling ideas at each other, they're game.

"What about swimming across, but with some sort of mobile cover protecting us?" they ask.

"Too conspicuous," Radley rebuttals, "Besides, anything we could fashion to float like that, on such short notice, would be too weak to withstand sniper fire."

"Hmmm..." Keera ponders, rubbing their pointer finger with their thumb to help think, "Maybe make a smokescreen?"

"Don't have the materials. We also don't know what other tech they might have that could see through the smoke," she says.

"A distraction? One draws their attention, while the others slip in?" Keera suggests.

"Would be suicide for the bait. And no one here's expendable. Unless... maybe Jack?" she adds, glancing over at Keera with a wry smile. They didn't know their distrust of their new companion still came through that strongly to her. Keera returns the glance and the smile.

Just then, Keera hears heavy boot-steps behind them, and they turn to see Jack strolling in. He's carrying something that Keera has to double-take at: two plates, each piled high with mounds and mounds of steaming, fresh, delicious-smelling food. "Does this make me less expendable?" he jests with his own smirk.

Radley asks, "Where... where did you get that?"

"Oh, this?" he asks, as if she could be asking about anything else, "I found it on the first floor."

"You just... found a bunch of food down there? Unspoiled?" she is still incredulous.

Jack starts handing out the food, "No, anything not in cans was well past expired," he explains.

The two cautiously take the plates, as if he's about to yell "sike" and snatch them back at any moment. Keera eyes him, then the food. It looks and smells delicious, even better than the few bits of cooked food they got while briefly staying at The D'acier. It reminds them of meals they had during community gatherings down in Canary Bridge. The desire to dig in is strong, but they hesitate. Jack is still on the fence, as far as Keera is concerned. About to get off it, but not just yet. They need the full story first.

"How did you cook it?" they ask.

"How about I just show you," he says, gesturing with his hand as he turns to leave, "Come on, can you walk and eat?"

Mine as well, they seem to both decide, as they follow Jack out of the room.

The bounty hunter takes them down, down flights of stairs. Keera misses the working elevators in D'acier. Along the way, Radley starts eating the meal. Keera looks at their own plate, shrugs, and digs in. It *is* delicious. Wonderful, warm mashed potatoes, crispy corned beef hash, and tender fried carrots. There's less butter than Keera is used to, but the seasonings present are making up for it and then some. It's so good, they can't help but let out an audible "Mmmm," of satisfaction. They notice Jack turning his head a bit behind at that, and they swear they see a slight smirk on his face. Keera suddenly feels a bit embarrassed and annoyed that they were acknowledged enjoying something. *Never again,* they vow.

Finally, at the bottom, the trio exit the stairwell and wander down more identical corridors. It takes longer than it should to dawn on Keera that they are actually on the first floor, an area that should presumably be underwater. Specifically, it takes until they notice the windows: everything is bathed in a deep blue-brown. Outside is a normal city street; in disrepair, totally vacant, and submerged in water. It's a mesmerizing sight.

Keera is snapped back to reality by Jack's voice, "Macabre, yet beautiful, isn't it? I watched it for a while myself earlier." The teen pretends like they didn't care. They don't feel a need to relate to this man. They can remain acquaintances. He's basically just a hired bodyguard, anyway. Soon he'll be on his way, absconding with any effort put into connecting with him. A part of them can't help but agree, though. It's a pretty cool view.

Jack takes them to a set of open double doors, with debris piled to one side. "I had to move some of this out of the way," he says, "Through here." Jack then ducks into the semi-collapsed doorway.

"How did you find this place? Keera says, following him and Radley in.

The bounty hunter taps his nose, "Followed the scent of rotting food."

Peering inside, this place looks out of time compared to the rest of the hotel. There is still some disrepair and decay, but not nearly as trashed and clearly looted as the rest of the place. Spotless white walls, stainless steel countertops snaking around the entire room, a space which is bigger than some apartments Keera has seen. Pots, pans, and utensils are everywhere, of every shape and size, all gleaming silver like the day they were abandoned. Everything is lit by dim blue daylight shining in through a handful of small windows near the top of the room. The expansiveness of this kitchen makes sense to Keera; they recall looking up as they descended the stairs, and had seen it go for quite a way. If the rest of this place was in as good of a condition as this place, this kitchen looked like it could start churning out food with minimal prep time.

Keera can tell immediately where Jack had been making their breakfast; a handful of cans lay open and stacked on a countertop near some burners.

Radley notices as well, and asks, "Wait, so you used these stoves?"

"Yep," he responds, fetching more cans from the nearby pantry. Keera can see from here it is packed to the gills with food.

Radley's expression turns stark. "You idiot," she scolds, "What if there was a gas leak?!"

Jack retorts, "Relax! Super sniffer, remember? Christ, give me some credit." He crams the cans in his bag as Radley rolls her eyes.

The two keep exploring while he packs some food in each of their bags. Radley inspects some other doors, more storage. Keera runs their fingers along the cool stainless steel counters. From behind them, Jack continues, "I think these stoves run on some source of gas independent from the rest of the building."

As if on queue, Radley calls out, "Yep, I see a room full of propane tanks here. Damn, it's like these bastards were ready for this place to go to hell."

"Maybe they were," Jack posits.

Keera idly wonders the same thing as they meander over to a heavy metal door. What did this city used to be? Was it like Brezio, a place people could stay if they wanted, but a bit rough around the edges? Or was it more refined, like a haven for weary travelers of the desert? Or, was this not even from this world, and appeared here during an incursion? Keera doesn't know if that's exactly how incursions work, but they're just daydreaming, anyway.

So deep are they in these musings that they almost don't notice Jack suddenly appearing to block their progress toward the door. "You don't want to go in there, little fox."

There's that "fox" shit again. "Why not?" they protest.

Jack taps his nose for the second time today. "Just trust me, if you can," he mutters.

Keera gazes at the door. They aren't sure what could be so bad that Jack wouldn't want them to see. But, if he knows from the *smell alone*... Keera will leave it be.

Instead, Jack and them make their way back to Radley, who is in the center of the space waiting. She looks pensive.

"Well, we've got all the food we could carry," he says, "We'll be set for the rest of the journey, and then some." Then, specifically to Radley, he asks, "Anything sparks any ideas?"

"No, I—" Radley starts, then stops. Something hits her: "Not until you just said that."

Jack cocks an eyebrow, "Hm?"

Ignoring Jack's response, she looks at Keera, "You had mentioned building a bridge earlier."

"Yeah, but it was a joke," they clarify, "I know we couldn't actually—"

"What if we could?" Radley asks, "Very quickly, and one with enough cover."

Keera is confused. Both of them look at Jack, who also seems to be out of the loop... until he isn't.

"Wait, you're not suggesting...?" he trails off.

Radley nods.

Keera feels so lost. They are racking their brain trying to connect the dots the other two have clearly already connected.

Finally, they exclaim, "Will you two just explain what you're thinking already? I hate this."

Radley, for the second time today, smirks.

***

"You know this is insane, right?" Keera asks, as they lug another heavy-as-hell propane tank into the lobby of the hotel. A very striking view: like the windows Keera had seen earlier, but with glass up to the ceiling of a twenty foot high atrium. Somehow, it has withheld against the immense water pressure of the surrounding lake for this long. However, if all goes to plan, that is about to change. "Like, not all of us have a bunch of super powers like you two," they add, placing the tank in a pile next to the others. The pile of propane tanks is centered near a rusted metal support that, according to Radley's estimation, should send this building collapsing into the central skyscraper if it gives way. Key word being "if."

"Don't worry," Radley reassures, "I'll be with you, and we'll make our escape to the other tower before this one even finishes settling."

"And Jack's just going to be on his own?" they ask.

Just then, the man saunters in carrying the last few tanks. "You sound so concerned for me, Snow Fox," he jests.

Keera rolls their eyes as Radley explains, "He has to trigger the explosion."

"Right, and I can fly up that stairwell faster than either of you, even with a bum wing," he says, then pats Keera on the shoulder, "Don't worry. I'll be fine."

They still aren't sure about any of this. But, they remind themself they are not as experienced in violent acts like explosions. So, they defer their judgment to the experts.

After everything is in place, they move toward the exit of the lobby. There, Radley hands her gun over to Jack. Before he lets go, however, she grips it, and looks him dead in the eye. "Don't lose it," she orders.

"I wouldn't dream of it," Jack replies.

He goes to pull the gun to him, but is still met with resistance. "I mean it," she asserts.

"I promise you, Radley of the Wastes, I won't lose your gun," he states.

"And remember," she continues, "Give us fifteen minutes. No less. I don't want to be caught in the middle of a collapsing building."

"Radley, I know the plan. Trust me, I know what I'm doing," Jack reassures her slowly and calmly. With an intense stare, she releases her grip on the gun. Radley is a severe person, but this is a new level from Keera's experience. Understandably so, but it's nonetheless striking. Finally breaking eye contact, she leads Keera out of the lobby and to the stairwell.

Looking up, Keera is a lot less terrified than when they were looking down. Instead, it's more stressful and tiring. They need to be at the top — all the way to the TWENTIETH floor in fifteen minutes. But, once again, Radley says it's doable, so...

They don't run, instead jog. Keera's heart is already ready to beat out of their chest by the tenth floor, but they aren't sure if that's because of exercise or the stress of it all. Probably both. Now and then, a bit of debris or rubble forces them to zig or zag around, or even vault over. This breaks their stride, but not too much. A few floors on, and a small chunk of errant concrete catches them underfoot, almost causing them to fall face-first into the cold, hard stairs. Luckily, they catch themselves on the railing, which unfortunately forces them to look down. This gives them flashbacks of the mountains and treacherous paths they walked back then.

"Careful," Radley calls back to them, only slowing down a beat.

"Thanks," Keera mumbles sarcastically to themself. Collecting themself, they have to work a bit to catch up with Radley.

Until Radley stops dead in her tracks.

Keera, confused, rounds the corner of the landing, and sees what has stopped their companion. And their heart falls all fifteen stories they have just climbed.

The stairs are out.

Keera shoots a wild look at Radley. "You didn't check the stairs?!" she exclaims.

"I..." Radley is dumbfounded, "I didn't think..."

Keera is incredulous. They thought Radley was an expert. That she had done something like this before, that she always thinks of every variable.

Radley shakes her head, snapping her out of her dismay. "No time for this," she asserts, "This place is going down in less than five minutes."

Keera swallows the angry rant that was building inside them. She's right. Not the time. They need to get up. Now. But, looking at the hollow space where stairs used to be, they can't think of anything short of flight. At least Jack shouldn't have a problem...

Suddenly, Radley exclaims, "The fire escape."

Keera can't believe what they're hearing. "You mean those stairs on the *outside* of buildings?" they ask facetiously, "The ones exposed to *the sniper?!*"

"It's the only option we have," Radley says.

"What— what if we just go back down and tell Jack to stop the detonation . If we go fast, we might be able to—"

"We don't have time to argue, Keera," Radley speaks firmly, intensely, "We have to go. Right. Now."

A low rumble shudders the floor.

Keera and Radley stop, eyes looking wide in all directions.

The rumble gets louder.

And the ground below them begins to tilt.

"Time to move," Radley orders, "Grab onto me." Keera holds tight. They take off through the stairwell exit.

Radley sprints down the twisting corridors, Keera held tightly in her arms. The two bounce from wall to wall, trying to keep as much momentum as possible while the floor around them angles forward. Keera holds firm, white knuckles on Radley's black leather jacket. Around them, loose hallway furniture is starting to slide with them, as if they are attempting to escape impending doom as well. Running with the tilt is easier, while running perpendicular to it is slowing her down. Radley stumbles, almost losing her grip on the floor or Keera, but she is fast. Very fast. The groaning and breaking around them has become louder, turning into a cacophony. Thankfully, soon, the two round a corner and spy a window at the end of the hallway. Outside, the central tower is visible, as well as the metal hand railing of the fire escape.

"Get on my back, and grab your leaf," she orders Keera. They hop out from her arms and jump onto her back, using her backpack loop and collar as handholds, while squeezing the leaf in their pocket until it feels like it's about to cut them. The mercenary draws her sword.

Radley dashes forward. Dodging left and right, around shifting furniture, opening doors, keeping her footing, she uses the momentum of the toppling building to propel her forward, until they're at the window, then SLASH! In a fraction of a second, she carves her blade through the windowpane, shattering the glass just as the duo jumps through.

They hit the railing. Keera almost takes Radley's backpack ass-over-teakettle into the water below. Their eyes bulge out of their head in terror, just as a protective arm from Radley flies back to stabilize them.

Radley wastes no time sprinting up the stairs. "Watch the tower!" she yells, over the sound of crumbling concrete and bending metal, "If you see something—"

"LOOK OUT!" Keera shouts, as they see the before-image of a bullet impacting Radley square in the head. Radley dodges just in time, the bullet just grazing her left cheek.

"We need something shorter," she says, not skipping a beat up the slanting stairwell, "Just yell the place where it's about to hit me."

"CHEST!" Keera shouts, a fraction of a moment later. In a flash, Radley's blade flies perfectly in place to block the bullet. Keera feels the metal projectile whiz past them into the railing nearby. They keep going, as Keera keeps shouting:

"HEAD!"

"HEAD!"

"CHEST!"

"RIGHT LEG!"

"RIGHT SHOULDER!"

"HEAD!"

The sniper is relentless. Not skipping a beat, each shot cracks through the air, just preceded by Keera's visions. With each of their warnings, the swordsman throws her sword in the path of the incoming bullet. At worst, it merely grazes the skin. They have a system, and it's working.

The floor below them starts to approach a forty-five degree angle. Adapting, Radley begins running along the struts of the railing, then leaping up to the next set of rails. It slows them down, but her balance and coordination keep their momentum. They need to get up, and fast. Out of the corner of Keera's eye, they notice the tower. It's closer than before. A lot closer.

"Uhhhh, RADLEY...!" Keera calls out. She looks where Keera is looking.

Just then, a bullet cracks through the air. Keera feels Radley buckle under them as she cries out in pain. Her right leg has been hit. "Radley!" Keera calls out instinctively.

"KEEP YOUR EYES ON THE FUCKING SNIPER!" she shouts through gritted teeth. Radley continues running, but she's now even slower. She can deflect the bullets, but running along the railing is proving more difficult. And the tower is getting considerably closer.

They won't make it to the top in time.

"We have to jump now!" Radley shouts, blocking a headshot Keera just called.

"What?! But we aren't there yet!" Keera protests.

"Hold on!" Radley orders.

Keera does so. The tower is feet from them. They're headed for the glassy outer surface. The teen closes their eyes, grips Radley as tight as they can, and braces for impact.

CRASH!

Showered in glass shards that cut their skin, Radley and Keera are flung into the interior of the new skyscraper, like they are shot out of a cannon. With them comes a shower of metal, glass, and concrete, sliding along the floor until all parties come to a gradual stop.

Keera instinctively curls into a fetal position, waiting for the rumbling and shaking to stop. Eventually, the world is still again, the only sounds being the ragged breathing of the two of them. Slowly, they lift their head, scanning their surroundings. It's an orderly office of some sort: a sprawling space with polished marble floors, geometric and drab gray desks, and a number of glass and metal partitions separating spaces from each other. Compared to the other buildings they've been through in this city, it looks to be in a better condition, barring the mess they just caused breaking and entering. Keera notes that the lights above them are still working.

The teen slowly raises themselves to their feet, being careful where they place their hands to not cut themselves more on the debris. Radley does the same, but a lot slower. Quickly, Keera scooches over to the woman and does their best to support her weight, helping her to a nearby chair. The woman sits with a huff, gritting her teeth. Looking down, Keera finally gets a good look at her leg wound: a gruesome red hole is ripped through her thigh. She can still move, which is good, but this will certainly slow them down.

Keera feels incredibly guilty. If it wasn't for their lack of attentiveness, this wouldn't have happened. They know Radley feels the same. So, the next few minutes are awkwardly quiet, as the mercenary bandages up her own wound.

Eventually, Keera decides to break the silence with an important question: "Where's Jack?"

"Probably a few floors up, wondering the same thing about us," she grunts, lifting herself to her feet.

"Should we go find him?" Keera asks.

"We're both going up," she says, not looking at Keera, "We'll run into each other. Come on, we have a job to finish." She stands, walking a bit better now, but the limp is still noticeable. Without another word, Keera follows Radley out of the room they entered, following signage toward the stairs.

***

ONE HUNDRED AND FIFTY FLOORS?! Keera thinks to themself. That is what the sign says, displaying the layout of the tower posted near the now-defunct elevators. Their heart sinks. They knew the tower was tall, but they didn't estimate quite HOW tall by looking at it. This is going to be one hell of a climb. If only the elevators were still working. They then think of Radley, and how much worse it is going to be for her. Regardless, she marches on, not skipping a beat. *I guess if she can do it...* Keera reasons. Already feeling tired, the teen trudges behind the mercenary, adding to the innumerable number of stairs they have climbed in the past twenty-four hours.

This sucks.

After what feels like an hour straight of climbing in silence, they reach a landing with no more stairs going upward. Thinking they must be at the top for a brief moment, Keera is devastated to see the number beside the door, representing the floor they have reached: seventy-five.

"Great," they say, "Only halfway. How do we get up from here?"

"Find the main stairwell. These buildings had to have something like that in the event of a fire," Radley explains. Keera wants to protest so badly. Their legs are on fire, and their pulse is in their ears. But they know they don't have that luxury right now. At least they are getting a break from the stairs for a little while.

With that, the two exit the stairwell and step into a hallway that looks remarkably like the one they left over five hundred feet below. Keera wonders why these massive structures, buildings that are monuments to their time, are filled with the most boring, repetitive layouts imaginable. If Keera was designing something like this, each floor would be like its own realm, full of distinct atmospheres, layouts, and functions for the city. Or, hell, they would've at least painted the walls a different color.

Near the stairwell, there is a map layout of their current floor, indicating which ways to walk to get to the main staircase. Radley jots down a crude map on a scrap of paper, and the two continue on.

Not long after they start their trek, do the two suddenly stop in their tracks. They hear something.

Footsteps. coming from up ahead.

Radley draws her blade, entering a readied stance. "Get behind me," she orders Keera.

The footfalls draw closer, a shadow rounding the corner. The two stop. They hold their breath. Ready for anything.

Anything except Jack.

The leather-clad vampire saunters around the corner, only to throw his hands up at seeing Radley pointing her sword at him.

"Friends," he says, "Don't be so happy to see me."

"Idiot," Radley mumbles to herself. She sheathes her blade and reaches out a hand toward the man.

Jack ignores the comment he certainly could hear, and retrieves Radley's gun from his bag, returning it to her. He then continues with, "Glad to see you both made it out alright. I was worried. You weren't at the rendezvous point. What happened?"

"Stairs were out," Radley states, "We had to improvise."

"Fair enough," he shakes his head, looking the two up and down. Then he notices Radley's new bandage.

"Courtesy of our friend," she says, gesturing up.

"Improvise indeed..." he mutters.

"What are you doing going this way?" Keera asks, then points past him, "Isn't the main stairwell that way?"

"Yes, but..." he says, nodding his head for them to follow, "I'll show you."

He leads the two companions down the route Radley had mapped out, ending at a door with "Stairwell A" on a small plaque above it. The door is propped open, allowing the group to peer in and see a mass of crisscrossing wires haphazardly strung across the interior.

"You've gotta be kidding," Radley groans.

"Yep," he says, affirming her fear, "Seems our friend had time to booby-trap the place."

"Is there any way we can get through?" Keera asks. They are not fully understanding the severity of the situation yet.

"Not unless you want to blow us all sky-high," Jack clarifies, "Each one of those strands is connected to a brick of C4. Explosives. One misstep and..." He makes an explosion gesture with his hands.

"Can't we cut them?" Keera asks, "You two have enough swords between the two of you."

"Not worth the risk," Radley growls, "Plus, if they're this thorough, they probably have fail-safes in place."

Jack adds, "They wouldn't block all the exits down from their perch, though. One of these stairways must lead up to them. Watch your step, though. There's bound to be more traps where these came from."

With that declaration, the group heads toward the shortest route to the nearest staircase on the map. Everyone's heads are on a swivel. Keera is particularly watching the floor for any more tripwires. The thought of causing not only themselves but also their friend's violent demise keeps them on edge the entire way.

As the group nears the destined stairs, only a few turns away, Jack pauses. His brow furrows. "Did you hear that?" he asks.

"Hear what?" Radley returns.

"I heard a beep just now," he clarifies.

Frantically, the group looks around for any sort of source of a noise like that. Keera has no clue what to look for, but with the consistently uniform architecture, they look for anything that seems out of place.

"There!" Keera shouts, as they notice a small metallic lump stuck to the wall around ankle-level. On it, a barely perceptible green light is flashing. Dread fills their veins as they worry about just what this small device might have triggered.

Squinting, Radley approaches it carefully, and bends down to inspect it. "It's a transmitter. Connected to a motion tracker," she says, "No way of knowing what it's connected to, though..."

"Well, we didn't blow up yet, so that's a good sign," Keera says, trying to lighten the mood. The mood is not lightened.

Then Jack sniffs the air, and his worried expression turns to horror.

"Gas," he breathes.

"What?" Keera whips their head to him. They couldn't have heard him right.

"Gas, in the vents!" he exclaims, "This whole floor is getting gassed! We have to move now!"

Without hesitation, the group bolts down the corridor. They try to watch for more traps, but they are now on a ticking clock, according to Jack. As they round one more corner, they see the door to the stairs. However, they also see what awaits them along the forty-or-so-foot long hallway between them and said stairs: a tangle of dozens and dozens of tripwires lacing the hall, like a deadly spider web. From floor to ceiling, the wires almost fully block the view of the door beyond. The group stops, stunned in silence. The worst potential outcome for their current situation.

"Shit," Radley breathes.

"Let's keep going. There has to be another way. Maybe we can reach a window before this place fills up," Jack motions to continue down the corridor, but Radley doesn't move.

"No," she protests, "We don't have time. We have to go through."

"Go *through?* Are you serious? Do you SEE how many wires there are?"

"There's enough space for a bird to fit through. You'll be fine."

"But what about you two?" Jack persists, "You're still not one hundred percent, and Keera—"

"We don't have time for this, Jack!" Radley shouts, "Get to the door, now! We'll meet you there!"

It's then that the group notices the air getting hazier with a sickly yellow fog. This is enough for Jack, as he nods sternly, compresses into a feathery silhouette, and flits carefully through the web of tripwires. In moments, he is on the other side, reverted back to human form, and looking back at the other two. The gas is growing thicker, forcing a cough out of Radley. She raises her shirt collar to her nose in defense, Keera doing the same. This is impossible, insane. Jack was right. There has to be another way! They want to trust Radley, but...

The swordswoman kneels before Keera once more, looking them in the eye. "Listen to me," she says in a calm voice, "You can do this, okay?"

"Can I?" Keera questions. They aren't sure on what basis Radley is basing this assumption on.

"Yes, I know you can. Just follow my lead. Do as I do, and we will be just fine," she says, "I promise."

Keera has been told a lot of things in their brief life so far. Mostly rules of what not to do, what they couldn't do because they were a kid or haven't experienced enough yet. But this... this might be one of the first times an adult has told them that they *can* do something. That belief lights a fire in their heart. They nod in agreement.

Radley sees this nod, and says, "Alright. Watch and learn."

Chapter 17

W ITH MOVEMENTS PRECISE AS a surgeon, Radley enters the tangle of wires.

Step right. Duck under. Turn right. Step left.

Her moves are almost dance-like. Measured like this is a routine she has performed countless times.

Duck again. To all fours. Crawl. Get lower. Army crawl. Stand up in place.

The entire time, Keera is watching in rapt attention. They have to remember every single move. *This is impossible*, they think. No, not the time to get distracted by pessimism. They have to focus.

Step left. Bend back. Step right. Step left. And turn, unbending while taking a final step right. And she's there.

Radley turns around, as steadily as she had been moving through the maze, and releases a breath she was holding the entire time. Her posture loosens, and she staggers a bit on her feet, but remains standing.

"Alright," Radley calls from across the gap, "Go for it."

"Are you crazy?!" Keera calls back, "I can't do all that!"

"Yes, you can. Just focus, and don't let your nerves control you," Radley refutes, "You say you have abilities, right? Well, use them."

Keera feels the fire inside them dwindle a bit, as the gaseous vapors continue rising. The yellow haze is becoming thicker. They shut their eyes. Focus. Remember what she did, what she said. Control your nerves. Don't let them control you. They take a deep breath, as deep as they can, feeling the gas eating away at their lung capacity. It's threatening to make them cough it up. They grip the leaf in their pocket, concentrating, as they take a step forward.

Right. Duck. Turn. Step—

KA-BOOM!

Their eyes snap open.

Nothing happened. They haven't moved. Keera blinks.

They did it! Their powers worked!

Keera is so elated by this, they almost forget they're holding their breath. They feel their lungs burning, and cough out the stale air. Gasping for breath, they catch the acrid air, sending them into a further coughing fit.

"Keera, pick it up!" Jack yells. They hear the two of them stifling coughs as well from across the corridor. They know they can't waste any more time. *Now or never.*

Keera takes one last deep breath, shuts their eyes, and starts moving.

Step right. Duck under. Turn right. Step left.

Their muscles are already trembling. But, with a small roll of their shoulders, they smooth them out, like a duck shaking water off its back. *Not right now.*

Duck again. To all fours. Crawl. Get lower. Army crawl—

BOOM! An explosion flashes before them. They freeze.

No. Don't crawl yet. Get even lower.

Army crawl. Stand up in place.

Keera feels themself teetering, trying to perform maneuvers their body is not trained for. They're sure their movements aren't as elegant as Radley's, but that doesn't matter. They feel their lungs start to ache. Only the results matter right now. *Home stretch, keep going.*

Step left. Bend back. Step right. Step left. And turn, unbending while—BOOM!

Unbending while take—BOOM!

Unbend— KA-BOOM!

Nope. This isn't going to work. They aren't built like Radley; they don't have the core strength or precision. Their lungs are groaning for new oxygen, but the air outside will surely send them into a coughing fit that will doom them all. They're bent back, teetering on the edge, feeling the cold metal wire grazing their chin. They need to think of something, quickly, or it's all over.

Fuck it, tuck and roll.

Keera falls, slamming their shoulder into the cold marble floor, pushing past the pain into a roll, hoping like hell they won't roll into the wire and...

They made it through.

Remaining un-exploded, the teen exhales the spent air with a forceful croak, and continues hacking as copious amounts of poison gas floods into their lungs. The corridor is now drowning in a thick sulfurous soup.

"Keera!" Radley calls. They hadn't noticed in their focused state, but Radley and Jack are coughing heartily now as well. The two kneel beside Keera as they open their eyes.

"Keera, are you okay?" Jack worries.

"I got her," Radley says, not waiting for them to respond, "Go, now!" She grabs the child in her arms, sprint to the door, bursting through into the stairwell. Keera gasps as they climb above the gas. Fresh air never tasted so good.

Chapter 18

KEERA AND THEIR TWO companions continue to plod their way up the seemingly never-ending steps. They are drained, both physically and mentally from the encounter downstairs. Luckily, the gas is not filling the stairwells fast enough to be a danger anymore, so the three can take their time and recover. The rotten egg smell still fills Keera's nose, and they can feel the rasp in their lungs. While all of this is making it hard for them to continue upward, the thing driving them, or more accurately distracting them, is their accomplishment. They actually *used* their ability instead of just hoping it will happen when they need it to. It can be controlled after all, and that thought alone keeps them from collapsing in a tired lump at the next landing. If this is something they can control, then Radley's contact can teach them for sure. Pretty soon, they won't feel like a helpless tag-along kid, and instead like a valuable member of this little troop they're gathering.

Suddenly, Jack motions to the other two; a signal to "quiet down and move carefully." Keera instantly tenses. *Oh no, what now?* As the trio carefully creep up the staircase, Keera sees the source of his caution: The end of steps, punctuated by a solitary metal door at the top. This must be it, where their assailant is hiding.

As they all reach the last landing, Jack peers up through the fogged window in the door.

"Can't make out a thing," he whispers, "But the space looks big."

"We'll have to be ready for anything. This bastard likely booby-trapped this place, too. And they still have that drone," Radley evaluates. She then turns to Keera, "Stay here."

This time, Keera doesn't feel the need to protest. They're worried about their guardians, but they also realize that they will only slow the two of them down here. Their ability to see the immediate future is useful in a pinch, but in their current tired state, they don't trust themself to remain aware of so many deadly factors all at once. Keera simply nods. If anyone can do something like this, Radley and Jack Cressfield can.

Slowly, Jack cracks open the door, peering out into a large dark space. He slowly opens it, doing well to keep the noises to a minimum. He slinks out, followed by Radley. Keera catches the door, so it doesn't slam shut. Radley turns back, nods, and follows Jack into the dark. Keera, at first, gradually starts shutting the door, but then stops. Curiosity is getting the better of them again. Leaving it cracked certainly won't hurt, they decide. Besides, if the two *do* need their help, they need to keep tabs on the situation. So, Keera holds the door slightly ajar, and peers through the crack to watch what events will unfold.

The room beyond the stairwell door is vast and cavernous. The ceiling is so high; it is almost not visible in the low lighting. All over, concrete and steel supports break up sight lines, like an artificial forest of leafless, precision-planted trees. The only light source is the daylight from outside streaming in from the massive windows opposite the stairs. These features give the impression this floor wasn't finished being built before the city was abandoned. A hollow cathedral. Completely silent, except for the careful footsteps of the two intruders.

Radley and Jack, weapons drawn and ready, keep close to the pillars for cover. They are constantly turning and checking every angle as they creep further and further toward the light. About half-way through, Radley suddenly raises a hand. The two duck behind the nearest pillar. The two peer out at something near the far end of the room. It's so far away, Keera can't quite make it out. It looks too thin to be a person. Some sort of metal stand, or chair or something? Radley's gaze darts away from the mystery object, scanning the space for something. Keera is confused until a familiar hum starts to echo from somewhere within...

CRACK!

A bullet pierces the silence, causing Jack and Radley to dive in opposite directions as it tears through the corner of the concrete pillar. They both dart off to separate sides of the space, disappearing from Keera's view. Then silence.

CRACK!

Another gunshot, this time closer, followed by the faint sounds of feet pitter-pattering away. Silence again. The whirring sound is getting louder.

CRACK! POW, POW-POW-POW!

Someone is returning fire.

THUD.

Keera nearly jumps out of their skin as a figure lands crouching directly in front of them from somewhere above. They almost instinctively gasp, but resist, knowing it will blow their cover. As the figure stands, Keera gets a good look at their assailant: They appear human, slightly on the short side, and slim of build. They possess short black hair, trimmed sharply a few inches from the shoulder, and creamy pale skin. Not much is visible, however, as they wear a skin-tight chrome body suit, with various black straps and harnesses, as well as two circular ports in the back. The reflective suit doesn't glimmer like a polished metal, but blends in, mimicking the person's surroundings.

As they stand there, surveying the arena for a tense moment, Keera holds their breath yet again. Any noise could tip off this adept hunter. Evidently seeing no viable prey, the figure sprints to the nearest pillar, making not a sound. As they turn around and press their back to the pillar, Keera gets a look at their face. Their face possess feminine features: sharp cheekbones and a rounded jaw, with eyes small and hard like bullets that are peering around the corner. Their skin is flawless, not something Keera would expect from a hardened soldier. This person looks more like a model from the old-world magazines Keera read down in Canary.

What certainly *does* distinguish them as a soldier, however, is the big fuck-off sniper rifle they are holding up, like a bannerette with no flag. The weapon itself is as long or perhaps longer than her, and it, too, is painted in a similar reflective way as her suit. A futuristic knight, or combat-astronaut.

Keera's mind is moving frantically from the close encounter, but they steel themself and take in the situation. Clearly, no one is aware where anyone is at the moment. This battle isn't like the others they've seen Radley fight. It isn't a rapid sword fight or a wrestling match with a giant monster. This is a silent, tactical encounter, where every shot counts, and locating the enemy before they locate you is paramount.

That's when it dawns on Keera. *They* know where the enemy is.

Keera needs to tell their friends and needs to do it fast. But how? They wrack their brain for ideas. If they make a sound, they would give themselves away, and be shot. They could create a noise some other way? They scan their surroundings, searching for anything that can work.

Then they spot it: A tripwire. Only about fifteen feet away, at ankle-level. Near the sniper. Perfect! If the explosion doesn't take this woman out, then the noise will draw their allies closer, and the distraction will give them time to get to cover. Now they just needed something to throw...

They peer around and notice a hefty hammer just to the right of the doorway, near a wheelbarrow and some other construction supplies. This should do. They carefully retrieve the tool, retreating with it back into the room. They test its weight and balance, like they knew anything about projectile motion. *Yeah, this'll do,* they decide. Returning their attention back to the target, they notice the woman has kneeled down and is peering down the scope of their rifle. She must see someone. Gotta move fast. Quietly, they cock back their arm, and grip the leaf in their pocket. Steady breaths. They start to see the after images of their attempted throws. Pretty soon, they land on the one that will hit the wire. *This better work...*

The hammer flies, spinning in the air.

Keera ducks behind the door frame.

KABOOM!

The explosion rocks the entire floor. So much so, the door Keera is hiding behind flies open, a cloud of dust billowing into the stairwell. Keera shields themself from the debris, and can't help but let out a cough or two as a new aerosol agitates their sensitive lungs. They step around the corner, scanning the space where the sniper once was. Through the smoke, Keera can barely make out the chunks taken out of both the floor and the nearby pillar. A few feet from the explosion site, they spot the form of the woman. Still alive, just winded.

Alright, Plan B: Run.

Keera sprints to the left, away from the sniper. They need to get as far away from her as possible while they can. Running along the stone pillars, they reach the one closest to the left wall. They round the corner, slam their back into the cement, and sink to the floor. Crouched. Panting. Eyes wide.

Silence.

Keera's breathing steadily slows, but they're still on edge. Sweat drips down on their forehead, and they wipe it away frantically. They don't dare peek around the corner for fear of getting their head blown off. They just sit there. Waiting.

A moment passes. Then another moment. And another. Nothing happens. Keera is starting to think they may have actually gotten her and seeing her moving was just a figment of their frantic imagination. They decide it is safe to just quickly peek. The sniper is gone. Blood rushes from Keera's face. *Shit.*

Just then, that whirring sound grows louder and louder behind them. They turn slowly, and in abject terror, witness that same drone that dogged them earlier. Keera spots a few hasty repairs done to the areas they broke before, as it hovers just feet from the teen. It spotted them. They freeze, unable to think. They know what happens next. No friends, no one to save them. They shut their eyes, preparing for the sound of a bullet firing in their direction...

When, suddenly, Keera is shoved over from the right, just before KAPOW! A shot rips through the air, and collides with the pillar, right where their head was a moment ago. Keera recovers from the impact, just as they're hoisted into their savior's arms.

"Gutsy, kid," Jack growls, "Stupid, but gutsy." He takes off with the child in his arms.

KAPOW!

Another shot just misses the two of them.

Keera looks back to see the drone following behind. Until a few lower-caliber shots ring out, connecting with the drone. Not enough to break it, but enough to get its attention, as it swivels and pursues the source of the shots.

After moving a suitable distance from where they were last spotted, dodging a few traps along the way, Jack skids to a stop behind another pillar. He places Keera down and looks them over. "You okay?"

"Yeah," Keera whispers, "You guys?"

He nods, "We're fine. They've gotten really close, though. Did you get a look at them?"

Keera says, "They have a shiny suit. Their gun is huge, it's like longer than the—"

"Did you say 'shiny suit?'"

"Yeah? Why? What does that mean?"

Jack curses under his breath, "I should've known. This seemed like her style…"

"You know this person trying to kill us?!" Keera says, a bit too loud, and Jack motions for them to simmer down. He peeks around the corner, checking that their position isn't compromised. Satisfied, he returns to the conversation.

"She's a special agent from Manhattan Gate," Jack says.

There's that organization again. How did they know they would be passing by here?…

Jack continues, "One of the best. We need to take her down. Now. The longer we wait, the sooner our luck's going to run out."

"But how?" Keera protests, "An explosion didn't even take her out."

"That suit must have impact reduction. Won't save her from a bullet or a blade, though, so we need to get in closer. If we can just find her…" Jack trails off. Then, his gaze slowly drifts back toward the teen. Keera can almost see as the dots connect in his mind. "You."

"What?" Keera questions.

"What you did before, drew us to you with an explosion. We're going to do that again, except this time, we will draw *her* to *you!*"

Panic erupts within Keera at this suggestion. "What? No! Hell no, I'm not making her shoot at me!" they respond, keeping their voice low.

"Don't worry. I'll be watching," he responds, "And you'll know that the shot is coming. All you have to do is dodge a bullet. Can you do that? Can you trust me?"

Not that long ago, they would've said no. But, just in the last few days alone, Jack has saved them numerous times. Jack Cressfield takes his jobs very seriously, and they get the sense he wouldn't put his paycheck in any danger he didn't think they couldn't handle. Keera nods.

Jack nods in return and pulls out a throwing knife from his boot. "Throw this," he instructs as Keera nervously takes it, "Don't worry, I have a spare." He puts a firm but comforting hand on their shoulder before darting off to hide behind another pillar.

This is insane. But, honestly, compared to a lot of the things they've done the past few days, this is about par for the course. *What are the odds my luck will run out this time?* they think sarcastically.

Shots echo from somewhere else in the space. Radley and the sniper must have engaged each other again. Keera peers around the corner, and sees nothing. Although that might not mean much in this situation, they take that as their cue. Sprinting to the next pillar, Keera is frantically scanning for any of the woman's traps. It doesn't take long to find one about twenty feet away. Reaching cover, they hold up the knife, eyeing its sharp point with trepidation. *Better get this right,* they think. Keera shoves their hand in their pocket, takes another deep breath, and focuses. They see flashes of futures where the blade bounces wildly one way or another, some where they slice their hand open. It still hurts like hell, but not for long as they flash to a new possibility. Then, they find the one. They cock back their hand, aim it *just* so, and... throw. Keera ducks behind the pillar, before another loud BOOM echoes through the space. They spin around the pillar, hiding from the center of the room, duck down, and wait.

The gunfire from Radley and the sniper has ceased. It's as if the entire world is holding its breath, the dust settling. Everyone is waiting for their moment.

Keera's heart is pounding in their chest, screaming at their brain, body, whatever will listen to not move. To stay hidden, where it's safe, forever and always. But their mind overpowers their fear. They have to trust Jack. They have to do this if they want everyone to leave here alive.

Keera steps out into the open, eyes searching for where the shooter is hiding.

They see a flash.

KABLAM!

Keera opens their eyes again. They just died. And now, they're alive again.

With panting breath, searching their memory of that brief moment. That flash, and where it came from.

There

They find it.

They know where the sniper is.

"Third pillar from the window, second from the left wall. She's there, she's there!" Keera calls out to any who are listening. They then step out, staring right where they know the sniper is hiding. Sure enough, there she is: crouched, aiming down sights, right for the child. They stare them down with a look that could be confused with rage. However, it isn't anger, but one of adrenaline-fueled determination.

Determination to save themself, their friends. Determination to end this whole protracted nightmarish ordeal. They stare her down, and they swear, even from dozens of yards away...

They swear they see the sniper hesitate.

KABLAM!

It misses.

Keera reaches up and feels the side of their face. Where the bullet grazed the side of their cheek, they feel a shallow cut. Looking at their fingers, they see the faintest drops of crimson. None of this is affecting them deeply right now. They have entered some sort of Zen-like state, emotions being suppressed in favor of survival. Returning their gaze to the sniper, they see the figure frantically reloading their weapon. Frantically. She really is rattled.

Just then, another figure in a trench coat dives at the silvered sniper from the left. Jack. She dodges out of the way, as Jack's sword wedges firmly in the concrete pillar she was perched behind. He wastes no time, though, and dashes for her again, leaving behind his stuck blade. She nimbly dodges back, almost cartwheeling backward to keep her backward momentum as he pushes forward. Then, another form that Keera hasn't seen in some time appears from the right.

Radley.

Shots fire, but the silver woman, instead of ducking away, dives forward and deftly moves Radley's arm, and by proxy the gun, to the side. The shots go wide.

This dance repeats. Jack dives in, she moves back. Radley aims, she moves in to deflect. Even outnumbered, the woman in silver's moves are precise. They have her on her back foot, though, and have collectively moved the fight toward the window. Keera keeps up, but at a safe distance, just in case they can be of help somehow. The woman's suit is being damaged by the onslaught, but she herself shows no signs of slowing down.

Keera suddenly hears, hidden beneath the noise of combat, another sound growing closer. Sure enough, from somewhere high above, flies into the fray, buzzing right past Keera.

What happens next occurs in a matter of seconds: the thing b-lines it for the sniper, while she creates some breathing room from both combatants. The drone then pivots in the air, hovers behind her back, and attaches itself to her around the shoulder blades.

The sniper then ascends into the air.

"Shite," Jack curses.

The pair dive behind the nearest pillar as the sniper rotates her gun from off her back and fires. Keera instinctively ducks back, too, before peeking out again. Now equipped with her mechanical wings, the woman gives chase to Jack; the vampire dodging in and out from between the pillars. "Get this bitch off me!" he calls out.

Radley follows the action. Firing at the flying woman, the sniper unfortunately dodges the shots. "I'm trying!" Radley responds, "I think the damn drone camera gave her eyes in the back of her head!"

"Fuck," Jack pants, "Then I'm taking this fight up high! Think you can keep up?"

"I can certainly try!" Radley growls back.

With that, Jack's form compacts into a raven, and he too ascends. The sniper is in hot pursuit. Radley, taking a moment, eyes up a nearby pillar, and runs straight at it. Keera is watching in rapt attention as she's able to get enough grip to ascend almost double her height, before springing to the next pillar behind her. She repeats this until she is high above Keera, level with the dogfight. She then springs to the next pillar, keeping up the momentum as she follows the others. Keera has seen this woman do a lot of shit, but it hasn't stopped being impressive to watch.

The combat-turned-chase is now a zig-zagging mess between the pillars high in the air. The silvery woman pursues the almost imperceptible blackbird, and a leaping Radley follows her. Occasionally, either the mercenary or the sniper fire off potshots at each other, but none connect. The shots are not accurate, but are attempts to break one party's rhythm, giving the pursuer a chance to close the distance. Everyone is fast, skilled, and focused. Little ground is gained or lost, but it is only a matter of time before someone slips up.

After another warning shot, Radley sinks her sword into the wall and hangs from it, giving her a moment to recover. Even from the ground, Keera can tell she is panting. She can't keep this up, neither can Jack. They've both been through a lot in the past forty-eight hours. They have to end this fast.

Radley looks down. She meets eyes with Keera. In that moment, they can see the desperation in their mentor's eyes. She's at her limit. In that instant, Keera knows what they have to do. They take a deep breath, stand, and give a stern nod to Radley. They hope this translates to their mentor as "Follow my lead." After a moment of hesitation, the merc steels her own expression and returns the nod. "Alright." Keera then scans the room for the flying sniper. There, near the front of the room. Perfect.

Keera sprints down the middle aisle, toward the door. As they do so, Radley calls out, "Jack, lower! I can't keep this up!" Radley slides down the pillar and disappears off to the right. Keera keeps running, waiting to hear the telltale sound of the drone lowering. Sure enough, it does, and Keera looks back over their shoulder to see the mechanical-winged woman chasing the bird behind them. The bird peels off to the left. *Nice, Jack.*

Keera then falls. It hurt more than they intended, but they had to sell it. They cry out in pain on the floor and look again to see how the sniper is reacting to this.

Exactly as they had hoped; hovering there about fifteen feet off the ground, the sniper has lost interest in the bird and the other woman. She has her sights trained on new, easier prey: Keera.

That's it... Keera makes an attempt to crawl away, clawing toward the door, their shoulder and knee burning from the impact. They can hear the cocking of the rifle behind them. She was taking her time with this shot, either out of caution, or to savor killing the one that got away. Keera didn't know or care either way.

Anytime now guys... The teen spins around, looking in fear up at the silhouette; an angel of metal and chrome ready to smite them where they laid.

"NOW!"

In a flash, Radley and Jack appear on either side of the woman. Jack descended from above and behind, while Radley from the front and below. The woman attempts to dodge, but both of the assailants' blades connect; Radley slashes apart the right rotor of the drone, while Jack's sword slices through the woman's arm. Together, they send her pinwheeling to the ground, impacting with a visceral THUD. *Fuck yes!*

The woman yelps and struggles to regain her footing, but Jack is on her in an instant. He places a boot on her and a sword at her throat. Cautiously, Keera approaches, as Radley steps forward and yanks the woman's gun from her hand. She then notices Keera approaching, and gives a nod. "Good job, kid," she says. Keera nods in return. A small smile curls their lips before they turn their attention back to their defeated opponent.

Keera is, at first, surprised. For having lost an arm, this woman isn't nearly as vocal as they'd think she would be. However, upon noticing the stump where her arm once was, a reason for this becomes clear. Instead of a gory mess that would probably give Keera a new nightmare for the next few weeks, there is instead a tangle of metal and wires protruding from the stump. There *is* a fluid that is leaking, but it is a greenish-white liquid instead of blood. Yet another strange development this former cave-dweller was not anticipating.

"She's an android..." Radley mutters. *Well, that would explain it.*

The woman, teeth gritting, still struggles feebly in her restrained state. The one drone propeller still whirs ineffectually, and she bangs her remaining fist on Jack's leg. Radley puts her boot on her arm and levels her gun at her head.

"It's over, Arianna," Jack growls, "Now, who sent you?"

"You know damn well who I work for, daywalker," she replies, venom coursing through a deep, precise voice, "What are you doing helping these two? Don't you want their bounties?"

"Got a better offer," he explains before pressing, "You didn't answer my question. *Who sent you?*"

After a brief moment of hesitation, angry eyes flitting to Radley, she responds: "Amphion."

Jack's head sinks. He sighs. This name means something to him, but nothing to Keera. They look to Radley, who seems just as in the dark as them. "Who's Amphion?" she asks.

Jack responds, head still hung, "The head of this region's Manhattan Gate Initiative chapter."

A weight hangs in the air with those words. It was all but expected it was someone from that dreaded organization that sent this assassin. But, something about putting a name to it...

"That's right," Arianna continues, "You all have been enough of a hindrance to his operation that he is determined to have you all terminated. And he will not stop until he has achieved this objective." Her attention then shifts back to Keera, "However... after he gets the data I've recovered, that may change..."

"Well, he can fuck off," Radley says, "In fact, I'll tell him myself if I have to."

"I doubt you will get that chance," Arianna returns coldly.

Radley crouches down, getting right in the robotic woman's face, "Oh yeah? Why do you say that?"

"Because I never fail a mission."

It is then that the ground begins to rumble.

Chapter 19

"**S**HE SET THEM OFF! She set them all off!" Jack shouts as explosions rock the skyscraper.

"Are you fucking crazy?!" Radley shouts at the mechanical woman. Her face doesn't react.

"Forget about her. We have to go, now!" Jack yells.

Go where?! Keera panics internally. Surely the stairwells wouldn't be viable at this point. They scan the space, looking for any other escape route.

"The window," Radley states.

"That's an option, HOW?!" Keera explodes.

The tower quakes. Debris crumbles and falls from the ceiling, pillars collapsing. All too familiar to Keera, freezing them in fear.

"It's all we've got," Radley says, "Hold on to me!" She grabs the stun-locked teen in her arms, and sprints toward the blinding light from the massive glass window.

Time slows. Shards rain down around Keera as it too gives way under duress. They shield their face from the wind, the rubble, and the shards, as Radley leaps.

And they're airborne again.

The sensation is familiar. But, as Keera peeks down, it becomes all the more terrifying to see the water far, far below. And it's getting closer. Keera can't help but scream, accompanying the chorus of rushing air and the roar of the massive skyscraper collapsing above them. The water gets closer, and closer, and closer, until impact. It all goes black.

***

The first thing Keera feels is coolness washing over them. It comes and goes in waves, at first convincing them that this is what blood feels like coursing through their system. In their beleaguered state, sensations seem alien. As they interrogate this feeling, the coolness shifts to a deep, burning pain. No specific source, just a general ache, like they've just been hugged too tightly for far too long.

Next, a sound comes. A sound which also confirms the source of the aforementioned coldness: lapping waves. Their eyes flutter open, blinded and blurred by a ringing in their mind. All they see is the sky. Slowly, like an old door whose hinges haven't been moved in years, they crane their neck to the right.

A wild, tangled mass of concrete, glass, and metal lies felled across the lake, encroaching into a few surrounding buildings. Smoke billows from all around the structure. Luckily, it is too far away to be of any concern. Turning their attention to closer matters, Keera notices they are lying on a chunk of the superstructure, severed and at an angle, protruding from the water. They are low enough that the waves just reach them at their height, but not enough to carry them out into the black water.

Keera is just done with all of this. Everything hurts. They wish this was all just a messed-up dream, and that when they blink next, they would be jolting up, out of bed, at home. But no, this wasn't a nightmare. They *actually* fell over a hundred stories and survived, all thanks to—

Where's Radley?

Keera sits up, despite their body's many protests, whipping their head around, searching for the woman. "Radley?!" they call out.

"Up here," a familiar voice calls out from behind them.

Keera whips around, looking up the slanted ramp. The mercenary is there, waterlogged, looking to be in similarly rough shape, but alive. She is sitting up on her elbows, staring up into space. Instinctively, Keera scrambles up the ramp and kneels beside the woman.

"A—are you okay?" Keera worries.

"Yeah, I..." she coughs, "I'll be okay."

The duo sit in silence for a moment. Nothing but the sound of lapping waves and the distant crackling of fire hold the space. With ordeal after ordeal that's only seemed to escalate over these past few days, the moment of silence is well needed.

Unfortunately, someone breaks the peace, calling from the top of the ramp: "Hey!"

The pair spin to see a familiar silhouette against the setting sun, with another leaning against him. "There you two are!" Jack exclaims, as she carefully steps his way down the decline, "I was worried I lost my paycheck."

"Good to see you too, Jack," Radley responds dryly.

As he gets closer, the features of the second figure come into focus: it's Arianna, with a tow cable wrapped around her torso, fastening her remaining arm to her body. "Found this one floating with the debris. Figured she would be a good source of information," he says. The robotic woman looks to be in rough shape, with tears in her suit, water-soaked hair, and even parts of the "skin" on her cheeks scraped away, revealing small bits of shiny metal.

"Not a good idea," Radley objects, "She could be in contact with her boss and give away our location."

Jack simply shrugs, "Well, then we'd both have information, wouldn't we? If anyone would know what to expect in the mythical Summit Station, it would be one of Manhattan Gate's top assassins." He smirks at the captive, who returns a look of cold malice.

"We'll see..." Radley eyes the entire situation, before slowly crawling to her feet, "In any case, we should rest here for the night, and get going in the morning. It's only a matter of time before Manhattan Gate comes to investigate all this."

Everyone silently agrees, and clamber their way up the ramp in search of a place to shelter for the evening.

***

The night is uneventful; the group sleeping in a decaying third-floor apartment. Arianna is bound to a radiator in the bathroom, to prevent any escape attempts as the other three sleep. She owed them that much after harrying them the previous night. For Keera, the night is still restless, however. Apart from the overall soreness from the previous day's events, a pervasive feeling of being watched also makes their night restless. Likely, it's just left over paranoia from earlier, but they can't convince themself of that.

In the morning, pastel golden rays and the fresh sizzling smell of Jack cooking some sausage and beans greet the party. After breakfast, the trio discuss their plan. The lack of a vehicle has increased the estimated travel time to Radley's contact by quite a bit. However, it is Jack that points out that, in order for this place to be as flooded as it is, there must be a source of all this water. And, sure enough, after briefly scouting the area, he finds it: a narrow canyon river that flows into the basin from the north-northeast. Vaguely the direction in which they are heading.

"Likely how our mechanical friend got here so fast," Jack posits, "Which means she likely had a boat... Give me a few, I'll try and locate it." Without waiting for a response, Jack takes off once again into the sky on the hunt for a boat.

Keera notices that, in his haste, Jack has forgotten to clean his cookware. The daywalker's impulsivity reminds them of how they were earlier in their journey on the surface. It also reminds them of how mad Radley gets when she witnesses such behavior, so they decide to cover for him a bit. Collecting the cookware, they carry it to the bathroom, where they know the water is still working.

As they enter the dimly lit space, however, they are frozen by two cold eyes staring daggers at them from the dark. Keera pauses, a prey animal noticing a predator eyeing them from the brush. They soon shake it off, reminding themself that Arianna is still restrained to the radiator. The air shifts from fear to awkwardness, as the child steps closer, placing the pots and such in the sink. They begin cleaning, still feeling the ivy stare to their right.

Keera isn't sure how to act in this situation. They've never been involved in taking a hostage before. Even though this woman had tried to kill them only hours prior, it still felt... wrong. Also "woman?" This being is obviously mechanical. Is it even a woman? Had Keera just assumed they were a woman by appearance? Given Keera's gender identity, this was a bit ironic, and added to their guilt a wee bit. Was this being even a person, technically? They've never seen anything like them before, but that is becoming the norm for Keera at this point.

"What?" Arianna asks dryly.

Keera realizes they've been staring at her the entire time.

They clear their throat before responding, "Uh. Sorry, I um, I've never seen—"

"—an android before?" Arianna finishes. Keera nods sheepishly. "Understandable. There are not many of us left, especially not in the bunkers."

"How do you know I'm from an underground city?" Keera is blindsided by hearing a reference to Canary Bridge.

"It's my job to know. That, and to shoot people," she states as a matter-of-fact, "Hey, could you do me a favor?"

"Why should I?" Keera's demeanor immediately turns cold. This woman is tricky. They have to remember that.

The android shifts a bit and gestures to a pouch on their suit. "There's a lighter and some cigarettes in there. Could you get me one?" she asks.

Keera hesitates. There has to be a trick here, they just aren't seeing it. Arianna notices and rolls her eyes. "Come on, kid, look at me. I'm already in pain from missing an arm. I don't need to add withdrawal symptoms."

Part of Keera doesn't think this thing deserves to feel any form of comfort right now. They're bad. They tried to do terrible things to Keera and the people they care about. But then they think back to Canary, and they remember that Bri's dad was a smoker. He tried to quit so many times, as parents who smoke often do. When he tried, however, he was always unfocused and angry. Not a state Keera wants to see a deadly assassin in.

Cautiously, Keera kneels beside the chained-up woman. They reach for the pouch, finding the two small box-shaped items, and retrieve them quickly, as if something in there was going to bite their hand if they lingered any longer. All the while, Arianna watches them. The bitter anger Keera thought they were observing from afar seems more like tired curiosity up close. Keera removes a single cigarette from the pack, prompting the woman to lean toward her, mouth slightly open, expectantly. This gives Keera pause again. What are they doing? If Radley caught them doing this, she surely would chastise them. But... something inside Keera is telling them this is the right thing to do. Even though this entity was recently an active threat, they don't have to match their cruelty. They can be better.

Carefully, the teen places the filter end of the cigarette between the woman's lips, flicks the lighter a couple of times to start it, and lights the cigarette.

Keera then stands again. They take a step or two back, not only out of mistrust, but also because of the incoming nicotine fumes. Arianna sighs, a waft of smoke billowing out like steam released from a high-pressure valve. "Thanks, sweetheart," Arianna says.

"Yeah, you're welcome," Keera responds, then returns to washing the dishes. They try to focus on the task at hand, but some subtleties in what the robotic woman just said keep nagging at them. With the air of awkwardness subdued and replaced with the smell of tobacco, Keera feels a bit more at ease to ask: "So, you said you feel things?"

Arianna lifts an eyebrow, "Don't you?"

"Well, yeah, but you're a robot."

"That's a pejorative term."

"A what?"

"A slur, dear," Arianna explains, "The word has Slavic roots in terms like 'forced labor' and 'slave.'"

"I—I'm sorry, I didn't know," they stammer. The uncomfortableness has returned.

"It's alright. Not many know," the android sighs, puffing on her cigarette, "But, to answer the question; I'm designed to feel. As a motivator. A camera with a microphone will observe passively. If you want it to be active — to find and seek out information or complete an objective in an efficient manner — you have to at least give it the ability to feel satisfaction. But, if you want it to be active in a *specific* way... you have to make it feel displeasure. All other feelings stem from those two origin points, really."

Keera ponders this for a moment. They weren't expecting a deep, introspective conversation about the nature of feeling this early in the morning, but here they are. "So the people who created you made you feel pain so they could control you?" they ask.

"Grim, isn't it?" she says. Keera swears they can see a slightly sardonic smirk cross her lips, though she might have just been adjusting the cigarette.

"Can't you just... I don't know, reprogram yourself to not feel the pain then? Like, delete that part of the code so you don't have to feel it anymore?" Keera posits.

Arianna shakes her head, "I don't know the inner workings of my mind any more than you do. And the people that do are long since dead." Just then, the cigarette falls from between the android's lips. It didn't seem intentional, and yet she expresses little remorse.

"C'est la vie."

Keera moves to retrieve it for her, but is met yet again with that cold, indifferent stare. A slight shake of her head "no."

A call from the other room breaks the tension; "Keera, hurry up! Jack found us a ride!" Radley calls.

"Yep, coming!" Keera responds. They give one last look at Arianna. Knowing what they know now, a lot of her demeanor makes sense. The cold, calculating nature, the reckless abandon to blow up a tower while still inside it, the rage at being held captive. She's in pain. A pain Keera will probably never truly understand. They decide to keep the cigarettes handy for her.

***

Zipping upstream in a boat, perfectly reflective like Arianna's suit, the three fugitives and their captive make their way away from the sunken city. Keera is glad to be moving again. Much like most places they visit on this journey, the city started as a place of beauty and wonder, only to be tainted by violence and trauma. So much so that, by the time they finally leave, they never want to see the place again. They hope this trend doesn't continue. They would like to find a place that they look forward to seeing again. A home. But, for now, they have to settle for looking forward to whatever lies on the horizon.

The river, unfortunately, gives only a slight view of any such horizon, as its steep canyon walls press in on either side like a massive vice. Rough stone walls, at least twenty feet high, extend up to create a jagged blue scar of sky above. The current is quick, but this boat has a powerful enough motor to make going upriver feasible. It is, however, not very quiet.

"If anyone is waiting for us up ahead," Jack says, helming the vessel, "They've probably already heard us coming."

"Right. Eyes up," Radley says, "I'll climb up to get a better view here soon. See how close we're getting."

"It would be easier for me to scout ahead. Just tell me what I'm looking for," Jack suggests.

Radley shakes her head, "Just focus on not crashing us into these rocks."

Jack sighs and gives a small shrug of the shoulders, "Yes, ma'am." He returns his attention to the river ahead.

Keera shoots a curious glance at Radley. They know she can be cagey, but that response made no sense. As a raven, Jack could see way farther, and could easily give updates and headings. Why shoot that down? Keera needed these answers.

A few hours later, Radley anchors the boat in a bend of the river where the current is slower. She is preparing for her ascent of the cliffs when Keera blurts out, "Take me with you."

They expect resistance. They expect the classic "No, stay here. Do what I say."

What she *actually* says blindsides Keera: "Okay, hop on."

Okay, Keera thinks, *Maybe we're done with this whole defensiveness shit. Maybe I can finally get answers whenever I want!* With haste, the teen hops onto the woman's back, and holds on tight, as the duo ascend the wall.

At the top, the atmosphere is much different: scorching bright sun, heat waves rippling over craggy stone planes, sightlines in all directions. The river is almost imperceptible from up here unless you are right on top of it. To the south, Keera can still make up the reflective surfaces of the tallest remaining buildings of the sunken city.

Radley pulls out a small pair of binoculars from a pocket in her coat and slowly scans the horizon back and forth. It's only the subtle roar of the river below and an occasional wind accompanies them.

Keera clears their throat, "See anything?"

"Not yet," Radley responds.

"If you let me know what you're looking for, I might be able to help," Keera suggests.

Silence.

Alright, guess we're doing this, Keera sighs, "Why don't you want help? First Jack, now me?"

"I..." there's a pause, before Radley finally mumbles, "I don't know what I'm looking for."

"Wait, what?!" Keera exclaims.

"The people I trained under, gnumans, are very secretive. They take measures to make sure they aren't found. And, since I'm not from this universe..." she lowers the binoculars, but keeps her eyes locked to the horizon, "I don't have a goddamn clue where they could be."

Keera is floored. They feel like they've been lied to. "Then what did you take us all the way out here for?" they question.

"I told you from the start, I had an idea where they *might* be," Radley responds, turning on Keera, "And besides, *you* were the one that insisted we try and find them. Don't go blaming me when what I warned you about comes to pass."

Keera scoffs. She isn't wrong, but they're still frustrated. "Then what are we even up here for right now?"

"A sign. Some type of marker I recognize. Anything. They're around here where I'm from, but things must be different here," Radley says.

Keera, feeling the wind fall sharply from their sails, gazes out into the vast rocky vista, as if they might pick up on something Radley didn't notice. They likely won't, but their mind just doesn't want to accept the idea that this trip was all for nothing. "What now then?"

Radley gives a pause, thinking on this for a moment, before decisively saying, "You go back."

This time, it's Keera that turns on Radley, "You can't be serious."

Radley says nothing.

"So that's it?" Keera continues, more and more rage burning in their throat, "All of that, all of the days spent on the road, all of the times we got shot at, everything, just to send me BACK?! What, am I just supposed to walk all the way back on my own?"

"I'll convince Jack to take you back to Adley's," she says.

"No," Keera is pacing now, "No fucking way."

"Keera, I—"

"No! I am not leaving you now! We went this far, YOU broke your promise, and now—"

"I didn't break my promise!" Radley's voice is raised now, too, "I said I would TRY to find my people, and I didn't, so now you are going somewhere safe, while I do what I have to do."

"What happened to us staying together?!"

"I DON'T WANT TO PUT YOU THROUGH ANY MORE BULLSHIT!"

That explosion echoes through the air and through Keera. Not only is this the loudest they've ever heard this woman in the short time they've known her, but this is also the most visibly distressed she's been. Keera watches her, wide-eyed, waiting for her to compose herself and continue.

"You have been through more than anyone should at your age, even in a place like this," she finally says, "And, if you keep following me, it's only going to get worse."

Keera feels like interjecting, but they can tell she has more that she needs to say, and protests might just shut her down again.

"Manhattan Gate. The group that keeps chasing us down," she states, "I'm heading to one of their most heavily guarded bases of operation: Summit Station."

"Why would you be going toward the guys who want you dead?" Keera asks.

Radley takes a deep breath, then exhales a deep, soulful sigh. One she's been holding in for a long, long time.

"My home is in Summit Station."

Chapter 20

"I don't remember much from my childhood. What I do remember are trees. Beautiful oaks, tall, powerful pines, and one beautiful birch that my mother and I would sit under. My mom would read me stories while I swung on a swing set. Stories of great adventures, of magic, and monsters. All kinds of exciting fantasies kids like reading about. We'd stay out there for hours, just her and I. Sometimes, I would close my eyes, and just listen to her voice as she read to me, with the wind rustling through the leaves and the sun on my face.

When it was time to eat, or if it started to rain, we would go inside. We lived in a small, single-story brick house, surrounded by a beautiful garden my mom tended. She was proud of that garden, and she loved to let me wander through it. I'd pick up pots and rocks, and find all the little bugs hiding underneath. And the house was beautiful, too. Simple, but homey. My mother liked to sew, so the place was covered in handmade blankets, doilies, and dolls that she made for me. And the food... fuck, the FOOD!

I didn't know a life outside that place. Every now and then, a man in a white suit my mom simply called 'the doctor' would come by the house. She played it off as normal. He never did anything too weird or bad, just checking vitals and asking how I was doing. Things like that. I was a kid. I didn't know any better.

At some point, I snuck away from my mom and ran to the end of the driveway. My mom never let me go beyond a certain point, and my curiosity was driving me crazy. So, I snuck out while she was doing some intense cooking or something.

When I got there, I found a wall. You could only see it if you stood next to it, and it was impossibly tall. I asked my mom about it later that day, and she refused to say anything. All she said was that we were safe here, and to not worry about it.

I thought about that wall from time to time. What did that mean about where we were? Was there more to the world than just us in this house? What was it like? But I didn't let that bother me too much. There wasn't much to worry about at that point, in that place, with my momma. It was perfect.

Until the day... we were attacked.

I heard them before they came. I was eating lunch at the dining room table, and she was cleaning up dishes. I could hear a faint booming sound in the distance. When I asked my mom, she told me not to worry about it. Probably just a storm moving through. But, I had looked out the window, and the sky was clear. Then, the booming got louder and louder and louder, and suddenly an explosion blew open one of the walls. My mother told me to run, so we did. We sprinted out the back, past the garden and the trees, into the apple orchard we had in the far back of the property. We kept running and running. I could hear the sound of gunshots behind us, men shouting. I looked back, and our house was on fire. My mom told me we couldn't stop. To not look back. To keep running.

We made it to a clearing, with a tire sunk into the dirt, or at least that was she had told me it was before when I asked. It turned out to be a hatch, and she opened it. Told me to get inside. I was scared and confused, so I hesitated. She told me she would be right behind me. So, I climbed inside...

I looked up, seeing if my mom was following. Then I heard a gunshot... and my mom stopped moving. She went limp, staring down wide-eyed in shock and pain.

She whispered down at me, 'Run. Radley, I love you.'

That was the last thing I heard my mother say.

I wanted to climb back up and hold her, hug her one more time. I wanted to wake up in bed like it was all a dream, and go running to her room, where she could hold me and tell me everything was going to be okay. But I couldn't...

I heard footsteps coming, and I knew I had to go. I climbed down the ladder into the dark; her face staring down at me. I can still see that image in my nightmares...

I ran. I ran through the tunnels, out into the world, emerging from some giant mountain I didn't even know I was in. I ran for days, before collapsing somewhere in the middle of the badlands. That's when the gnumans came across me.

They brought me back to their clan, nursed me back to health. Afterwards, most of the elders wanted to throw me back into the world. But one elder, Davanti, argued for them to adopt me. I don't know why. I think he saw something in me even I didn't see at the time.

So, I stayed, and was trained in their ways. This included their unique fighting style, which involves using a blade only for defense. It is an ancient, sacred custom. To use a blade to draw blood is to dishonor it, yourself, and your entire clan. After arduous training, training that pushed my body to its breaking point and then some, I was given the privilege to have a blade of my own.

I named her *Clover*.

Davanti also helped me unlock and hone my time manipulation abilities. Gnumans came to this universe long ago to help contain EUEs, keep them from destroying it even more than they already have. So, they have knowledge most don't about the nature of time and space. This made him an ideal mentor for me in many ways. He was the one who taught me to be tough and stood up for me when others tried to come after me for being different. We were close, him and I. Loved him like a father...

A few years passed. To remain useful, I had joined the clan's security force. I quickly rose up in the ranks due to my abilities until I was almost the same rank as my master. As such, I was often given a squad of my own to lead on missions. I was still young and bold, though, and my cockiness sometimes showed in my mission planning. One particular assignment was to recover some goods stolen from our traders by some no-name thugs. Unfortunately, by the time we got to the bandits' hideout, it was already under siege. By Manhattan Gate.

I, not knowing what this meant, saw an opportunity. To use the other raiders as a distraction, slip in, grab the goods, and get out. Unfortunately, I underestimated Manhattan Gate soldiers. As we were escaping with the gear, a squad of them found us, and... it was a massacre. I'd never seen such tactics outside gnuman ranks before. Random raiders used simple guerrilla maneuvers, overwhelming with force or with speed. These guys utilized both with precision and discipline. I lost my entire squad that day... I would've died, too. But one of the soldiers recognized me. It seems word got out of the woman so fast she could cut bullets, and someone from Manhattan Gate took interest in that...

I was knocked out, drugged, kept floating between a state of consciousness and unconsciousness for what felt like days. The next thing I clearly remembered was a dark, metal room with blaring bright lights beaming down on me. I was restrained, and too tired to try and escape. Then, some men in white medical gear came in. Started poking and prodding at me. Soon, the pain started. Agonizing, deep pain, as they stabbed me with needles, took knives to my skin and stitched them up. Any number of painful things. I screamed and pleaded with them, but they didn't care. For days, maybe weeks, all I felt was pain. Every time I thought I was getting numb to it, a new torture would come, and would start the process all over again.

At some point, my mind was so desperate to escape this hell that it retreated into my memories. Back to my home. With my mother. I remembered the smell of the trees and the leaves rustling in the air. I remembered the feeling of soft blankets she had sewn for me. The sweet taste of her apple pie she made from freshly grown apples. The wonderful rainbow of her beautiful garden. I remembered her smile. And I so, so desperately wanted to be back there. I wanted to be away, far away from here. I wanted none of this to have happened the way it did, my mother to be alive, our home to be my safe place again, I wanted to be home, *our home!*...

And everything went white.

The next thing I knew, I was lying in a crater. I had no clue where I was. Around me, the medical equipment was destroyed, walls and windows smashed, a big hole blown in the ceiling. But there were no bodies. As I looked around, the only thing I could find of my equipment was my sword, *Clover*. So, I took her, and ascended out of the hole, and into the light.

I was in the middle of nowhere. Desert, in every direction. I'd been hardened by this point, though, and was able to make it to the nearest road and hitchhike my way to the nearest settlement, which happened to be Brezio City. There, I tried to find information about my clan. That's how I met Adley. She was a down-on-her-luck crime boss at the time, and the two of us struck a deal: I worked for her, and she let me do my own investigation on the side. That arrangement worked well for a few years. Well, for her, anyway. She became the queen of Brezio, while I still hadn't found anything about my clan.

Eventually, I made my way out to the badlands again, and I stumbled across that place where I woke up. It was the same as I'd left it all those years ago: a hole in the ground, sand piling in, rubble everywhere. I decided to explore the place a bit more this time. While sorting through the piles of rubble and sand, I found documents about various other Manhattan Gate projects. One in particular caught my eye.

It talked of an experiment being conducted on a woman, age thirty. They believed something about her would unlock supernatural abilities in her children. And the document mentioned a child...

It was me. The document was talking about me and my mother. I couldn't believe it. It seemed like I had traveled back in time. But, that's impossible, since the year was still the same. The only conclusion I've been able to come up with is that I jumped timelines: crossing over into another parallel universe where everything was similar, but not the same. Events were somehow delayed in this universe versus my own.

If that was true... Then that meant there was a chance. I had a chance to save my mom, to save *myself*. And maybe... maybe I could see it all again. The house, the forest... and my mom.”

Radley lets that thought hang in the air for a while for Keera to process, her gaze drifting down to the sand. She then continues: “So that’s what I’m doing now. Summit Station is where she is. Where we are. I was making my way there when I came across you and your town under attack. And well... you know the rest...”

Keera sits there beside this woman, as she retreats once again into her memories. They knew this whole time that Radley had to have had a sorted past, but... to hear it all laid out before them, was... intense. The pair sit in silence for a while. The teen isn’t sure what to say. They have no more questions, it’s all been said. They suspect now why Radley doesn’t want them to follow her. Not because it’s dangerous, or Radley prefers to work alone. That is a given. No, it’s not that.

This is personal for Radley.

Her quest is to right the wrongs of a past already written, a desperate attempt of a broken woman to put it all back together again. Both her past, and herself. She needs to save herself, in more ways than one.

Keera looks at their savior. The hollow desert wind sweeps up Radley’s long white hair with it, creating waves like linens on a clothesline. They see more than just a dark and brooding woman who refuses to be known, now. They see a woman alone and grieving losses greater than Keera has ever experienced. And it’s at this moment that Keera knows what they must do.

“What do you need from me right now, Radley?” they ask.

“I don’t need...” Radley starts, but then stops herself. “I... I need you to be safe.”

Keera nods thoughtfully. “Okay,” Keera responds, “And you’ve proven time and time again that the safest place for me is by your side. So, I’m staying.”

Radley looks to the child. For a moment, there is anger. Anger at the child’s defiance. But that feeling quickly fades, as she regards them for a moment, the same wistful expression she had as she recalled her trauma encompassing her. Keera is even convinced they see a tear begin to well in her eye before it's swiftly rubbed away.

The warrior nods, with a resolute smile, as she gets up and makes her way back down the cliff face to join the others.

Chapter 21

"FREEZE!"

Before Radley and Keera can turn around from descending the cliff, a gruff, masculine voice shouts at them. Slowly, Radley sets the teen down, raises her hands, and turns around. Keera sees this and does the same. In doing so, they observe the scene that was obscured to them up on the ridge. Both Jack and Arianna are standing in the boat, hands also raised. Along with them is another figure, about seven feet tall, and dressed in an all-black tactical suit. They are pointing a combat rifle directly at Jack. They are wearing a strange, protruding gas mask that obscures their face. For a moment, Keera is confused how one person can hold up a group of such capable warriors.

Until they hear the telltale clacking of shifting weapons being pointed at them from the left and right. Slowly turning their head, they see another, slightly shorter figure in the same gear and the same weapon, pointing a gun at them, and another astride Radley.

Then they see the ones on the walls.

Gripping the stone walls above them and across the way, are another half a dozen soldiers, hanging by one hand while pointing weapons with the other. There are almost a dozen heavily armed soldiers pointing readied weapons at their small troop.

"Weapons on the ground!" the figure in the boat barks. His voice is muffled by the mask, but amplified by an in-helmet microphone. The group complies, detaching and dropping a good deal of weaponry, firearms and blades alike.

The individual turns to Radley and says, "You too, drop the blade!"

Keera notices, sure enough, Radley had not dropped *Clover*.

"I said, drop it!" he barks again.

Radley, instead, responds by speaking in a language Keera has heard before. It's guttural and punchy, with not many hard fricatives. The figure, shifting a bit, responds in kind with similar sounding words. This back-and-forth occurs for a few minutes. The exchange doesn't seem tense, at least from what Keera can tell from Radley's face. That's not much to go off of in this situation, though.

At a certain point, there is a pause. Then, the figure shouts something to the rest of the soldiers. Collectively, they all lower their weapons, the ones on the walls ascending to the top. The two nearest the group collect the weapons on the floor, and gesture for Radley and Keera to step into the boat. They comply. The two of them sit beside Jack and Arianna as the largest soldier starts the boat.

Jack leans over to Radley, whispering, "So... What just happened?"

"They're taking us to the gnuman settlement," Radley responds flatly.

"Wait, really?!" Keera exclaims, trying to keep their voice down. She nods. The teen then asks, "So... Are these..."

Arianna chimes in, "Gnuman? Yes." Her head nods down, and Keera follows her gaze, noticing the person's legs. They are double-jointed, like deer or horse legs. And, instead of ending in feet, they have two thick, cloven hooves. The gnuman revs the engine and speeds upriver.

"Well, that... worked out, didn't it?" Keera says. They aren't sure if this cynical world is getting to them or not, but they are choosing a more cautious optimism for this situation.

"Keep your guard up," Radley mutters, attempting to hide the words under the roar of the boat engine, "Something seems off here."

And there it is, Keera thinks, as they speed toward somewhere unknown to them. Things are never that easy up here, that much they've learned so far.

***

A good few hours pass until they reach a cave. About ten feet above water level, there is a thin, almost invisible gap in the rocks. It is just enough for someone to fit through, and just conspicuous enough to go unnoticed if one wasn't looking for it. The gnuman parks the boat directly below the opening, which emphasizes the natural rock-ladder that leads to the entrance. Again, something one wouldn't notice unless they were looking for it. One by one, the group ascends, with their armed escort holding up the rear.

While the entrance is cramped, the cavern quickly opens up into a passage that can be comfortably moved through. A warm flickering glow produced from cheap incandescent lights illuminates the slick, jagged walls. Keera has a flashback to the old abandoned mine back home, but they quickly repress that again. Like Radley said, keep your guard up.

The tunnel snakes on for a few hundred feet. This is clearly a natural cavern, but it feels intentional. Like some subterranean force had the foresight that people would need to move through this crack, so it made sure to give them just enough space, as well as relatively even footing. Slowly, the cavern widens, and as they round a left bend, and are greeted by the abrupt sight of a sturdy metal door.

"This is it," the gnuman says, pushing to the front, and producing a small card of some sort.

Radley turns to the group and whispers, "Before we go on, I have to say this: Do not mention that I'm an EUE. Gnumans are sworn to stop anything from other worlds from invading this one. So, just don't mention it, and let me do as much of the talking as possible." She locks eyes with Keera and Jack, waiting for an affirmative from both before proceeding. Keera is suddenly a bit more nervous about this whole thing. If they can't use Radley's connection to the gnuman in another universe, this might be tricky. They also find this prejudice a bit hypocritical, given that gnumans themselves are not from this world originally. But, they won't judge a people they've never met before. They'll just have to wait and see.

The gnuman swipes the card over a small panel beside the door, changing it from red to green. They then open the door with a loud CA-CHUNk, revealing a clean fluorescent environment beyond. Stepping aside, they gesture for the others to enter. They comply.

The difference between the exterior and interior of the gnuman base is stark. Marble-white floors, cold metal walls, and harsh blue light encompass the hallway in every direction they look. This all reminds them of the skyscraper they just fell out of yesterday.

The two other gnumans appear from rooms along the flanking hallways. Without their masks on, Keera can view their features, which are jarring at first glance. Both possessed a head like a goat or a wildebeest, with long snouts, covered in brown or blonde fur, and with two curved horns at the top of their heads. They look at each other, nod, and say something over a radio on their lapel. Then, one of them says to the group, "The woman and the child, with me. The other two, Torval, take them to the holding cells."

"Holding cell?" Keera blurts out, only to be immediately silenced by a severe look from Radley.

"A temporary measure, while our commander speaks with you two," he says to Radley and Keera, before gesturing with his rifle, "Now move!"

The group complies. Keera darts a worried glance back at Jack. "It's alright, little one," he says in a quiet, soothing tone, "I'll be fine. A bunch of overgrown lambs couldn't hurt Jack Cressfield." He smirks, which Keera returns to him, but there is still trepidation. None of this seems right. Radley had made it clear these people were militant and devoted to their beliefs, but she also hasn't seemed to let her guard down yet. Reluctantly, they follow Radley and the goat man that had brought them here down the leftmost corridor, while Jack and the bound Arianna continue forward with the other two.

They are led down a myriad of twisting, brutalist tunnels, all lit by the same cold fluorescent light. Even the lights in Keera's cave-home were more inviting than these. They don't pass many individuals roaming the halls, but they do pass various doors, all labeled either by number or by utility, like "conference room" or "janitor's closet." The few people they do pass look a lot like their escort: burly gnumans wearing the same tactical gear and wielding the same weaponry. This doesn't feel like a place anyone would live in, to Keera. But they are deep into the bowels of this place now. No turning back.

Eventually, the gnuman stops in front of one of the many doors. This one is labeled "301 - Sgt. Davanti." The door slides open with a hiss. Their guide gestures for them both to enter, and so they do. He shuts the door behind them, leaving them to take in the space beyond.

For all the buildup to this moment, the scene isn't all that impressive: the two find themselves in a well-decorated office, complete with the normal trappings of said space. Bookshelves, potted plants, chairs to sit in, and an enormous desk in the middle back of the room. All very well made, to be sure, but still *just* bookshelves, *just* chairs, and *just* a desk. It is so... pedestrian. Everything, except the massive goat in a military uniform, sat on the other side of said desk. He is tall, even taller than the two gnumans Keera has already encountered. His fur is a slightly lighter shade of tawny blonde than the other two, and he sports a prominent scar that obliterates his left eye. Behind him, on the wall, a huge greatsword is mounted horizontally.

Presently, Devanti is scribbling something on a piece of paper when he looks up to see who's entered. A grumbling growl emanates from his throat. "Who are you? What do you want?" he questions.

Keera sees Radley's shoulders fall a little. "My name is Radley. This is Keera. We've come for the gnuman's help."

The goat man turns to a computer on his desk, and begins clicking through pages. Both the mouse and his pen are comically small compared to his big, meaty hands. In fact, nothing in this room seems to be made for him, not even his fancy suit. Nothing except the gigantic sword on the wall seemed like his by choice.

"I don't see an appointment for you on my calendar," he says.

"We don't have an appointment," Radley responds, "We were searching for you, because we are aware gnumans are wise and skilled fighters. And I— we hoped you would be able to help this child." Radley gestures to Keera. They give a sheepish wave. Davanti barely acknowledges this, instead glancing between them and his computer screen.

"You will need to make an official inquiry with the recruitment department before any formal training interviews can be conducted," he grumbles, "I can get you the correct forms if you like."

"Forms?!" Radley asks. Her expression has grown only more and more confused the longer they've been here. It seems she has finally cracked. "Since when do gnumans deal in forms? Since when is there a recruitment department?!"

"That is how it has always been done," Davanti huffs, "For someone who has never been here before, you certainly seem to act like you know quite a lot."

"I know because I have—" Radley stops herself. She takes a breath before continuing, "I've lived alongside other gnumans before, and they did not operate this way."

"So you're admitting to working with defectors?" Davanti questions, a surprised gaze landing on Radley.

The air in the room shifts. Radley's brow furrows. Keera can see her gears turning, trying to process the implications of that phrase.

Radley starts, "I..." But no more words come. She is stun locked.

Keera feels that if someone doesn't step up now, they could be kicked out, or worse. So, they build the courage, and speak: "I can see into the future."

"Keera!" Radley whispers.

"What did you just say?" Davanti asks.

Keera, ignoring Radley, continues, "I can see into the future. Only in flashes, and only when I concentrate, or am in a stressful situation, but still. Started happening weeks ago when I found a weird tree in a cave below Canary Bridge. I don't know why, I don't know what's happening to me, but we were hoping you would be able to help us, help me figure this out."

Keera's heart is racing, as they catch their breath from that outburst. The whole time, Davani's attention was darting back and forth between them and his computer. Now, he analyzes something on the screen, takes a deep sigh, and says, "Alright. I think we can help you."

"Really?" Keera exclaims. They are so ready for something good to happen, they drop their guard, allowing their excitement to peek through.

Davanti nods and stands, hands on the table. It was easy to tell he was large when he was sitting down, but now, the duo get an obvious demonstration of his seven-and-a-half-foot stature. "Yes," he huffs, "In fact, I believe we can help each other... Keera, and Radley."

The teen looks at Radley. Her tense stance has not changed.

"In fact," the gnuman continues, "I believe the Manhattan Gate Project would like to learn a lot about the both of you. Torval!"

Keera's blood runs cold, face going pale at the mention of Manhattan Gate. They are so lost in the horrid realization that they react well after the *whooshing* sound of the door opening. They only just glimpse of the three armed gnuman closing in on them, one grabbing Radley and plunging a needle into her neck. Before they can run, call for help, anything, they, too, are injected with something cool and numbing, sending them back into a state of unfeeling darkness.

Chapter 22

THE NEXT SPAN OF time comes to Keera in blurry vignettes. The first that comes is a hallway floor flowing past them, like a gray marbled river. A pair of hoof-clad legs kick out along the bottom of their vision.

Next, they feel themself lying on something cold and metal. They feel uncomfortable, like their body isn't in a position it wants to be in. Their surroundings are dark and unfocused. A muffled shouting throbs and rumbles through their mind, masculine and deep. They can't make out the words, sounding as if underwater. But they are angry. Then the whole world rumbles and shakes. The deep, bone-rattling rumble is too much for their senses, thrusting them back into unconsciousness.

When Keera comes to again, everything is still shaking, but less painful than before. They can make out shapes that their brain can turn into recognizable objects: The four dark blobs sitting high above them must be Davanti and the three other gnumans who ambushed them. They recognize the brilliant gold fur of the one that stabbed them. On the ground, at their level, they recognize a dark and silver blob lying motionless. It's Radley. Then, further away, the pale and black blob has to be Jack. One of the gnumans seems to have a hoof down on his back, like furniture. Then, slumped against the far wall of the space, is the unmistakable silver and white blob of Arianna. None of their compatriots were moving. Keera dares not try to, either.

"Father," a booming voice echoes from the blonde gnuman, "Don't you feel this to be wrong? Only the woman is an EUE."

"All of them are abnormalities, and are wanted by Manhattan," Davanti responds.

"But we are not Amphion's lap dogs, like Vertex and his lizard thugs," the other argues, "We agreed on this partnership because we had a common goal: collect and contain Extra-Universal Entities."

"We would've been thrown in cells like the rest if we hadn't," Davanti almost steps on his son's words, "Or have you forgotten already?"

There is a pause, the blonde gnuman remaining silent.

"Why the sudden change, Torval? What about these in particular is turning you... soft?" Davanti asks.

"That one's just a child..." Torval mumbles. Keera swears he is looking right at them.

"What was that?" Davanti asks.

"Nothing, sir," Torval answers. Keera can feel the darkness at the back of their mind pulling them away yet again, the world fading.

Davanti lets out a huff before saying, "For this show of weakness, you will oversee their transfer. Understood?"

"Yes, sir..." Torval says quietly, his voice almost lost to Keera.

"What was that?!" the father bellows.

"Yes, sir," Torval asserts, just as Keera drifts off back into unconsciousness.

The next thing Keera witnesses is being high in the air yet again, staring at a concrete floor, stationary. Around them, they can hear sounds from various sources. Laboriously, they lift their head, trying to make out as much as they can. They're in a larger, but still industrial-looking space. Behind them, a military cargo truck is parked, as well as three gnumans, each holding one of their companions. To their right, they see other smaller black-suited shapes, more human in size and shape. They are head-to-toe combat armored, holding weapons as well.

Somewhere behind them, where they can't see, someone starts slow clapping. "Well done! Well, well done, Davanti!" a voice says. Slow, deliberate footfalls bring the clapping closer, until the source is revealed to Keera.

They see a man clad in an emerald green three-piece suit. On his feet are a pair of spurred, pointed cowboy boots. He wears a wide-brimmed, black cowboy hat, out from the bottom of which hangs long greasy black hair. Keera can't quite make out his face, as he turns to inspect the other three.

"Now, what DO we have here...?" he says, starting with Arianna. "Ol' reliable, miss Ari Mayhart herself. Not that reliable, it seems. Looks like they did quite a number on ya. Maybe it's about time we... decommission you, old-timer."

"No... please..." Arianna's voice sounds modulated and weak.

Suddenly, the man's hand shoots out and smacks her across the face. "Shut it!" he snaps, "You've sealed your fate, bitch."

He then continues his slow, jingling jaunt down the line of prisoners. "Ah, Jack Cressfield. Seems like you got involved in something that didn't concern you. Wonder what that mistress of yours will think about the trouble you've been causin'?"

"Fuck you..." Jack growls, and spits in the man's direction, before receiving an echoing slap of his own.

"Damn, am I going to have to show every one of you the back of my hand? The lip on some people, I swear," the man exclaims.

Then, he moves to Radley, who is notably more still than the others. "And you. You've been causing quite a commotion ever since you crawled out of your hole," he muses, caressing a gloved hand across her cheek. He continues, "You are the most intriguing specimen I've come across in a long, long time. That is..."

Slowly, the man turns, his face finally revealed to Keera under the dark, wide brim of his hat. If the teen had more energy in this moment, they would have screamed. Instead of a face, Keera is met with a jaundice, skin-wrapped skull, complete with exposed teeth, a void in place of a nose, and lidless, unblinking eyeballs. As he moves in close, inches from the poor child's face, they can see, even through delirium, how every twitch, every flex of a muscle pulls and stretches the taut skin this way and that. And the smell. The stench of rot and decay emanates from his disgusting visage.

"... until you came along," he finishes. Up close, Keera can tell there is some level of voice modulation happening somewhere in his rail-thin neck to allow him to speak as if he had lips. It isn't at the forefront of her mind, however, as they are currently being appraised by the grotesque man's bloodshot eyes. "After analyzing the data from your fight with the robot, it seems you possess some... unique abilities, little miss. Something I've never seen before... And I intend to find out just what makes you tick. By any means."

He steps back, thankfully, and turns to Davanti, who has been standing at attention off to the side. "Get the kid and the rest to the holding cells," he orders, then gestures toward Radley, "This one's still out cold. Take her straight to surgery."

"Yes, sir," Davanti responds, and he orders the rest to move out. Keera wants to scream. They try as hard as they can, but all they can muster is a pitiful whimper. The sudden movement of the gnuman carrying them is a shock to their systems, however, and sends them drifting back into unconsciousness. But, not before they feel the rumbling, and hear the familiar voice of the gnuman carrying them say, "I'm sorry, little one."

As Keera's mind finally clears, their body is wracked with aches and pains. Their eyes ease open, to find themself on a concrete floor. The lights above are as cold and foreboding as they have been lately. The rest of the space gradually comes into view, revealing it to be a small cell with a simple sink, dinghy cot, and an even more disgusting toilet. Gross blue light barely creeps into the space through a set of thick iron bars.

As they sit, stiffness slowly being shed from their body, their hazy memories from the last few hours solidify. They remember the horrid man with a skull for a face, the gnumans arguing, Radley...

Radley!

Keera jolts up from the floor instinctively, and throws themself at the bars, despite their protesting muscles.

"Radley!" they shout, rattling their cage to no avail.

"No use, kid," a familiar voice emanates from the shady cell across the way. Peering past the blinding fluorescence into the darkness, they can just make out the hunched form of Jack, leaning against the wall. "She's not here."

"I know! They're going to cut her open. We have to help her!" Keera asserts.

Jack responds, "They confiscated everything from me. We aren't going anywhere, unless you can convince big guy over there to give you the key." He gestures to the right of Keera's cell. Following his gaze, Keera lands on the imposing Torval, standing at the ready, holding a rifle.

"Keep it down!" he bellows.

"Or what?" Jack retorts, standing and stepping closer to the bars. "Step into the ring, big guy. Promise, I don't bite."

"Back away from the bars," the gnuman says, taking a step forward as well.

Jack, unfettered, continues, "I thought Radley said you were an honorable people. Since when has ambushing and drugging opponents been considered 'honorable?'"

"We do what is necessary to accomplish our mission," Torval responds.

"And your mission involves kidnapping women, children, and disabled robots? Got it," he shoots back.

A familiar crackly voice responds from the cell next to Jack's, "I resent that." Keera peers over to see Arianna slumped over on her cot.

"Yeah, well, no one asked you, snake," Jack retorts.

"How am I a snake?" she says, even though talking sounds like a laborious action for her now.

"Don't give me that!" Jack says, "Your data is the entire reason they're going to dissect Radley and Keera like fucking pigs! You knew this would happen, that's why you came willingly."

"I... I didn't think they would decommission me," she trails off.

"Right, and *that's* why you're sorry. A couple of selfish assholes, the both of you!" he storms away from the bars to pace his cell.

"*We're* selfish?" Arianna retorts, "Aren't you the one who's just here for the money? Didn't you also try to kill those two, only switching sides because you got a better offer?"

"Please," he says, but Arianna keeps going.

"No. no, I know what you did. You're no better than the rest of us, you hypocrite."

"I knew I should have put a bullet through you the second I had you pinned, you mechanical bitch!"

"You wouldn't have gotten the chance if it wasn't for a CHILD!"

"That child had you dead to rights i—"

"BOTH OF YOU, SHUT UP!" Keera finally bellows. The room goes quiet. Once the bickering is clearly done, they continue, "Arguing isn't going to help anyone. If anything, it's just giving me a headache..." Keera slumps against the wall. The crushing feeling of helplessness, coupled with the side effects of the knock-out drug and the arguing, has left their head in a vice. They rub their temples, the silence feeling like a refreshing ice pack.

"You're already sounding like her," Jack mutters.

"What?" Keera asks.

"Radley," he clarifies, "You sounded just like her just then."

A small smirk crosses Keera's face, only to be swiftly wiped away by the pain and worry yet again. Keera intuits they are all experiencing a similar sensation of helplessness. They came all this way, through all the adversity and hardships, just to end up caged like animals. For Keera in particular, it feels especially frustrating, as they were so close to potentially learning more about their powers, or at the very least, finding a way to harness them properly. But no, instead they are stuck where they started; surrounded my metal and stone, trapped, unable to escape.

"For what it is worth, I do not agree with what is to happen to all of you," Torval murmurs.

"What do you mean?" Keera asks.

"I do not agree with turning you all over to Manhattan Gate to be dissected," he elaborates. Keera finds his opinion rather hypocritical given their current situation. Torval continues, "Ever since we gnumans arrived to this world, we had a mission: to contain any Extra Universal Entities that invaded this universe, protecting the inhabitants from a threat they have no defense against."

"Great job at that, by the way. Only one of us here is an EUE," Jack interjects.

"Even so," Torval explains, "We do not torture any EUEs we capture. Instead, we capture them and study them through observation. Only if the subject proved uncontainable or an immediate danger would we seek termination. This arrangement, that we have made with Manhattan Gate, is... wrong."

Even with an alien visage such as Torval's, Keera can see the frustration on his face. The feeling that something is wrong, the desire to act. They know that feeling all too well. Then it clicks.

They see a way out.

"Then why do you do it?" they ask, "Why do you do what they tell you to do?"

The gnuman pauses for a moment, clearly surprised at the mere question. "I..." he eventually starts, "I must. Gnumans are loyal to each other, to our clans. And *especially* to our families."

"I take it the commander is your dad?" Keera asks. He darts a suspicious glance in their direction before relaxing and solemnly nodding. "Is that loyalty more important than your mission, then?" they continue.

"I... am not sure. The two have never been in conflict before," he says.

"I get how hard that can be," Keera sighs, "I really wanted to see what was outside my hometown. But my community wouldn't allow it. My parents were also very against it. I loved my parents and my people a lot, but they were stopping me from doing something I felt I *had* to do. Something that felt right."

"This is not some simple want," Torval rebuts, "My clan has gone against the duties mandated of us by our forebears. We have lost our way."

"Then isn't that an even better reason to not go along with all this anymore?" Keera suggests.

Torval glances to the floor. Keera can practically hear the pitched combat in his mind before he speaks next, "What did you do?"

"What?" Keera asks.

"How did you resolve your own... moral conflict? Between yourself and your community?" he clarifies.

"Well, my town was destroyed by a group affiliated with Manhattan Gate," Keera states somberly. They don't know if this is something they've said out loud before. They continue, "So I didn't really have a choice. But, I feel like if that hadn't happened... I would have still left town someday. Like, even though a lot sucks up here. I've almost died so many times in the last few weeks, I've lost count. I've been hunted by a bounty hunter, lizard people, an assassin, and a bunch of big monster men with guns. No offense to everyone." The collective acts a tad guilty for a moment, but Keera continues on, "But, even then, it's still worth it. Seeing new sights, new wonders I would've never dreamed of down there. Knowing I can go anywhere I want, be anything I commit to being. It's just... pure freedom. I've known for a while this was my destiny, what I was meant to do: be a wanderer. And I don't think I could've lived with myself if I didn't follow my own path."

Keera feels a weight lift from their shoulders. They aren't sure how long they've been carrying this, how long they were suppressing this part of them that is clearly true. But now, having expressed this, shedding the regret from their past, and dreaming of an unimagined tomorrow, they feel elated. So much so, they almost forget they're in a jail cell right now.

"I... admire your strength, little one," Torval says, looking at the young teen directly for the first time, "You possess a conviction to yourself and your ideals that many do not. Including myself, it seems..." He trails off, his sorrowful gaze drifting back to the floor.

Then, suddenly, as if struck by a bolt of lightning, Torval shoots to attention, determination flashing in his eyes, "But that ends today!"

Keera's eyes widen, and both Jack and them rush toward the bars in anticipation. "So, what are you saying?" they ask.

"I am rejecting the orders given to me by my father! I will no longer stand idly by, while gnumans are used as pawns by a selfish and unholy organization! I will follow the mission as ordained to me by my ancestors, and carry out their wishes everywhere I go!" Torval declares.

"Hell yeah, man!" Keera cheers. On top of this, meaning they might have a chance to escape, they are also simply excited to see a fire light inside this creature's eyes.

"I reject your will, Manhattan Gate! I reject your will, father! And, if I am exiled for this, THEN SO BE IT!" the gnuman bellows.

Jack and Keera can't help but celebrate with Torval, this agentless soldier driven so passionately by the thought of becoming his own person. It is, indeed, infectious.

The moment of celebration passes, leaving Keera and Jack standing awkwardly as Torval continues to revel in his newfound rebellion. "So," Jack interjects, "Are you going to let us out, or...?"

"YES!" Torval shouts, and moves to unlock the cells. Both Keera and Jack breathe a sigh of relief, and after some brief jangling of keys, the pair is free again. Torval then moves to Arianna's cell, unlocking it as well. However, there is no rapid movement toward freedom like the others. Keera cocks their head.

"I will retrieve your equipment. Wait here, then we will find your friend before it's too late!" the goat-man exclaims. He jogs to a door at the end of the hall, disappearing out of sight.

Jack moves toward Keera, and places a hand on their shoulder. They look up at the vampire. They can tell, now that they're up close, that he is beaten and bruised. But, behind all the damage, there is a confident smile beaming down at them. "We'll get her back, little fox. Don't you worry," he says. Keera nods.

Then, their gaze shifts back to Arianna's open cell. She has still not moved. Curiosity once again has gotten the better of them, and they peek around the corner. There, they see the slumped form of Arianna, right where she has been the whole time. Since she doesn't properly breathe, Keera thought the worst. Until a cold, indifferent eye darts up to meet theirs.

"What?" Arianna asks.

"Aren't you coming?" Keera asks.

Arianna squints at them, "Why would you want me to be a part of your little prison break? I tried to kill you, remember?"

Keera shrugs. "Yeah, well, so did he," they gesture to Jack, "But he got over it."

"Wait, you're not serious," Jack interjects, "She works *for* Manhattan Gate!"

"Right, so she knows this place inside and out, I would imagine," Keera explains. Jack furrows his brow, looking between Keera and the android. Keera groans and rolls their eyes, "Come on, Jack. Look at her, she has one arm! What's she going to do against the two of us and a giant goat guy?"

Jack takes one more look at Ari, sighs, shrugs his shoulders, and mumbles, "Alright. Get up, shinny."

"You're still assuming I want to leave," she says.

"Would you rather stay and be dismantled, or break out and maybe find a way to repair yourself?" Keera asks, absolutely done with her angsty attitude.

A beat passes, until Arianna finally agrees, standing and joining the other two.

"Good," Keera says, letting out a sigh they didn't know they were holding in. *I didn't think that would work,* they think. They then continue, as they hear the thundering hoofsteps of Torval returning with their belongings, "Now, we have just one more we have to save."

Chapter 23

KEERA CLUTCHES THE LEAF in their pocket, as they slink through the maze of metal corridors. The edges and the texture of their souvenir is so familiar to them now. It is almost comforting to fidget with. They can use all the comfort they can get right now, because even though they are *attempting* to move quickly and quietly as a unit, one member in particular makes this difficult. Torval, naturally leading the charge, is doing his best to be quiet, but his enormous form and hooved feet are working against him.

"How much further?" Jack whispers.

"The operating room is two more rights, then a left. Wait!" Torval instructs, throwing out an arm to halt them. He peers around the corner. Keera hears footfalls and chatter grow louder and louder, and then softer and softer. "Okay, go!" Torval orders. Keera can feel the adrenaline pumping through them once again. They don't like the brief despair that had taken hold of them in the cell. They're realizing in this moment that they would rather actively risk their own safety to be free than to put up with being trapped and helpless. Not something they would've thought of themselves back home, but here they are.

As they round the aforementioned left, Torval stops at a door. It's just like every other door they've passed along the way, only with a small sign next to it saying "Operating Room 1."

"This is it," Torval proclaims.

"What sort of resistance should we expect?" Jack asks.

"None," Arianna states.

Jack whips his head to her, "What? How do you know?"

"This is Summit Station," Arriana says matter-of-factly, "There's hundreds of feet of rock, dozens of concrete, and several of steel between the outside world and this room. If they make it past them, and all the security at the entrances, they've earned it."

Jack looks to Torval, and the goat-man simply nods in confirmation.

"Even still, be on your guard. We don't want the entire might of Manhattan Gate bearing down on us. Get in, get her, get out. Got it?" Jack says.

The group nods affirmatively.

He puts a hand to the button that opens the door.

"Ready... And... BREACH!" Jack yells.

The door flies open, the group flooding in. The space they enter is dark, and it takes everyone a moment to adjust to this. Their eyes quickly are drawn to a bright spot beyond a window: a group of three people in white are illuminated by a bright overhead lamp. They are all hunched over a waist-high table. The party freezes. The doctors don't seem to notice them, or the door opening. *Good, let's keep it that way,* Keera thinks. But, then, another thought enters their mind: *Oh no... are we too late?*

Keera frantically searches the darkness for a way inside. As their eyes adjust, Keera spies a door to the next space. They tap Jack, motioning to it. He locates it as well, gives a nod, and motions for the rest to move up.

After everyone is in position near the door, Jack locks eyes with all of them and gives a countdown.

They burst open the door.

"GET AWAY FROM THE TABLE!" Jack shouts.

The three people in white step back, one yelping out of surprise. Immediately, their hands fly up in surrender, some holding small scalpels and medical tools. Each of them is wearing a medical face mask. Keera can still tell they're terrified just from their eyes.

"I said MOVE IT!" Jack responds, brandishing one of his blades at them. This snaps them out of it, and they scuttle away from the operating table, into the dark of the rest of the room like roaches. As they part, they reveal Radley. She is stripped of her combat gear, and is instead wearing a flimsy baby blue gown with the chest exposed. They can see a thin line from her collarbone down to the middle of the sternum.

Jack and Keera rush to her side, and simultaneously breathe a sigh of relief. The line is dotted and drawn with a medical marker. Not an incision. "Radley, Radley, wake up," Keera jostles her arm. She doesn't move.

"She's heavily sedated," Jack explains.

"You need to wake her up, now," Ari warns, "It will only be a matter of time before they notice we're not in our cells."

Jack whips to the people in lab coats, "You! Wake her up!" he shouts, pointing at one man. Then, he points at another, "You, grab her things!"

The pair scramble, clearly not used to being threatened at sword-point. The one told to resuscitate her rifles through a small toolkit, and produces a needle. He approaches Radley, only for Jack to grab his wrist. Arianna promptly moves to check what is in the syringe. She explains, "It's a dopamine stimulant. He's doing what you told him to, let him go." Jack's severe look shoots to the android. She rolls her eyes, "If I'm lying to you, and she dies, you can throw me on that table and dismantle me yourself."

Jack takes this as a sufficient offer and lets go of the doctor's arm. The man in white, still wearily side-eyeing Jack, proceeds to slip the needle into Radley's neck. Squeezing the plunger,its contents drain into her veins.

He removes the needle.

Everyone in the room holds their breath, all eyes on Radley as she lies there. Still.

Suddenly, the mercenary jolts upright from the table, nearly toppling it over, gasping for air. Instinctively, Keera rushes to grab her hand, gripping it tight. She looks around wildly, panicking at every face she sees surrounding her.

"Radley, Radley, it's okay," Keera soothes desperately, "It's okay, you're okay. It's us, we're here."

Steadily, her breathing calms, and her eyes finally fall on Keera beside her. With no hesitation, the woman leans forward and embraces Keera in a tight, trembling hug. Keera is stunned. So much so, they don't hug back at first. Radley does not cry, does not break down in their arms. It is a silent, strong, desperate hug. Like someone clinging to a rescue ladder after being lost at sea for days. And, Keera, realizing this, returns the hug with warmth and compassion, until the death-grip melts into a soft embrace.

"We thought we lost you," Keera whispers.

"Me too..."

After a brief moment, Arianna interjects, dramatically cleaning their throat, "While this is nice, we are still on a ticking clock, everyone."

At the sound of her voice, Radley shoots her an angry glare, "What is she doing here?" then she finds Torval in the darkness, "And you. You're the one who knocked us out!"

"It's a long story," Jack says, "But the short of it is, they're on our side now. Helped us get to you."

Radley eyes the two fresh additions wearily, before a light squeeze of her hand from Keera softens her expression a bit. "Fine," she huffs, "If either of you try anything, you'll both be eating bullets."

As if on cue, the other researcher fumbles, dropping some of Radley's equipment, as she returns with it.

"Right, very scary. Now, get changed, we need to go," Jack orders. Then, to the researchers, "The three of you: go in that room, lock yourselves in, and don't even THINK of leaving until you know we've been gone for at least five minutes. Got it?" All three nod, and run into the side room the researcher just obtained Radley's belongings from. The door locks with a barely audible *click*.

"You should've just killed them," Radley states.

"They didn't hurt you. They were just doing their job," Jack says, "Come on, we can live to regret having some morals later." With that, Jack and the others scamper out into the hall to wait for Radley to change.

A short time later, Radley emerges from the darkness, clad in her black coat, black military getup, and *Clover* over her shoulder.

Keera can't help but smirk a little. They never thought they'd see this badass woman again, but there she was. Tall, dark, and ready to kick ass yet again.

"Where to?" Radley asks plainly, to no one in particular.

"Front door is this way," Torval gestures down a hallway.

"Are you insane?" Arianna disagrees, "Do you intend to fight your way through an entire battalion? No, there is a safer exit out through the maintenance tunnels, at the lowest level."

"The elevators will likely be heavily guarded. They would not expect a frontal assault," Torval says.

"Listen here, goat-man," Ari gets in his face. Or, well, two feet below his face, but as in his face as she can be, "I've known this place inside and out for over a *century*. I know best how to—"

Just then, the lights around them switch to an ominous red emergency beacon. A loud siren blares, and the group readies themselves instinctively.

"Oh shit," Jack exclaims.

"They must've noticed we're missing?" Keera guesses. Jack nods.

Then, to Ari and Torval, he asks, "Which is closer, elevator or exit?"

"Exit," Torval responds.

"Then, that's our out, let's move," Jack says, and takes off down the corridor, with the rest hot on his heels.

Arianna scoffs, jogging behind them as well, "You both are seriously braindead if you think you can fight your way out of Summit Station!"

Suddenly, Radley stops. Keera turns back. She looks like she's just seen a ghost.

"Where did you say we were?" she asks, eyes wide and severe. The rest halt as well.

"Summit Station," Arianna repeats.

Keera and Radley lock eyes. They can see surprise and desperation in them.

"Come on, Radley, we have to move!" Jack calls. She ignores him.

Keera wants to shake their head no. They want to tell Radley they don't have time, that this place is about to be flooded with Manhattan Gate soldiers, plus who knows how many gnumans. They want to say they'll come back later, rested and with a plan, not having just been beaten and drugged. That they'd come back once they've mastered their powers, so they can fight alongside them all effectively, too. They want to say they're sorry, but it's for the best.

But they can't. They know too well what this means to Radley.

I guess we're doing this.

Keera takes a deep breath and nods to her companion.

They will follow her to the end.

CHAPTER 24

A SQUAD OF MANHATTAN Gate soldiers ready themselves in front of the elevator. Some crouched, some standing, all staring down the hallway, as gunfire and shouting echoes from somewhere down the corridor. One or two of them shift nervously. They don't know what to expect. All they were told is that highly dangerous prisoners have escaped, and are likely heading for the access elevator.

Just then, a woman with white hair, dressed in all black, and wielding a pistol and a sword rounds the corner. The squad commander shouts, "Fire!" The squad unloads a volley of suppressing fire, as the woman ducks back behind the wall. They have their orders. They cannot reach the lower level. This squad is the last line of defense, and they must do so with their lives if necessary.

***

"Elevator's up ahead. Got another squad," she says to the group. Then, to Ari, "You're sure this is the only way?"

"All high security projects are kept in the lowest level of the facility. If your home is still here, that's where it will be," Arianna confirms.

"Alright then. Torval," Radley redirects her focus, "You and I will act as a shield. Don't let a single bullet past you. Jack, once we're close enough, disarm them. ONLY disarm, we don't need you going feral on us. Let Torval and I take care of them."

The two men nod affirmative.

"Alright, ready... go!" she shouts. The group charges around the corner.

"Fire, open fire!" the commander at the end of the hall shouts again, and a torrent of bullets fly toward Torval and Radley. As this happens, Torval produces a massive greatsword, as wide as a door, and holds it in front of him. It's so wide that it acts as a shield as he charges forward, with Radley deflecting bullets with her blade beside him. Not a single bullet gets through as the group charges forward. Keera hears it all: gunshots, metal hitting metal. They can smell the gunpowder in the air as the group closes the gap between the two groups in a matter of seconds.

They are on top of the squad now, Jack nimbly leaping over the two front liners, flipping in the air, dual blades drawn, and landing in the middle of their formation. The soldiers, surprised by this, turn and try to react. But, the daywalker is just too fast; with a few elegant swings, weapons are knocked or sliced from soldier's hands, leaving them defenseless, as Radley slides in with her pistol, and Torval grabs the semi-auto rifle from his back. Together, the two swiftly dispatch the entire squad.

Everyone is left catching their breath, standing amid the bodies. All except Ari, of course, who uses the down arrow to call the elevator. The group collects themselves while they wait.

"Grab some of their ammo. No telling how many more will be waiting for us down there," Radley orders, "Take their radios, too. We can use those if we get separated."

"For what it's worth, I still think this is insane," Arianna states.

"No one asked you," Radley says.

No one dares take Arianna's side on this one, not even Torval. He barely knows Radley, but he can tell just by how the others reacted when they said what they were doing, that this woman is driven by some powerful force they do not want to get in the way of.

Radley turns to him, "Torval, you know this place. What should we expect?"

"I do not travel to the bottom floor," he states, "Only gnuman with top level clearance, like my father, are permitted entry."

"Right, I told you already," Arianna says, "Top-secret projects that *I* don't even have the clearance to know about. This is most likely a death trap."

"Can you get us past security?" Radley asks, in a way that it feels more like an ultimatum.

"I don't know what we will be going up against, so I can't guarantee—"

"Can. You. Do it?" Radley interrupts.

Arianna pauses, clearly taken aback by the fire in the other woman's eyes. She glances down and notices something sticking out from one of the dead soldier's pockets. Fishing it out, she produces a fresh pack of cigarettes. She looks to Keera. They remember they had the lighter last, and return it to Arianna, who promptly lights one up. The android takes a long drag and releases a cloud from her lips. Her shoulders relax.

"Alright, now I can do it," she says, the panic and irritation in her voice having dissipated with the cigarette smoke.

Radley nods, just as the elevator dings, the doors opening.

Down we go, Keera thinks.

The ride down is tense. Crammed in a metal box, descending hundreds of feet below the earth, Keera can almost hear their heartbeat echoing off the walls. They still have no idea what is waiting for them down below Summit Station. Apart from hunting down EUEs, they have no idea what Manhattan Gate actually does. And on the top-secret floor? What are they doing here? It is almost enough to make Keera nauseous. But, the teen looks to Radley, as they have for these past few weeks, and finds in her expression pure determination. Perhaps even a bit of anticipation. That's why they're here. They can't forget that. Radley needs this closure, something Keera only wishes they could have. If they can't have it themself, then the least they can do is to be there to help them obtain it. Some well deserved inner peace. Hopefully.

The elevator doors slide open. Floor B34. A subterranean chill wafts over the tense group. Keera shivers. Everyone steps off the elevator as the door shuts behind them. Ahead, a long, double-wide hallway stretches for hundreds of feet. Squinting, Keera can just make out a door on the other end.

"Let's get moving," Jack says, "That elevator will be back down here with squads of soldiers pretty soon."

With that, the crew begins the long jog to the other end. Their footsteps echo all over the corridor. By the time it returns to them, it sounds like rolling thunder in the distance. Coupled with the chill in the air, these sensations bring to mind the calm before the storm. The entire group must be feeling it, too, as no one says a word.

When Jack does speak up to Radley, he does so in a hushed tone. "Once we get there, what's the plan? Do you have an out, an exit strategy?" he questions.

"We'll use the maintenance tunnel I escaped through as a child," Radley responds, not losing her focus on the horizon.

"What if this place's layout is different, like the gnuman clan was?" he asks.

"Then we fight our way back to this elevator," Radley says flippantly, "Why do you care? Your mission is done once I get to that room."

"I..." he pauses, clearly wanting to say something else, before shaking it off and saying, "I'm simply looking out for myself." He looks to Keera. They can see the concern in his eyes. Concern that goes deeper than Keera can understand as a child.

Just then, Keera hears a gentle click beneath them. Time feels like it slows to a crawl. A mass of heat and light erupts from underneath their feet. The blast is so strong; it sends the entire group flying in all directions, with Keera going straight up into the ceiling, crushing their spine, and shattering their skull on the unforgiving ceiling.

Keera's eyes fly open. Jack is saying, "I'm simply looking after my—"

"MINES, WATCH OUT!" Keera shouts. The group skids to a halt. Just in time, as Keera notices an almost imperceptible red blinking light where their foot would have landed, indeed had landed in their vision.

"Did you just?..." Jack asks. Keera nods.

"Incredible... so this was the ability Amphion was intrigued by," Torval surmises.

"Stay alert," Radley states, "There's bound to be more—"

Indeed, there is more, as the panels of the walls, ceiling, and floor erupt outward, pushed aside by familiar, scaly skinned hands. A horde of lizard-men pours into the tunnel from hidden compartments, hissing and shouting, as they surround the party.

"Fuck," Jack exclaims.

"What's the play here, merc?" Arianna calls out.

Before she can answer, however, a deep, guttural laugh echoes through the corridor. Silence befalls the lizards. From behind the crowd, a tall, thick-bodied form emerges. His massive shotgun is in hand. And, as his face comes into view, a toothy smile curls his reptilian muzzle.

"Well, well, well... Seems the boss was right," Vertex jeers to his audience, "Our group of lab rats wanted the cheese at the center of the maze. Greedy little rodents, caught in a trap." His gang cackles as he continues. "The boys upstairs won't be too happy. They still wanted you alive. But, after you HUMILIATED me, slaughtered dozens of my men, well... I can't promise I won't take at least ONE of your heads for my wall..." He aims his shotgun threateningly with one arm, toward Jack. "I'm looking at you, pretty boy."

Jack grits his teeth. The reptile continues grandstanding while the bounty hunter whispers over his shoulder to Radley, "We can't let them slow us down, or we'll have more problems to deal with."

"We need to punch a hole in their line, then have someone cover our asses while we retreat," Arianna chimes in.

"Let me be the rear guard. This overgrown lizard doesn't look so tough," Torval suggests.

"His scales are impervious to bullets," Radley says, "No, we need you to help clear a path. All we need is a distraction..."

Keera searches for a way to help. It isn't long before they notice something: "The mines. They haven't gone off yet."

"I'll trigger it," Radley decides, "Torval, get ready to block the blast, then push forward. Everyone else, stay on his ass."

Nods all around.

"Enough chatter!" Vertex calls out, "You are surrounded! I'll give you one last chance: surrender now, and I will only kill the daywalker."

"You know, if you would've given me that offer a few days ago, I might've actually considered it..." Radley says, "But you trashed my friend's night club. So fuck you. Torval, now!"

With that, the goat-man slams his sword into the floor. Everyone rushes behind him.

"SEIZE THEM!" Vertex shouts.

The lizards charge, but Radley is faster: An explosion rocks the tunnel, sending lizard-men flying in all directions. The party grips one another, anchoring themselves behind the wall that is Torval. As soon as the dust settles, the gnuman retrieves his sword, and everyone charges into the smoke and the rubble left by the blast.

The few lizard-men who manage to scramble to their feet first are effortlessly shoved aside by the giant goat man, or dispatched by the mercenary or the bounty hunter. Keera, for their part, just keeps running, while doing their best to watch out for more traps. Soon, they clear the debris and the crowd to find themselves within a few yards of the exit.

"YOU MORONS!" Vertex shouts from among the crowd of dazed and confused gangsters, "Don't let them get away!"

The horde of weapon-wielding mutants scramble to their feet and charge. They will be on them within moments.

"Go," Jack says.

"You can't take them all, not on your own," Radley urges.

"This tunnel is narrow enough to keep them from surrounding me. I'm doing my job, buying you time. Now GO!" Jack repeats, turning to the attackers, swords drawn. Without another word, Radley steals her composure, and gestures for the rest to follow. Keera hesitates, but is dragged along by the arm as Radley pulls them onward, through the open door. They don't even have a chance to say anything. The last thing Keera sees of Jack is his blades carving into the first few assailants.

"COME AT ME, YOU ARSEHOLES!" Jack shouts.

The door shuts.

Keera turns on Radley, "We have to go back for him!"

"He'll be fine," she says, "He's been holding back the entire time we've known him. Without us around, he can really let the beast out... and at the very least, buy us some time."

Keera can't believe this. They trust Radley and her fighter's intuition, but this... this isn't like the Radley they've come to know. She's been cold, but never the type to essentially sacrifice someone. Still, they trust their savior... So, Keera nods, and they push onward into the facility.

Beyond the door, the group follows more snaking hallways and corridors, reminiscent of those they first encountered in this facility. They rush past offices, meeting rooms, and break rooms. What dark secrets are held in those filing cabinets and on those computers? No one can say. Those aren't what the party is here for at the moment, however. They're after one specific secret.

At the end, they reach a door that looks promising: along the wall leading to it are signs reading "Test Chambers A-F."

"That way," Arianna says.

"I thought you didn't know anything about this level," Radley questions.

"I didn't think I did..." the android says, scanning the area, "But I recognized this hallway... this door. I... I don't know why, it just... feels like a fragment of a memory..." She snaps out of it as she realizes the others are staring at her. "Anyway, we have to move. If Vertex and his goons knew we were here, then others are likely lying in wait, as well," she says.

"Maybe because someone tipped them off..." Radley says, glaring at her.

Arianna rolls her eyes, "Oh, come off it! I have as much to lose here as you do, sweetheart. Both of us are getting torn apart if we're caught down here. Now, unless you want to have it out right here right now, and let everyone down here know where we are, so they can come snatch up the victor, I suggest we get a move on!"

Radley huffs. Slowly, she peels her gaze away from the android and to the door. She readies her blade and her gun. "Eyes up," she says, and opens it.

The group enters into a large, utilitarian space. A metal box, a couple hundred feet forward and to the sides, and about half as much vertically. Taking up a majority of the space are a number of odd, geometric pillars of steel. Some are only a few feet high, while others are a couple of stories. Gray sand makes up the uneven ground, undulating to simulate hills and valleys. Along the perimeter, a concrete, walkway-sized border frames the entire room, leading around to a door on the far side. Between the concrete and the sand, there is a yellow and black painted section, with words appearing periodically throughout. They say the phrase "DANGER: DO NOT ENTER WHEN LIVE TRAINING IS IN PROGRESS" in bold, white lettering. Carefully, quietly, the group keeps close to the outer wall, following the concrete path around the outside. Radley and Torval take turns aiming forward and toward the center of the room.

About halfway across the room, Radley raises a hand. The group halts.

"What was it?" Torval asks.

"I saw movement. There," Radley gestures to the center. They all look to where she is pointing: a space between two larger pillars of metal, with another pillar jutting out at roughly a forty-five degree angle. Keera doesn't see anything.

Silence. The group all diligently scans their surroundings.

Suddenly, Arianna calls out, "There, under the overhang!" just before bullets impact and explode the wall behind them. The group dashes to the nearest cover, sliding past the warning sign, slamming into a waist-high barrier in the sand. Bullets continue to fly over them, everyone keeping their heads low as possible. Keera, instinctively, covers their ears.

"WE'VE GOT GNUMANS!" Arianna shouts above the fire.

Just then, the fire halts. The group is panting.

"How many did you see?" Radley asks.

Ari peaks above the barrier, only to initiate another hail of gunfire. Luckily, they duck back down just in time, and report, "About a dozen. Grouped up squads of three or four around the center."

"There were only about six guns firing at us just now," Radley says. Keera has no idea how she can tell that simply by the sound. For all they could tell, there could be a hundred men shooting at them. "That means..."

"... Half of the units are engaging in suppressive fire, while the other half are moving in close, from either side," Torval finishes her sentence, "This is a tactic we employ when we believe we outnumber, but do not outmatch, our enemy."

"Then let's show them just how outmatched they are," Radley says, "Torval, provide covering fire. I'm going to make a run for closer cover and cut them off before they surround us."

"I was hoping it wouldn't come to this, not so soon..." Torval says.

"You changed sides the moment you let us all out of our cells," Ari says.

The gnuman raises his voice, "Just an hour ago, they were my brothers! My family!"

"And now they're your enemy," Radley returns intently, "But you're still a gnuman soldier. You made your decision. Now live with it, and cover me."

Torval is shocked by the severity in the woman's eyes. As he sits there, processing the thorough verbal lashing he was just given, a familiar gruff, gnuman voice calls out from the center of the arena: "Torval. I know you are with these traitors, these abominations. I don't know in what way you have been manipulated, but if you turn them over now, we can look past your transgressions."

They all know who is addressing them. "I joined them willingly, father," Torval responds, "You and the others have strayed from the righteous path bestowed upon us by our ancestors! In siding with Amphion, you have betrayed the tenants we must follow to call ourselves proud gnumans."

"The goals of Manhattan Gate are parallel to those of the gnuman. In order to accomplish our goals, free of interference, we must be willing to adapt, to find allies who can further our goals," Davanti explains.

"You sold our people as soldiers for soft beds and lavish meals! We send Extra-Universal Entities to be *slaughtered*! Father, that is not adaptation. That is BLASPHEMY!" Torval argues.

"You would prefer to side with anomalies, with back-stabbing traitors, and *murderers,* over your own flesh and blood? My son... you surely have lost your way, and I have only myself to blame for that," Davanti says.

Torval stands defiant. Keera and the others peer around the obstruction, and can make out the large, yet refined figure of Davanti a few yards away. He is standing, arms behind his back, chin up, as if he were addressing a soldier, not a child.

Torval speaks, "I can no longer follow you, father. For it is you that have lost your way. But, on one matter, we can agree: you only have yourself to blame."

Torval's proclamation hangs in the air like the final tolling of a church bell, as both sides eye the two gnumans. Both are full of stubbornness and disappointment for the other. The frustration is palpable.

Finally, Davanti lets out a defiant snort. "Very well," he says, "If you wish to live your life beholden to gnuman tradition, then I will allow you a Rite of Excommunication."

The three with Torval look perplexed. "What's a 'Right of Excommunication?'" Keera asks, whispering to Radley.

She doesn't seem to know the answer either, but Torval steps in to elaborate: "It is tradition that if a member of a gnuman tribe wishes to leave, he must face an elder in combat. They must either force the elder into submission, who will allow them to leave freely, or... they must die."

"What?! That's stupid, you can't do that!" Keera pleads.

"I must. My father is right. If I wish to walk a righteous path, I must not allow myself to decide what customs I choose to follow, and which I ignore" Torval looks to Davanti, "Unlike him."

Torval steps away from the group. Keera's hand instinctively moves to try to stop him, but Radley catches it and holds them back. A stern shake of her head subdues them. Instead, they watch with sadness as their newfound friend approaches his father.

"As I am your son, however," Torval says, "Would you permit me the honor of modifying the conditions of our duel?"

"Name your conditions, and I will decide," Davanti states.

The son responds, "I fight not only for my freedom, but for the freedom of them as well." He gestures back behind him to his three compatriots. "If I succeed," he continues, "All of us go free. If I fail, well... I will no longer be able to stop you from recapturing them."

Davanti eyes his son, then the others, calculating something. Finally, he responds: "Agreed."

Torval turns back to the group, "Go now, I will buy you more time."

Without a word, Radley nods, and the three start running toward the exit. A few gnumans move to block their exit, but Davanti holds up a hand, "Let them go. This will not take long," he says, removing his commander jacket, revealing a combat-ready tactical suit, his greatsword on his back. He unsheathes his silvery blade.

As they run for the door, Keera looks back one more time at Torval. He meets their distraught, pleading eyes and nods reassuringly. The nod is so small and imperceptible, Keera is sure it was meant just for them. A private reassurance that steadies the teen as they exit the room. Then, Torval unsheathes his own blade, and the son prepares to charge at the father just as the door shuts, severing Keera's view of them both.

The dwindling group of Keera, Radley, and Arianna make their way further into the facility. Yet more corridors of metal and fluorescence. Keera is beginning to worry about just how far into the belly of this horrid beast they will have to travel. Knowing their friends are in the midst of pitched combat behind them also adds to the stress of it all. They are regretting siding with Radley on this. But they have gone too far and sacrificed too much to turn back now. At least, that's what they tell themself as they enter yet another large chamber.

The space is similar to the one they just left, only larger in every dimension. Namely, it is a great deal taller, with scaffolding zigzagging its way along every wall. They entered the room on one such scaffolding, leaving them about three stories above ground level. These features are not the focus of the group as they enter, however. Rather, these are smaller details they each discover independently, after taking in this area's centerpiece.

Suspended in the air, strung up by wires and cables, evoking a cross between an insect caught in a spider's web and a crucifixion, is an amalgamation of metal and scale. The body resembles that of a monitor lizard: stocky torso, clawed reptilian limbs, a long tail that reaches the floor, and a relatively small head that hangs limply from a serpentine neck. Beyond that, this figure is very different from your standard monitor. First, parts of it are coated in thick plates of steel. Apart from a few joints showcasing scaly skin, these plates create what looks like an effective, if not crudely installed, suit of armor for this inanimate creature. A few features seem to replace or are added to this creature's anatomy as well. At the end of its tail protrudes a massive metal sphere covered in six-foot-long spikes. In addition, in the place of its right arm, a giant gun of some sort has been grafted onto it. The whole thing is one large, grotesque sin, against both biology and engineering. A monster Keera cannot look away from.

"What is that?" Radley wonders, horror filling her gaze.

"I... I have no idea," Arianna states, her brow furrowed.

"How could they have kept something this big a secret down here for so long?" Keera asks.

Radley's apprehension fades, before she responds, "Whatever this thing used to be, it's dead now. Look." She gestures to the lower level of the facility. Massive pools of red-brown liquid have formed below the creature. These puddles seem to flow down through maintenance-hole-sized drains in the floor. As they observe this, the smell of rotten flesh suddenly hits Keera, festering in the air. They instinctively cover their nose and let out a grunt of disgust.

"Pretty easy to hide a corpse deep underground, even one this size," the mercenary states, "Come on, we don't have time to—"

"Welcome ladies!" a voice through some speakers rings out throughout the chamber, assaulting their ears, "I had a feeling you would be making your way down here."

"Who are you? Show yourself!" Radley calls.

But Keera already knows who this is. They recognize the accent and the same sinister undertone he possessed back when they were floating in and out of consciousness. The green suit. The skull for a face.

Keera breathes, "It's Amphion."

Chapter 25

"Show yourself, coward!" Radley yells.

"Radley, we don't have time for this!" Keera says, "Jack and Torval are fighting for their lives right now!"

"Why so much ANGER, my dear?" Amphion jeers from the loudspeaker, "I'm not the one going around interrupting YOUR operations. I mean, sure, I put a hit on you, but only after you provoked me."

"You kept me in a box all my life!" she shouts back, "You're the reason my mother and I were here when this place was attacked. You're the reason she's dead!"

"I don't know about any of that, but I understand the importance of family. And I won't deny that something about me seems to have lit a fire in that belly of yours. Hot enough to burn through dozens of my men. Certainly has allowed me to obtain a great deal of data on your abilities," he says.

Radley grits her teeth. Keera grabs her arm and shakes her a bit, attempting to snap her out of it. "Radley!" they plead, "We have to go!" But Radley yanks her arm away.

"Fight me!" Radley yells again.

"Now why would I do that, when you clearly want to see the skeletons I have buried down here?" he muses.

With that, the lights flicker in the room. The walls and floors shake as loud grinding and hissing emanates from the ceiling above. Following the source, the group sees the cables from which the giant corpse is suspended begin to slack, steadily lowering it to the ground, until it is lying in an unceremonious heap on the floor.

As the form settles, Keera spots movement up and across the room from them. In a glass-encased observation room, they can barely make out the black cowboy hat and green suit jacket.

"There!" Keera yells, pointing.

The rest spot him, just as he says, "So instead… why don't I show you what they can DO?"

Amphion slams something on the console in front of him, and suddenly the room is alight with flashes and sparks, as electricity courses down the thicker metal cables into the dead creature. Its lifeless body twitches and contorts, tail and limbs wriggling as they are electrocuted. The surge then stops as abruptly as it began, and the creature lies still again.

"My apologies," Amphion urges, "He's a little shy. Come now, Argee, don't make Papa look silly in front of COMPANY!" He slams down on the board again, shocking the corpse again. The smell of cooking flesh mingles with that of rot, smoke rising from the entity. It twitches again, and as the shocking stops, flopping over again.

"Wake up, you dumb fucking LIZARD!" he growls, sending a third and more severe shock through the creature's body. Ozone has begun pouring from the creature's orifices, as it curls in on itself like a dying spider, a high-pitched bellowing emanating from its tortured body. After what feels like ages, the electrocution finally stops, and the creature lies still.

Then… it twitches.

And shifts.

Lights illuminate all over the creature's body. Tubes and wires pump and pulse, as some engine deep within the lizard groans and rumbles to life. This steam-powered monster begins to rumble to life, and Amphion cackles over the intercom.

"What the hell…" Radley breathes.

From the control station, Amphion maneuvers more switches on his console. "Now, RGX, up 'n' at 'em! Let's send father a message!" he declares. The thickest cables attached to this thing's back go taught. Slowly, they raise this corpse up, into a facsimile of an awkward standing position. With the gun arm, the creature is lopsided, and its head hangs limp like an elephant's trunk. Cables attached to the head pull it up, aiming it at the intruders. Its head is armored, with two glowing red lights where its eyes should be. It lets out another agonized screech and raises its massive gun arm. A high-pitched whining builds, and a similar red glow begins to emanate from the barrel.

"RUN!" Arianna exclaims. The three dive out of the way as a concussive blast impacts the spot where they were standing. The blast shunts Keera, slamming them into the wall, before falling to the floor of the scaffolding. They struggle to push themself up, a ringing in their ears as they search for the others. Radley is closest to them, staggering to their feet. Arianna is on the other side of the impact site, lying still.

"Arianna!" Keera calls. She doesn't respond.

Keera feels the floor under them shift. The sound of metal groaning.

"We have to go, NOW!" Radley yanks Keera up and pulls them along as the scaffolding begins to collapse. Looking back, they watch as the metal below Ari's body gives way, and the android plummets with the rest of the debris. They scream in their head to stop and save her, but they can't. They suppress tears and jump onto Radley's back as the mercenary picks up speed. All around them, metal supports and railings are crumbling. The two reach the stairs, also crumbling before them. Deftly, Radley slides down the rail of the stairway, kicks off, grabs a support pole that descends all the way to the ground, and slides down, down, down as the structure crumbles beside them. Keera grips for dear life, plummeting almost three stories. They're getting real fucking sick of falling from high places.

They look down; the ground coming fast. Their instincts kick in, telling them to leap from Radley at the last second, tuck, and roll away from the falling debris. They do so, and apart from some stumbling, they successfully land next to Radley. Keera catches their breath. They feel kind of badass.

That feeling leaves them rather quick as they're reminded of the android. "Where's Ari?" they ask, scanning the rubble for any sign of her.

Thudding footsteps shake them to their core, breaking them from their search. Looking up, they see the hulking cyborg monster towering above them. It is still some distance away, but it is way more terrifying from ground level. Its head lulls in their direction, and another hollow metal screech signifies its violent intent.

Radley stands and puts herself between Keera and the monster. "We've got bigger things to worry about," she says, "Stay behind me."

"You can't take that thing on by yourself!" Keera argues.

Radley shrugs a shoulder, "Only one way to find out."

Within a few shaky steps, the creature is upon them. It raises its front leg, aiming to squash them both like bugs. Radley shoves Keera back, and dives away just as the foot lands with a thud between the two of them. Keera rolls over, looking up at this putrid thing standing above them, dripping fluids and grinding laboriously. Its cold, soulless eyes stare through them. Keera sees no intent, ill or otherwise. No animal instinct, either. It is merely doing what it's being puppeteered to do.

The creature begins to sway toward them, only to be halted by the BANG BANG BANG of Radley's pistol shooting it in the side.

"HEY, AMPHION! OVER HERE!" she shouts. The creature slowly rotates toward her. "PICK ON SOMEONE WHO CAN FIGHT BACK, YOU COWARD!" More shots ring out, not affecting the creature in the slightest.

"Hmm, good point," he muses, "It'll be much easier to capture the other one alive with you out of the way..."

The creature raises another clawed foot, but Radley nimbly dodges. Another stomp, another dodge. Even the giant worm Keera saw her fight before was faster than this thing. She's too fast for its lethargic movements. The merc dashes forward, fires some shots into this thing's exposed scaly skin, then darts back, its claw trying to sweep her away.

"What's wrong, too fast for ya?" Radley jeers, "You know, for being a top secret project, I expected more."

Keera hasn't seen her this arrogant before. Normally, she is all business. What could her angle be? Whatever it is, it seems to be doing something, as Amphion's frustrated growl comes from the speakers. Just then, the creature begins to sweep around, the massive mace on the end of its tail scraping across the metal at increasing speed, toward the two of them. Keera sprints toward the rubble for cover. They duck behind a fallen i-beam, and spin around just in time to see the sphere impact Radley, sending her careening into the left wall. She lies there for a brief moment, before staggering up and shaking her head, dazed.

Amphion cackles, and Keera watches as the creature lumbers toward Radley, faster this time, preparing to drop the barrel of the gun-arm onto the wounded warrior.

"RADLEY, LOOK OUT!" Keera calls out. This snaps her out of it. She raises her blade just in time to catch the descending column of steel from turning her into a puddle of blood. The entity pushes down with more and more force, but Radley holds strong, the metal floor buckling beneath her. Radley lets out a cry of rage. With pure, unbridled determination, and a surge of strength, Radley shoves the big gun to the side, forcing it to embed itself into the floor. The creature screams in desperation, as the cords attached to its arms try to pull the gun free, but to no avail.

"Won't you just DIE already!" Amphion yells. He slams something on his console.

With that, the jaw of the creature flies open, cracking bones, and aims directly at the mercenary. Without warning, a cloud of fire belches from the back of the creature's throat, forcing Radley to dive away once more. The fire is thick and smoke-laden, not clean like a gas fire, black smoke rising up from the corners of its mouth, as it swivels its head around to track Radley. More and more belches of flame keep Radley on the defensive, only occasionally allowing her to duck in for a shot or two before being forced back by another gout of flame.

Keera, watching from the rubble, hears some shifting behind them that pulls their attention away from the fight. They spin around and see a mangled feminine form pinned under a fallen staircase.

"Arianna!" they exclaim. Without a second thought, Keera rushes over to her side. They need to get her out.

"Keera, Keera no," Arianna breathes. Her voice is even more modulated now, the words wheezing out like a dying radio broadcast.

"It's okay, Radley is distracting it, I can help you," the teen says, as they shift to her pinned side and attempt to find better handholds.

"No," she reiterates, "I— I can't feel my legs. Leave me, let me go."

"I'm NOT leaving you!" Keera cries out, "I'm going to lift. When I say go, shove as hard as you can, push yourself away."

The woman looks at Keera, and the teen acknowledges her face for the first time: much of the artificial skin is scraped away, exposing shining metal, and synthetic blood leaking everywhere. She's missing her right eye. "No, Keera, please, I can't—" she starts.

"You will. Everyone's going to make it out of here! Now, are you ready?" Keera says. They don't wait for a response: "Three... two... one... push!" With all their might, Keera hoists up the metal staircase. They cry out in pain, muscles groaning, feeling the sharp metal dig into their hands. Even though they aren't superhuman, like so many other members of their group, their meager human muscles lift the rubble about an inch. That is just enough, as Ari pushes down with her one good arm, shoving her way out and away from the rubble. As she clears it, Keera promptly drops the stairs with an unceremonious clatter.

They breathe heavily, the both of them. A streak of milky white liquid smears out from under the rubble, ending at what is left of Arianna's lower torso. Everything below her chest is gone, with a mess of wires, metal, and tubes dangling from her cavity.

Ari slowly turns her head to the kid. "Why...?" she groans.

"I can't lose anyone else. Not even you," Keera says.

Interrupting the moment, the sound of wrenching metal can be heard, as the creature has managed to remove its metal gun-arm from the floor. It thrashes, screaming once again, this time even louder, as the mouth is stuck open. It is whirling around in circles. Confused, Keera searches the battlefield for Radley, only to find her relatively diminutive form clinging to the back of the creature. The head and tail attempt to reach her, but they do not have the flexibility. The mercenary slashes and hacks at every wire she comes across as she moves upward, carving a path to the base of the neck. She steadies herself next to one of the thicker cables, the one holding the creature aloft. *Clever,* Keera thinks, as they realize what their caretaker is about to do. With one swift chop, like that of a practiced woodsman, *Clover* slices cleanly through the small-tree-trunk-sized cord.

Immediately, the portion held by the cord goes limp, as if its spinal cord was severed. This throws Radley off balance, but she remains standing. The creature bellows. Either in pain or involuntarily, Keera can't discern. It is, however, still able to stand, its back arched downward, supported only by its wide-stance legs.

"Oh, no you don't, you bitch!" Amphion jeers. Suddenly, previously sealed hatches on this creature's back open up, and four giant, slimy tentacles erupt from within. Each one, as wide as the cable Radley just cut, flails wildly, trying to smack Radley off. She attempts to deflect them, but they flank her on all sides. One errant swing of the fleshy tentacle connects, sending her spiraling off, a few dozen feet away from Keera and Arianna.

"Radley, get up!" Keera yells.

The mercenary stands, using her blade for support. She looks battered and bruised. She grits her teeth at the entity. Then, regarding her compatriots on the sidelines, she makes a mad dash for cover, sliding in beside them.

"Are you two alright?" she pants.

"Been better," Arianna moans.

The merc regards the android, and a flash of sympathy rolls over her expression. She shakes it off. "This thing is tougher than I expected," she states, "Its armor is strong, and it has so many defenses, it's getting hard to anticipate what it'll throw out next."

"We can't waste time with this," Keera urges, "Arianna's bleeding out, and can't have much time left."

Radley pops her head up. The creature isn't moving, but it is readying its gun arm into a position in which it could use it. She then scans the room. Then stops. "There, the drainage hatch," she exclaims, "We can get out through there."

"We aren't as fast as you, we'd never make it," Keera objects, "And you won't be fast enough either if you have to carry both of us."

"Leave me," Arianna says.

"I already told you, we're not leaving you here to die!" Keera reiterates.

Ari shakes her head, "No, not to die. Well, perhaps after, but that all depends how this shakes out, really."

Radley turns to her, "What are you going to do? You can barely move."

"It's mechanically controlled, right? And you severed one of its data cables?" she asks. Radley nods. "Get me up there. I should be able to interface with it. At minimum, I'll buy you enough time to get down the hatch."

"Ari, no," Keera objects.

"Let me do this, kid," she urges, "At the very least, it'll make us even."

Keera shakes their head, "But—"

Radley interrupts, "Can you do that?" Arianna nods. "Alright," Radley declares, "I can get you on its back, but I'll have to leave before those tentacles knock me off. Keera, as soon as you see her plug in, run for that hole." She points to the nearest drainpipe, a few yards away.

Keera hesitates, but the roaring of the creature behind them snaps them out of it. It's aimed at them. "Go!" Radley shouts, hoisting the mangled torso of Arianna onto her back and sprinting toward the creature. Keera's eyes go wide: the gun is charging.

Keera scrambles to their feet and sprints out from cover just as a streak of red light impacts the rubble, exploding it in all directions. They are just able to clear the blast. The teen looks back, as heaps of metal are now raining down from the impact site. They desperately dodge chunk after metal chunk landing around them. They're now out in the open. Fully exposed. Can't stop now. Keera makes a beeline straight for the hole.

Meanwhile, closer to the beast, Keera notices Radley reaching the base of the monster. She is forced to duck and dodge as well, avoiding claws, tails, and tentacles. Leaping toward the cannon, she runs along its length, then jumps for the shoulder. She grips onto the metal paneling as Ari clings to her back with her one arm. The creature tries to snap and swat at them, but the angle is just awkward enough where it can't reach, allowing the two some time to clamber up onto its back. She sprints along the tortoise-like spine, dodging tentacle after tentacle, until they reach the base of the severed cord. Radley has just enough time to set Ari down, before a meaty tentacle wraps around Radley's waist, and hoists her up and away. She shouts, in pain and frustration, as she's flailed around by this beast. She fires at it, to no effect.

"Round two didn't last very long, did it?" Amphion laughs, "Now, I think it's about time we finish this— wait. What's happening? My controls!"

Keera, reaching the hole, turns to understand what's happening. The beast is frozen. Its neck is locked up, muscles twitching, as if it is being tased. Its horrible cry loops like a skipping record. The teen then notices what's causing the creature's distress: connected by the bottom of her severed torso, attached to where the data cable used to be, is Ari. Even from here, Keera can see she's gritting her teeth and shaking, much like the creature.

"What are you doing to my creation?!" Amphion yells.

Ari, with much effort, raises her clenched fist. With a bellowing scream, echoed by the scream of the creature, she opens her hand. As she does, the tentacle releases Radley, the mercenary falling to the ground. She staggers to her feet, takes a moment to regard the monster and Ari, then sprints toward the hole Keera is posted up beside. Both Arianna and the monster cry out in unison, wracked with pain. It's as if both of them are fighting for control of one another, and neither is letting up. Within the struggle, the arm cannon goes off, blasting a hole in another wall. The place begins to rumble and shake from all the damage sustained over the course of the battle.

Radley reaches the hole, and without a second thought, jumps down into the darkness. Keera takes one more look at Arianna, writhing in pain on this creature's back. *Thank you,* she thinks, before diving in after Radley.

Chapter 26

A IR RUSHES PAST AS Keera slides down into a dark, rank, slimy void. They hear Radley clattering down the pipe ahead of them. Down, down they plummet, until eventually they finally drop with a splash into a large body of liquid. It's not deep, and Keera quickly finds the surface, gasping for air. The air that comes is even more vile than that upstairs. So vile, they almost throw up right then and there, but they hold their composure.

Scanning the area, they realize they are in a trench of this awful liquid, surrounded on both sides by walkways a few feet above the waterline. Further out, there are footpaths and canals criss-crossing in a checkered pattern, with lights placed periodically along them. They're in some sort of sewage system.

Realizing this, Keera wades through the water to the nearest concrete island, and hauls themself up onto it. They fall into the pillar and gasp for air. They're tired, they're hurt, they're nauseous. And they just want to go home.

It is then that they hear the sound of sloshing water, and Radley hauls herself onto land next to them. She is also short of breath, but the determination has not left her face.

"Alright, we're almost there," she says, "I recognize these sewers. If we follow them to a maintenance shaft, we should be able to—" She stops.

Tears are streaming down Keera's sewage-covered cheeks.

"Hey, hey, look at me," Radley whispers, grabbing the teen by the shoulders, "This isn't over yet. Once we find what we're looking for, and we save whoever is there, we can all have a big long cry together. Alright?"

"What are we doing here?" Keera sobs, "What is all this for? What do you expect to find down here?"

"I... Hopefully where I grew up. And my mom. And, maybe, even a young version of myself, safe, just how it was before," she says.

"But you don't know it'll be like that! You don't know that there's anything down here! And you have all these people who care about you, all these people risking their lives for you, and for what? For a dream, for a... for a fantasy?!"

"That's all I have!" Radley screams. Silence. Keera's eyes are wide, staring at the woman, her knuckles tight on the hilt of her blade. She continues, tears welling in her own eyes, "For twenty years. Twenty. Years. All I've had were those fantasies, those memories. They were the only thing holding me together, keeping me going through all the shit I've endured. And, now that I'm here, I... I have a chance. I have a chance to see it all again, and that is a chance I *have* to take. I didn't ask any of you to come along. I didn't want to get anyone hurt. I knew this was my mission, my... death wish. But you chose to stick around. Even when I warned you not to...!"

"That's because we care about you, Radley," Keera insists, "You are a strong, caring, good person, even when you try and pretend not to be. We want to help, *I* want to help you, like how you helped me. But... you can't keep going like this! You have to know when to quit."

Radley stares through the floor, the tears threatening to overflow onto her cheek. Instead, she grits her teeth and wipes them away. She stands, and with an all too familiar distant look, says to Keera, "Like I said, you can go if you want. All of you can go. I won't stop you." With that, she starts walking away down the tunnel.

Keera is shaken. Even after everything, after rescuing them multiple times, and after she showed she cares, this woman is ready to throw it all away for a memory. Keera feels even lonelier than they did back home at this moment.

KAPOW!

Just then, a shot echoes through the catacomb-like tunnels. This knocks Keera out of their emotions, once again on alert. Scrambling up, they peek around the corner. Radley is hugging the wall one row away, peeking out into the canal as well.

"Well, well, well," a familiar, semi-mechanical voice rings out, "Looks like the rats finally made their way to the sewers." The sound of deliberate, spur-clad footfalls accompanies it. A few rows away, a familiar green suited silhouette strides slowly down the walkway.

Amphion.

He continues, "Your little friend upstairs sure did a number on my beautiful Argee. But he did a number on her, too. In fact, my constituents are probably about wrapped up with the rest of your little band of freedom fighters as well. So, why don't you go ahead and consider giving yourselves up? Maybe I'll make sure they die quick, painless deaths."

"How about you fuck off," Radley responds from cover, "And get the hell out of my way!"

"Oh no, little missy, you don't understand," he says with a sigh, the jangling getting closer, "You aren't *allowed* to leave here. You've seen too much."

"I don't give a shit about your giant Frankenstein's monster," Radley yells.

The jangling of footsteps stops. "Really?" he asks. Amphion sounds genuinely surprised, "Hm. I would've bet a pretty penny that you were working for my uncle."

Suddenly, Radley darts out from behind cover, gun and blade drawn.

"You would've lost that bet," she says. And fires. Center of mass, point blank.

The man staggers a bit, hand gripping for his chest, eyes wide. Then, he looks to his hand. Even from here, Keera can tell there's no blood on it, no hole in his chest.

"Nice try," he says. And fires back.

Radley just manages to block the bullet with her blade, and dives to the right, behind the pillar on the other side. Keera sees the perpetual grimacing smile peer out from under his hat, as he lowers his massive silver pistol. He cackles, continuing his slow walk toward her.

"Gonna have to remind myself to give the boys in the lab a raise!" he explains, tapping something on his belt, "This high-frequency emitter does wonders at making your bullet sail right through me without making contact. Feels funny, and usually, it gives folks who use it cancer. But when you're me, that's not that big of a concern."

Radley ducks around the pillar just in time as he reaches her row.

"Come on now, where is everyone?" he says, as he continues making his way down the walkway. He's getting closer to Keera.

The teen ducks around the corner as the jangling spurs get louder. They have to go, now. They have to link up with Radley. As quietly as possible, they scurry around the pillar and dart across the alley, leaping over a small rivulet of sewage. A loud KAPOW rings out as they hop the gap, and they cover their ears as they keep running.

"And there's the other one!" he says.

Keera keeps running to the other side of the space. They can't stop. KAPOW, KAPOW! Shots impact concrete as they jump from platform to platform, sprinting, just trying to get to whatever is farthest away from this madman.

"Stay STILL, little brat!" he shouts behind them, "Or am I going to have to bring out the big guns?" Keera turns as they hear a whistling sound. They see the gun begin to glow blue. Instinctively, they duck behind the next pillar, just as a thundering KA-RACK sounds, blue light ripping through the upper portion of the concrete support. Oh fuck. They need to get out, now.

Keera keeps running. Up ahead, fading in from the dim light, Keera sees a door up ahead. It's ajar. Without hesitating, she pushes through the heavy bulkhead door into the narrow, pipe-lined hallway beyond. They hardly get a chance to look around before they're grabbed by arms in the dark, brought low, and have their mouth covered. Keera yelps reflexively, but quickly recognizes the insistent shushing of Radley. Slowly, the mercenary releases a hand from the teen's mouth as they calm their breathing. The two make eye contact. Radley gestures down the hallway to the right. Even though Keera is sure she is leading them further into the facility, and not an exit, the sound of rapidly gaining spurs keeps them compliant. They nod and follow.

Keeping low and quiet, the two turn left, then right, then left again. These corridors are even darker than the sewers, which help in avoiding their pursuer, but makes it hard for Keera to keep track of Radley. Luckily, the woman's long white hair stands out just enough for them to follow as they sneak through the snaking passageway.

After yet another left, the pair comes to a ladder. By this point, Keera can't even hear the jingling sounds behind them anymore. They breathe a sigh of relief. Radley motions for Keera to follow, and begins ascending the ladder. Could this be it? Could this be the same ladder Radley climbed down to escape in another universe? They're still skeptical, but the confidence with which Radley made her way through these tunnels makes them think she knew where she was going, that this was all familiar to her. Only one way to find out. Keera ascends up after Radley.

Chapter 27

Light washes over the snow-haired climbers as Radley opens the heavy metal hatch. It is bright, white, and clean. The air is cool and smells crisp, yet stale. Carefully, Radley peaks out from the hole.

"Are we clear? What is it?" Keera asks.

There's no response.

The mercenary instead creeps up and out of the hole. Keera follows directly after, nervous. As they reach the last rung, the first thing that meets their eye level is grass. It's short and brown, like a manicured lawn in a drought. The sky above is less of a sky, and more of an endless white void. There's no sun, no definite clouds, not even a hint of blue sky. Just a perpetual gray-white.

Keera is similarly speechless as they emerge fully from the hole. They're in a forest, much like what Radley described in her memories. Only, instead of a verdant apple orchard, every single tree they can see is dead. Barren sticks erupting from the dirt, like gnarled capillaries petrified by the air. There is no wind. No sound or rustling. Only a thick fog hangs in the air, mirroring the gloominess of the sky.

"Is this...?" Keera can't even bring themself to finish the question.

Radley still doesn't respond. Keera glimpses her face as she surveys her surroundings. It's pure fear. Fear holding back a leaking dam of emotions, threatening to burst their way through with each rapid breath she takes.

Just then, she starts walking in a direction. Keera, naturally, follows. The pace starts slow, but builds in speed into a steady speed-walk. Then into a jog.

"Radley!" Keera calls after her, "Radley, what's going on?!"

Nothing. The jog turns into a sprint. They abruptly leave the treeline, entering a vast open field, with only vague silhouettes in the edges of the fog. Keera is having a hard time keeping up, and eventually they lose her to the fog as well.

"Radley!" they call. No response. For a moment, they consider stopping, but think better of it. She was running straight. Just keep going straight.

Sure enough, pretty soon, the form of Radley reappears ahead of them. She is still. Standing, facing something in the fog. This stops Keera in their tracks as well. "Radley?" they ask. Slowly, they approach. She isn't moving, not responding. They reach her and step in front of her to see her face.

Tears are rolling down her cheeks.

Keera's heart sinks. They have a feeling what she's seen. But something within them hopes their intuition is wrong. So, slowly, they turn and witness it.

Through the fog, clear shapes have emerged. More barren trees. A white wooden trellis sits over a large plot of gray tilled soil. Like a strange grave marker. Beyond, the edges of which are disappearing into the mist, is the silhouette of a single story farmhouse. Brick walls, chimney. Homely and quaint.

The roof has caved in. The windows are shattered. And the walls are covered in scorch marks.

A choking sound emanates from Radley behind them. Keera spins to see Radley. The warrior woman is sobbing. Her body heaves and jerks with each shaky breath. Her face is contorted and stretched in one of pure agony.

Keera reaches out a weary hand, "Radley, I'm sorry..." As soon as her finger makes contact, the woman aggressively yanks away. Her arms wrap around herself, holding desperately, as if she could explode from the inside at any moment. The teen retracts their offered comfort. Sympathy pangs roll through them like waves.

They want to comfort her, but they know she can't be touched right now. Instead, they stand beside her, looking out at the abandoned home with her.

Radley falls to her knees. She hunches over, irrigating the dead soil with teardrop after teardrop. The sobs are turning into wails of pain until eventually culminating in a scream. A primal, vocal-cord-wrenching scream of years and years of hurt and regret, all exploding at once from this single woman. The echoes of said scream ricochet off the hidden metal walls, ringing. Like church bells.

Slumping over, head hung low, tears still falling from her cheeks, Radley gasps for air. Eventually, her quiet, shaky voice speaks, "I thought things would be different here... I—I hoped... Why? Why here, too? It's— It's not FAIR! IT'S NOT FAIR!" What weak composure she had breaks again, and she sobs to the earth. All Keera can do is watch. This poor woman, who had saved them and pushed them through trial after trial, is now reduced to a broken heap on the ground. The weight isn't lost on them. They did all this, sacrificed friends. Fought, bled. For what amounted to nothing.

This brings to mind Keera's own pain. They instinctively grip the little gold leaf in their pocket, remembering their family, and the home they lost. What it felt like kneeling at the edge of the crater where they used to live. Two souls, overflowing with pain.

Both are lost in a sea of fog and grief.

So lost are the two of them that they don't hear the footsteps approaching behind them.

"Oh good, I don't even have to ask you to get on your knees," Amphion says.

The two whirl around, but not fast enough.

KAPOW.

As if in slow motion, Keera witnesses blood explode from the kneeling woman. Her face is one of shock, tears staining her cheeks. She falls backward to the ground, her unblinking eyes staring up into the bright white void.

Keera is stunned.

"There, was that so hard?" the skeletal man says. He smugly blows the smoke from the barrel of his pistol.

Keera's breath quickens. "You..." they whisper.

"Now, let's get you back to the lab, little miss," he says, the jangling approaching. Keera's gaze is locked on the dead body of Radley.

"NO..." they breathe. Tears roll down their cheeks. Something is burning up inside them.

"Don't make this harder than it has to be, darling," Amphion jeers.

Keera whirls on him, "NOOOOO!" Their scream cuts through the air like a fiery blade. The air ripples, rings, and tears.

And then it all goes black.

Keera's eyes snap open. They see Radley. She is on her knees.

The teen stammers, "Wait, I—"

They're interrupted by familiar words from behind them: "Oh good, I don't even have to ask you to get on your knees."

They spin around faster this time. He's there again, gun raised at Radley.

"RADLEY, MOVE!" Keera shouts. But they're too late. The same thing happens: She spins. He fires. She falls.

"There, was that so hard?" he jeers again, for the first time.

The rage bubbles up again. It gets hotter and hotter and hotter until—

Their eyes open.

They've looped again.

I need to be faster this time.

Without waiting for him to speak, Keera whips around and sprints at the skeletal man, just as he appears from the fog.

KAPOW.

Keera feels a searing pain in their chest. The force of the impact sends them staggering back. Gripping it instinctually, their hand comes away drenched in crimson. They fall to the dirt.

Their vision blurs. The last thing they experience before everything fades is Amphion kneeling over them, saying, "Such a shame. You brought this on yourself, child."

Then they wake again.

Okay, can't bum rush him. Think Keera, think. If they can't attack, then maybe…

They whirl around again, but this time, they hold their arm up, blocking Radley. "WAIT!" they yell.

Amphion pauses. Radley spins around, shocked at the sudden turn of events. She's still too emotionally broken to respond coherently, however.

"Take me, let her live," Keera pleads.

Amphion pauses for a moment, cocking his head in thought.

Then, he shrugs, and says, "Nah."

KAPOW.

Keera feels Radley's blood spray all over them. They are shaking. Slowly, the grotesque cowboy struts over to them and puts a hand on their shoulder.

"Let's go," he says.

In a fit of sudden rage, Keera swings wide, a haymaker connecting to the man's grotesque face. Amphion staggers back, shocked. He's bleeding. Keera looks down at their hand, noticing they were still unconsciously grasping the timestopped leaf in their fist. The tip is red with his blood.

"SHIT!" he cries, "You little BITCH!" KAPOW.

Keera awakes once more. This seems hopeless. The leaf worked, but they have to get close, and they can't get close without being shot.

And then it hits them.

"Oh good, I don't even have to—" the man's voice comes from behind them.

"RADLEY, ROLL!" Keera calls out.

It all happens in a matter of seconds. Radley rolls. Draws her weapons. The bullet fires. Keera spins. They throw the leaf. Then silence. Everything is frozen in time.

Steadily, Radley stands.

And Amphion falls to his knees.

He screams in agony. "Wha—what the hell—" he cries.

Before he's able to raise his gun again, Radley is on him. The gun is knocked from his hand. She levels hers to his temple.

He hisses, "I—I can't be shot."

"Wasn't a bullet," Keera says, "You wanted your specimen? There it is." They gesture to his leg. Sticking out of it is half of the golden leaf. He attempts to move, but the leaf stays stuck in space. It slices his flesh with each minute movement.

His groan of agony morphs into maniacal chuckling. "I must admit, I'm impressed," he chokes, "But also surprised. Of all the things here, didn't think THIS would be what you were lookin' for."

"What happened here? Where are the people you kept in this place?" Radley shouts, grinding the barrel of her pistol into his skeletal head.

"Shut down, by order of the council," he says, "The subject was to be terminated."

Radley grits her teeth. "Who's on this council? What did you do with them?!" she presses further.

"Don't you recall what I said about family?" he chuckles.

"I swear to fuck, I'll blow your goddamn head off, you fucking piece of shit!" she shouts in his face.

"That thing still won't hurt me sweetheart," he jeers, smiling his lipless grin up at her, "No matter how close you get, that bullet will just pass right throu—"

He stops, mouth agape. Keera's eyes go wide.

Slowly, the teen approaches. They can see a thin, bloody blade sticking through the man's torso. Radley is clutching the hilt of *Clover*, its blade deep in Amphion's chest.

Keera is speechless.

"You... You don't know what you've done..." Amphion chokes, blood gurgling its way up his throat, "They'll come for you. My brother, my uncle... my father. You're about to be at the top of Manhattan Gate's most wanted..."

Radley twists the blade in his chest. He lets out a surprised yelp, and the life leaves his lidless eyes. Amphion slumps to the ground, falling from the sword.

"Good," Radley says.

Keera is frozen in place. The implications of everything that just transpired spin around in their head.

But Amphion's last words come to the forefront, and as the merc turns, bloody blade in hand, once again facing the wreckage of her home, Keera asks, "What... what do we do now?"

Radley looks to her blade, holding it in both hands like a dead body. Then she abruptly stabs it into the dirt.

Without turning to Keera, Radley reaches down, picks up Amphion's weapon, and responds:

"I am going to kill them all."

EPILOGUE

A MAN SITS IN a dark room. A small cone of blue light emanates from a monitor atop a mahogany desk, illuminating him as he gazes out a window. Outside, a roiling sea undulates far below. Only the faint reflection of the moon on the waves betrays the vast water before him.

He sighs, smoke rippling off his cigarette. The man reaches up and runs his hand through greased black hair. Not out of nervousness or anxiety, but merely to maintain its perfect shape.

Just then, the door opposite the window opens. A figure dressed in red robes enters. His hair is stark-white, and he possesses a beard that reaches the middle of his chest. "Sir," the second man says, "News from Summit Station. Amphion has been—"

"I know," the first man responds in a deep, smooth voice, like indigo velvet.

"Zethus is already mobilizing units to pursue his brother's killers. Should I intervene?" the man in red asks.

"No," the first man says, "Let him have his crusade. About time the boy shows some initiative."

The man in red nods, then turns to leave. But before he does, he turns back to the man behind the desk. "Oh, I forgot to mention: Survivors of the massacre report that two of the attackers possess... unexplainable abilities."

"Not surprising. Amphion was always fascinated by EUEs. Was only a matter of time before one of the more deadly entities got to him," the smoking man says.

"There's more," the man in red states, "These two also possess white hair."

The smoking man freezes. Slowly, he turns to meet the gaze of the other man for the first time. Caught in the light from the monitor, glowing golden eyes squint across the room.

"Do they now?" the golden eyed man questions.

"Does that change your orders?" the red-robed man asks.

"No, but keep an eye on them, Nereus," the first man says, as he slowly turns back to the window. The waves are picking up now, and the moon is nowhere to be seen. A storm is coming.

"The defect might just have stumbled onto something... intriguing," the figure concludes.

The man in red nods, and exits the room.

Golden eyes stare out at the crashing waves. A flash of lightning briefly illuminates the man's scarred face.

"What did you find, little Amphion?..." the man questions the growing tempest.